WHAT CAME BEFORE

Initially trained as a lawyer, Anna George has worked in the legal world as well as the film and television industries. She studied Professional Writing and Editing at RMIT, and has written feature film scripts. She lives in Melbourne with her husband and two children.

WHAT CAME BEFORE

ANNA GEORGE

VIKING
an imprint of
PENGUIN BOOKS

VIKING

Published by the Penguin Group
Penguin Group (Australia)
707 Collins Street, Melbourne, Victoria 3008, Australia
(a division of Penguin Australia Pty Ltd)
Penguin Group (USA) Inc.
375 Hudson Street, New York, New York 10014, USA
Penguin Group (Canada)
90 Eglinton Avenue East, Suite 700, Toronto, Canada ON M4P 2Y3
(a division of Penguin Canada Books Inc.)
Penguin Books Ltd
80 Strand, London WC2R 0RL England
Penguin Ireland
25 St Stephen's Green, Dublin 2, Ireland
(a division of Penguin Books Ltd)
Penguin Books India Pvt Ltd
11 Community Centre, Panchsheel Park, New Delhi – 110 017, India
Penguin Group (NZ)
67 Apollo Drive, Rosedale, Auckland 0632, New Zealand
(a division of Penguin New Zealand Pty Ltd)
Penguin Books (South Africa) (Pty) Ltd
Rosebank Office Park, Block D, 181 Jan Smuts Avenue, Parktown North, Johannesburg, 2196, South Africa
Penguin (Beijing) Ltd
7F, Tower B, Jiaming Center, 27 East Third Ring Road North, Chaoyang District, Beijing 100020, China

Penguin Books Ltd, Registered Offices: 80 Strand, London WC2R 0RL, England

First published by Penguin Group (Australia), 2014

10 9 8 7 6 5 4 3 2 1

The author would like to acknowledge the following sources: Hepburn, K., 1991, *Me: Stories of My Life*, Penguin Group, London; and Lumet, S., 1995, *Making Movies*, Bloomsbury Publishing Plc, London.

Design by Laura Thomas © Penguin Group (Australia)
Cover photograph by WIN Initiative/Getty Images
Typeset in Adobe Garamond by Laura Thomas
Printed and bound in Australia by Griffin Press, an accredited ISO AS/NZS 14001 Environmental Management Systems printer.

National Library of Australia
Cataloguing-in-Publication data:

George, Anna.
What came before / Anna George.
9780670077731 (paperback)
Suspense fiction.

A823.4

penguin.com.au

MIX
Paper from responsible sources
FSC® C009448

For Jason

'My name is David James Forrester. I'm a solicitor. Tonight, at 6.10, I killed my wife. This is my statement.'

He plugs his mouth with a cigarette as the dictaphone hovers. He lets his car steer itself. He's thinking about the difference between admitting and confessing. Admit to one element of a crime too many and you've confessed. Murder included. That much he can remember.

He stops the tape.

In the middle of Tennyson Street, his car is travelling so slowly it's about to stall. Seddon, in Melbourne's inner-west, is silent around him. He stares at the ubiquitous picket fences and rose bushes. The weatherboard period houses, all like hers: double-fronted, two-toned and immaculate. Once, this sameness had made her laugh, him too. During its decade or so make-over – from industrial, working class to young professional – Seddon seemed to have consulted the same housepainter and landscape gardener. 'A busy pair,' she'd called them, 'with a limited palate.' But tonight, looking at the tricked-up houses, all he sees are grim replicas of his crime scene.

He closes his eyes and his car shudders; dies.

The dictaphone slips from his fingers and bounces against the steering wheel and into his lap. Its door springs open and the tape pops up. He smokes. He thinks of the story he has to tell, and of his pain. Usually he can order his thoughts without seeing them, usually he can recall names and dates without notes. But can he tonight? When the mistake's fresh and his hands are hurting? Maybe not. But he has to try, before his words are skewed and his memories muddied. Before his guilt becomes fact. He retrieves the cassette with its ribbon unspooled. What he feels, he realises, is sick.

He shoves open his door. The cold hits his face as he hawks onto the road.

At least he knows his way around a statement; in more than twenty years he's taken thousands. While his interviewees tend to be merely grouchy bankers, the principles are the same. Suing or being sued is an emotional business. And he's become a professional hand holder. He tells their shaky chins to put it simply, their own way, but that, he can see now, is a tough ask. In the twilight, he hawks again and sits up. His thoughts clear. He'll structure the thing chronologically. That way, the acts constituting his crime won't be tackled for hours. Besides, what came before is often more telling than those acts. What came before shapes the liability, reveals it. It's only once the damage has been done that anyone bothers about what came before.

With his gut churning, he restarts the car and rolls it along the kerb. He parks outside Tennyson Street's only brick-veneer house, inserts his pinkie into the wheel in the centre of the cassette and turns, like he's cleaning his ear. He watches as the tape smoothly coils. And an image comes. This picture is key to their story, maybe as defining as this wintry night. As much as it hurts, he can't avoid it. She's straddling him, long, gleaming and naked.

1

It was mid-August, almost exactly two years ago. He was buying a ticket to see *Talk to Her* as part of an Almodóvar retrospective when he saw her, alone, two people away from him in the queue. He recognised her immediately, though he'd only seen her once before. He watched her read up on the Spanish director. Up close she wasn't, technically speaking, beautiful. Her face lacked symmetry as her nose turned to the left and one eyelid was heavier than the other, but her face was so much better for these flaws. He admired her olive complexion and her hair, no longer solicitor-sleek and shoulder length, but now the mop of an urchin. It was this change, he suspected, that created her spectacular new look. In her heart-shaped face her pale eyes were enormous and ethereal.

If he had a type, she was it. He introduced himself and they chatted. After the film, she agreed to join him in the crowded bar across the road from the Sun Theatre. They were discussing Almodóvar's early work, when, somehow intuiting his tiredness, she nestled behind him and swept her hands across his shoulders, then rested her fingertips at his nape as if asking permission. When he didn't speak or step away she began massaging, her long fingers working the skin beneath his hair.

'Is that better?' she whispered.

Ah, yeah, he thought. He wasn't game to speak. It was such a rash yet fitting act, shattering something between them that might've taken hours, if not days, to demolish.

By 1 a.m. they were kissing in a taxi on their way to her place. Her little house was a cream-and-green Victorian affair, ornate, high-ceilinged. And he liked it, especially the decor with its old-world Eurasian flavour. She had an eye for second-hand art deco furniture and Chinese engravings, sideboards and lamps. The rooms were furnished with green and blue Turkish rugs and paintings of the sea and trees by artists he didn't know. In every room, bookshelves overflowed. He would never have expected a young, single person to occupy such a house. Although she'd told him she'd only recently bought it, nothing about it was half done, nothing uncommitted. By the time she opened her fridge, which was loaded with fruit and vegetables, he felt intimidated.

'Want an omelette or a plate of antipasto?' she said.

'No, thank you.'

His nerves left him then with nothing but his smile. She'd been this way ever since he'd introduced himself – open, warm, uncomplicated. So unlike his expectations of her; he couldn't work her out.

She led him through her lounge room, which was lamp-lit

and heated by a gas log fire, into a dining room housing a honey-coloured timber dining table and chairs. He managed to admire the setting and she seemed pleased.

'Recycled Victorian ash, courtesy of Film Victoria and its script development program,' she said, moving towards him. He must have looked confused. 'The funding was meant to get my script, *Daisy*, from draft one to two.'

That had been her first direct allusion to her new career. During the evening, though they'd found a shared passion for art-house movies, they hadn't discussed her role in the film industry.

He made appreciative noises as she unbuckled his belt. The chairs' cushions were covered in fine olive suede. The suede was silken against the skin. Conducive, he supposed, to scriptwriting.

By 1.30 they were both naked and she was astride him on a dining chair. Her breath was humid on his neck and her grip tight, enveloping, the way he liked it. Practically everything she'd done had been the way he liked it: perceptive and playful. They'd been at it for twenty minutes. Dictating the pace, she was curved on top, her slender arms locked across him. Beneath her fingers, from his shoulders, hair sprouted. There was hair on his back too. Hair tinged with ginger. He'd been watching her when his shirt came away, and her initial reaction had been akin to shock. But now, in the light of the gas fire, he saw her admiring the red-gold glistening on his skin.

'It wasn't there when I got up this morning,' he whispered.

'I like it.' She rocked slowly upon him. 'And I like your teeth and their gap, and your lips . . .' She traced them with a fingertip. 'Just enough to see when you smile, and just enough to . . .' She kissed him softly, and he stifled a groan. 'And I like your kinky hair,' she said, snagging her fingers in it, 'with its gingery highlights. It matches the hair on your back.' She grinned.

Unused to coital chitchat, self-conscious, he kissed her. But she was enjoying herself. 'No one feature of your face is particularly striking,' she said, pulling back, 'but all together it's compelling.'

He stared, stunned by her scrutiny.

She laughed. 'David, it's a compliment.'

She returned her focus to their bodies. Flattered and relieved, he watched her. Before long, their breathing was rapid and in sync. With his eyes shut, he felt her every detail: her thigh muscles above his, her tongue's tip at his ear, her hand at his neck. Any second now he would come. He opened his eyes to verify she was flesh, and not the look-alike he'd dreamed about four years ago. He rolled his hips and, within her, another chamber yielded. She moaned. Leaned back. He took in her flushed neck and her blue eyes pale and bright against her treacly skin. He tried to hold on. It wasn't easy. Then, as she gasped, he became aware of the perspiration above her lips, under her breasts, between her thighs. It was as if she was melting. All over him. He was reluctant to interrupt but he felt obliged.

'Ah,' he said, 'I think you're urinating on me.'

The room was silent but for their breathing and the purr of the heater. Neither of them moved. He kept his gaze on hers, praying he hadn't snapped the slender thread she'd spun around them.

'What did you say?' she whispered.

'I think you're ur—'

'What?'

She raised herself up, her inner thighs dripping. His groin was saturated and half the suede was soaked. She touched the cushion. Sniffed her fingers, her big eyes wide.

'I could do with a towel,' he said. He couldn't read her expression, but her cheeks were burning. 'It's okay,' he said with a gentle smile. 'Just very wet.'

Before he could speak again, she streaked to the door.

His pulse was still galloping as he examined the evidence. He dabbed at the chair, paused. Since his wife left, he'd bemoaned the inverse relationship between hygiene and sex. Often it was better not to identify flavours. If only he hadn't been quite so blunt, though – his fingers were at his nostrils when he glanced up to see she'd reappeared, bearing towels. Looking impossibly tall, she hesitated at the doorway.

'Well?' she said. 'What's the verdict?'

There was no avoiding it. He sniffed. 'Odourless,' he said with relief. 'Definitely.'

'Ha, I never doubted it!' she said, beaming. But relief crossed her face too, as she tossed him a towel.

In her galley kitchen, he was propped on a bench and eating vegemite toast. The condom had been binned, the cushion leaned towards the gas fire.

'Four years ago,' he said, 'I'd just started at Freeman & Milne when I stumbled across your farewell drinks.'

She finished her toast with gusto. 'I know, and when Andrew Milne began my legal eulogy, you fled.'

Surprised and flattered again, he could only nod. She'd been a senior associate then, up for partnership, and he was a freshly minted partner at the firm. When he heard she'd resigned, he'd been bemused and impressed. He'd taken a dozen years to achieve what she had in five, aged barely thirty. Hearing about her then, he'd assumed that she'd been educated at the right private school and reared in a leafy eastern suburb of Melbourne – that greatness had always been expected of her. That she was leaving the law was, he'd assumed, the most unexpected thing about her. About that he now knew he was wrong.

On safer, drier ground, they discussed his colleagues and her former bosses. The upper echelons of the legal profession, the elite inbred. There were few they both knew and liked – despite the two hundred–strong professional staff of Freeman & Milne.

'I always felt like the odd one out in that place,' she said.

At the sink she filled her teapot and smiled. He remembered then the sight of her, years before, in that boardroom. Encircled by mid-career lawyers, she was like a beacon in a sea of grey: animated, tactile, aglow. And now he knew why. Lawyers could be split into three groups: the minority of believers who loved legal practice; the agnostic majority who stayed (or sometimes left but came back) because they didn't know what else to do; and the lucky ones, the atheists, who left because they had another calling. She was, he realised, one of the latter. Back then, in that vast boardroom, she'd been alight with happiness. As she was tonight. A reminder to him of his flat-footed agnosticism.

Wrapped in a navy towel, he felt himself emitting a low-burning energy. 'You're intense, aren't you,' she said, 'like a blue flame.' He couldn't help but smile. She was pouring black tea, letting the steaming liquid arc from pot to mug. He touched her cheek with the back of his fingers and she over-poured, a reaction he found ridiculously gratifying. He thought he saw her blush, but in the steam couldn't be sure.

'Has it happened before?' he said.

She sipped her scorching tea. 'No.'

Leaning against the fridge, clad in her towel, with her straight back and long feet, she was a stately teenager at the school fence.

The sort of girl he'd always liked but rarely approached. Definitely top-shelf.

'Well then, I'm flattered,' he said. 'I've only ever heard of female ejaculation.'

This time her colour was unmistakable. 'I couldn't have done it without you.'

He laughed, at her jangling bravado and blush. She could say almost anything and he'd be amused.

'And I'm sorry we were cut short,' she said.

'Don't be. I'm completely satisfied.'

Mastering her embarrassment, she abandoned her tea and busied herself with dishes. He hopped from the bench to take a soiled butter knife from her hand. In front of him, barefoot, she was still tall. He liked that she didn't need to incline her head to meet his eye. He was aware anew of her breath: fresh, familiar, vegemite.

'What are you doing in ten hours?' he asked, entwining her wet fingers in his.

'Working.' She stepped away. Dried her hands. 'Don't take this personally, but I've pegged you as my first one-night stand.'

Frowning, he dusted his fingers against his chest, causing crumbs to cling. He wondered whether to parry: *I wasn't suggesting otherwise*, etc. 'And why's that?'

She hesitated. 'To see what it felt like, I guess.'

'And what does it feel like?'

'Exciting, fun . . .' She held his gaze. 'And finite.'

He gave her twenty seconds to change her mind. Or at least come clean about his effect on her. When he stepped towards her, she ran her hands through her mop of hair. When he brushed his fingers against her cheek again, her face became pink, again. Beneath his gaze, her lips were trembling.

'Tell me,' he said, 'have any of your other relationships begun like this?'

She mouthed rather than said: 'No.'

'And have any of your other relationships worked?'

Shaking her head, she was that stately schoolgirl again. 'But you're divorced,' she said, inching from him, 'and you're old and you're a lawyer.'

He blinked to mask his surprise. 'Ouch.'

'And,' she said, clearing her throat as if to garner authority, 'there's nowhere to go after a beginning like this.'

His red-brown eyes danced. 'Of course there is,' he said. 'We can go anywhere – anywhere, that is, with plastic lining.'

Her laugh was a loud, clear sound in her kitchen. And he rang with it.

He doesn't know where memory is stored: right side of the brain or left, or somewhere in between? But tonight his temple throbs, as home movies nearly two years old play in his head. Stricken in his driver's seat, he's swept up in a collage of her: grinning over her laptop, baking vegetable lasagne, weeding her tomatoes. In their twenty-two months together, her moods went from joyous to despairing. But in the beginning, she was luminous. He closes his eyes. Regret is distant but visible on the horizon.

He pictures her the morning after her first one-night stand. Slipping from his arms, she wrapped herself in a towel. And he watched. Without makeup, her cheeks and lips were rose pink and her blue eyes were startling against her mussed fawn hair. She was the most naturally colourful woman he'd ever met. Flashing him a grin, she swept up her clothes. Although it was a Saturday, he sensed she was late for her desk. But his weekend was, as usual, fairly empty.

'Tell me, why romantic comedies?'

The question took her by surprise and he was pleased. The night before, he hadn't mentioned her sassy romantic comedy, even though it'd been a critical and box-office hit. That morning, when she re-tucked her towel, he gathered she was vacillating about him. He smiled his best sultry smile.

'I blame Katharine Hepburn,' she said, with a sigh. 'I grew up watching *The Philadelphia Story*, *Woman of the Year* and *His Girl Friday*.'

'That was Rosalind Russell.'

Heading for her ensuite, over her shoulder: 'Yes, I know. I blame her too.'

Cross-legged and naked on her bed, he sang out, 'Screwball comedies, eh? Howard Hawks, George Cukor, the sparring and reversals?'

She paused. 'Yes, that's them.' She refocused those big eyes on his. 'As a teenager I thought that was the only way to relate to the opposite sex. For years, I've been waiting for some fast-talking man to realise that he can't live without me.'

She paused, seeming surprised by her answer. He watched her think. He'd been trying to work out her solo status since the night began; there was always a reason for it. This was the closest she'd come to an admission. As she stood, framed by the doorway, he appraised her. Her understated beauty and intelligence. Once, he would've tried to draw her.

'So,' he said, 'now you make romantic comedies to give other people false hope?' He took her cocked eyebrow as a gentle concession. 'There must be a law against that.'

'Actually,' she said, 'those films give me solace.'

'Do they now?' he said, his confidence growing. 'I get it from boxing, and Goya.'

When she smiled, he rose from the bed.

Her eyes grew serious. 'David,' she said, then paused. 'Have you actually seen my film?'

'Yeah,' he said, 'twice. I liked it. And call me Dave.'

Gently, he kissed her curving lips. Cupped her warm head beneath her hair. Untucked her towel and pulled her back onto the mattress. To his relief, she let herself become entwined in him again. Six hours later, he left.

In his car, he groans and the black box clicks. Jesus, she was a gift. One of the two women in his life he's loved. The enormity of what he's done hits him. He is many things, he thinks – a drunk, a prick – but not a killer. He wouldn't believe it if it weren't for the evidence. The scratches on the back of his hands are deep and long, exposing the meat within. He'd been leaning, his hands tight around her long neck, his thumbs pushing down. That was all it took: his body weight and his two thumbs. Even with her hands on his, digging.

In his right thumb is one of her fingernails. A pink, jagged crescent. He plucks it out and that pressure in his abdomen bears down. Hard.

He blasts out of Tennyson Street, heading for the Yarraville Gardens. The bliss of a toilet. Or shadowy bush. The pain tightens and he lurches. He fears he won't make it. Three long minutes later, the gardens come into view and he brakes, thrusts open his door and runs. In the near distance is the Port of Melbourne with its cranes and containers. *What a goddamned place*, he thinks. *The scrapyard of the city.*

The concrete toilet block is icy and lit by a single bulb. He throws himself into a cubicle, yanks down his pants and erupts. The deluge is brief and fierce. Not the relief he expected. Perplexed, he hunches over the old wooden seat. He closes his eyes and sees himself. Bent and trembling, hot and cold. Totally fucking out of control.

Without warning, his guts burst into his throat. It's the perfect ambush. He swivels but doesn't make it, splattering the cement floor. Mid-retch, he flushes to expel what he can of the stink. He kicks up the seat and retches again. Too late he remembers the two glasses of red wine and her homemade tzatziki; it's all tasting far worse the second time. And the third. Had he eaten lunch he would've had a better chance. Breakfast too could've plugged him up. As it is, he's going to relive last night's Chinese, dim sims and all. He retches, his arse jutting from the cubicle like a pasty, ginger-haired invitation. He yanks up his trousers and belts them, mid-heave.

Thirty years of drinking to excess and he's never thrown up like this. He wipes his face with waxy toilet paper. Breathes. Waits. Heaves. It's as if a gremlin is sitting in his belly and hurling the contents up at him, handful by handful.

He stares at the foul toilet floor, then at the splatters on his shoes. He frowns. They aren't vomit, or bile, or even shit. His trousers too – at the cuffs – are darkly soiled. His gaze inches up his legs, and he groans. His knees have matching stains and his blue shirt is a butcher's apron.

2

Elle Nolan is on her laundry's cool tiles. She is also on the ceiling, where she's feeling gloriously light, as if she is a balloon. Floating and hyper-alert, she is unafraid. And calm. From within her darkened house, she can smell marinara and hear the Buena Vista Social Club. It is not the music she would have chosen. In the laundry, she can see one of her nephew's socks and her long-lost silky g-string atop her wall-mounted dryer. And, two metres below, she can see her body. It is twisted, on its side, beneath a green towel. Though she feels sorry for it, she's in no hurry to have it back. Fragments of memory return to her: a shove, his hands, her screams.

So this is death.

Briefly, she wonders if her father and grandparents are going to appear, open-armed, like tardy ghostly hosts. And where's the swirling light or beckoning tunnel? She waits; nothing happens. Then, unheralded, in a fraction of a second, she sees the sweep of her life – its triumphs and mistakes. There she is as a ten-year-old, wearing a hot pink netball skirt in that ramshackle house in Kew; at twenty-one, with her father in their flat in Elwood; at thirteen, as a scholarship girl on day one at Melbourne Girls Grammar. MGS becomes Monash University becomes Freeman & Milne becomes the VCA Film School. Sundance Film Festival. The faces of friends forgotten merge with those of her boyfriends and her ensemble casts. She sees Mira; her brother, Jude; Doris; and her mother. Amid the busyness, she detects a thread. One portion of her life, in particular, is repeating. Looping. Almost as if, she thinks, she has something to learn.

She sees herself the Wednesday after she met David Forrester. At 9 a.m., she was at her desk, pale sunlight framing the script in her hands. Where her last screenplay had centred on the idea that 'courage is rewarded by lucky coincidences', this one mused that 'love can transform even the most reluctant lovers'. The focus on transformation was apt, as it was the core of romantic comedy. But of the depth of love's power she was less certain. Could it make a critical woman tolerant, or an indifferent man passionate – permanently? She was still deliberating when the parcel arrived. In it were two things: a familiar business card and Katharine Hepburn. Youthful and beautiful, rosy-cheeked and aristocratic, gazing out from the cover of *Me: Stories of My Life.* Flattered, Elle fanned the pages beneath her chin and thought of David Forrester, and Cary Grant.

Since she was twelve she'd had a crush on Cary. A crush spawned by midday movies and *Holiday*, a crush she'd not entirely outgrown. Over the decades it had extended, courtesy of *An Officer and a Gentleman,* to Richard Gere and, later, thanks to *Out of Sight*, to George Clooney. And now, of course, Ryan Gosling. Aged thirty-four, she still found those on-screen heroes and their great loves trumping her reality. Or at least she had – they had – until last Friday night. Since then, to her surprise, she'd thought often of David Forrester: his wit, enthusiasms and looks. Even his scent, delightfully melon, had stayed with her. In a handful of days he'd become larger than life. Perhaps she'd been wrong to let him go.

Examining his business card, she flipped it over. In a corner, in blue pen, was a dining chair. She spent the day smiling and annotating her script. She wrote until she couldn't resist the minute black numbers for another second.

By 5 p.m. she was driving to meet him in Middle Park. En route through Seddon, she found herself considering cafes for their breakfast the next day: Le Chien, or perhaps Sourdough Kitchen. Unpretentious and thriving, they were typical of her suburb and she hoped he'd like them. The northern underbelly of a highway, tucked between the cafe culture of Yarraville and the Vietnamese markets of Footscray, Seddon was a secret kept by a shrewd few. A secret she was looking forward to sharing. She remembered then, at the Sun Theatre, when she'd told him where she lived, he'd said, 'Sorry, where?' As if Seddon had been created early one morning when the rest of Melbourne was facing the sunrise. As if Seddon were seven hundred rather than seven kilometres from the CBD. On Williamstown Road she laughed, charmed again by his bayside ignorance.

Ten minutes later, snared in five lanes of traffic halfway onto the

West Gate Bridge, she sobered. Sirens were wailing and smoke was wafting from the north. Craning, she tried to peer beyond the safety railings to the world below. Her best friend and ex-sister-in-law, Mira Raison, and her two preschool sons lived in a narrow worker's cottage on Hyde Street in Yarraville. Their home, a car's plunge from the bridge, was nestled between the Mobil terminal and a colony of electricity pylons. Unable to see the pylons through the smoke, Elle's worry grew. Switching on the radio, she learned that a grassfire was burning but contained. As the tension left her chest, she retrieved her telephone from the console. *Mira.* She hesitated.

Amid the crawling cars and thinning smoke, she thought anew of David. She thought of their sex and banter and film talk: a potent and unique combination. But then, with Melbourne's cityscape jutting out in front of her, she thought of his suits. And his clients, and those unforgiving billable hours. Her excitement ebbed. That was a world she thought she'd left behind.

She thought then of her mother. Elegant yet dour, her mother had spent years waiting for her father, a beloved English teacher, to come home each evening. Elle's earliest memories were of her mother banging pots and slamming cupboards a tad louder than necessary. When Leo Nolan did return, around seven, to their draughty house in Kew, a light would go on in Isla Nolan. As a child, Elle realised that parts of her mother were sealed off from her and her younger brother, Jude. And, as she grew, observing her mother's brooding unhappiness, Elle made a decision: when she married things would be different. She would marry a man who 'brought up' the children with her. A man who could be beside her at three in the afternoon on a Tuesday. Perched on that bridge, eyeing his fifty-floor office tower, Elle feared that man was not David Forrester: a *salary man*.

Elle returned her phone to its console. If she spoke with Mira, she would mention David. But sharing him today felt premature. The traffic moved, taking her with it. She was tempted to do a U-turn but her old Valiant was swept over the bridge towards Fishermans Bend.

At Middle Park, the silken bay was animated with racing boats. Yachts clustered in the mid-distance like miniature swans. Ten minutes late, Elle parked and slumped low in her bucket seat. She could just make out the leader of the flock and, fleetingly, she wished she was aboard. Six metres away, David sat cross-legged on a concrete wall and watched the faraway race. She took in his square shoulders, long limbs and tousled hair lifting with the breeze. His nearness returned her to the touch of his lips and the brush of his skin. His presence filling her dining room, her kitchen, her bed. She sat, motionless, listening to her heart thud.

On the horizon, the purple in the sky was tapering now. On his concrete shelf, David rubbed his brow and checked his watch: it was 6.18. The possibility of being stood up was, she suspected, taking shape in his mind. And no doubt he had left Freeman & Milne early for her. She sighed. Four years ago, when she had resigned, she was aware of him. The firm was not known for its lookers, but a pacing Mr Rochester in its corridors was something else again. In the three weeks he was there before she'd left, she'd learned that he was a night owl who eschewed small talk and was estranged from his wife. Shortly after, she'd heard, divorced. Behind him in the lift, she'd noticed his suits were often crumpled and his socks odd. Glimpsing him at his desk, circled by files, she'd gleaned he didn't smile often, for there was a glowering quality to his demeanour. Even then, she had been intrigued.

Across the mouth of the Yarra, refinery chimneys were rising from the water like a distant charcoal kingdom. One light-studded spire rose and plunged as constantly as a slow heartbeat. She concentrated on its rhythm to clear her head, calm her body. She was so, so tempted. She told herself that his glowering demeanour suggested that he was actually unhappy. An occupational hazard. And she was done with unhappiness, giving it up the day she was accepted to do her masters at film school. She told herself they were indisputably from different tribes now . . . Through her grit-speckled windscreen she sneaked another look. David's fine forehead was in his hand. It was nearing 6.30 and the sky's show was almost over. Curtains of darkness were being drawn around him. She watched as he stood tentatively and stretched, showing, she thought, his age.

Three things occurred to her then: if she didn't leave immediately he would see her; it was fear – not his profession or his working hours – rooting her to the car; and, crucially, David Forrester was the most exciting man she'd met in years.

In less than a second, she climbed out. The evening was surprisingly mild. Encouraging. She intended to move slowly and not bed him again – at least, not that night. At a trot, she approached him from behind. She was forty-five minutes late now.

'Wow,' she said loudly, 'you're still here.' Seeing his rugged looks up close, she fought the urge to kiss him. 'I'm so sorry.' She remembered herself, told a half-truth. 'The traffic was shocking.'

'That's okay.' His voice creaked.

'There was a grassfire beneath the West Gate, banking up the cars,' she said, grateful for this fact. She turned to the west. 'Did you see the smoke?'

'No,' he said sheepishly. 'I didn't see a thing.'

'That's odd, it's right there.'

Together they stared across the bay but the smoke had diffused in the night sky. The bridge remained oblivious to the recent drama and was bejewelled as usual with fixed and gliding lights.

'I'm glad it didn't jump the fence,' she said. 'My nephews live across the road from the Mobil terminal.'

'Ludicrous place for children.'

His tone pricked her. 'Not everyone can bed down in Middle Brighton.'

She fell silent. Standing so close to him, she could detect a whiff of alcohol. Perhaps he was nervous too. She surrendered their flagging conversation and took him in. Orange sneakers, washed-out jeans and a misshapen red windcheater covered in Spanish. His style, eccentric and chaotic, seemed fitting. And this clearly well-loved outfit was far preferable to his suit.

'I don't know about you,' he said, 'but I'm starving.' He sprang over the concrete wall to retrieve a backpack from the sand; from it a French stick and wine bottle protruded. 'I hope you like cheese.'

'Absolutely.'

'But first things first.' He tugged something from the backpack's pocket. A modest bottle of sandalwood massage oil. 'For a woman who thinks too much.'

She felt herself blush, and he grinned. Wordlessly, they unpacked what he'd brought: a rug, still sporting its price tag; cheese and bread; pears and chocolate; wine and water. They worked fluidly, without touching. Once the rug was laid, he poured water and passed her a plastic tumbler. His grin at her was so broad that her breath caught in her chest. The sky was turning petrol blue and the air held notes of spring. The moment was like a snapshot. Heightened and pure.

—

Two hours later, David was leaning against a pillar on her porch and watching her. Their evening, having transcended its jitters, was at its next juncture, but she couldn't find her house key. She hesitated, awed. He was framed by the budding white star jasmine that overlaid her porch. It was intoxicating: his glowing brown eyes and creamy, gapped teeth. His maleness. Neither of them spoke. But as the seconds grew she couldn't keep the smile from her face, and neither could he. He seemed to read her and, silently, he made his move. Pulling her gently to him, he kissed her. In the fragrant evening their lips were an even better fit than they had been days before. Pressed together, they filled the gaps in each other's bodies.

After a moment, she withdrew from him and took his thick wrist in her slender fingers. The feel of him excited her, perhaps too much. She thought of what she had learned since their night together. According to Wikipedia, 'Female ejaculation (commonly known as squirting and gushing) refers to the expulsion of noticeable amounts of clear fluid by human females from the paraurethral ducts through and around the urethra during or before orgasm. The exact source and nature of the fluid continues to be a topic of debate among medical professionals.' He'd celebrated her body's cloudburst, and was if anything gratified by it. She'd appreciated his gallantry and felt indebted to him for it. But tonight, with his keen eyes on hers, she couldn't avoid the fact: she'd been mortified.

Her chest thudded. *Whatever happens,* she thought, *I'll cope.* She gestured him inside.

'Another one-night stand?' he said, lightly but unmoving.

She ruffled her hair, mildly panicked, and he smiled. Until now, neither of them had mentioned their first night together, not directly. She shook her head before locating her key and unlocking her front door. When she let the door swing open, he didn't move. Simultaneously, she became conscious of her excitement and his reticence. So she kissed him, insistently, until they were panting. Then, rising to the occasion, she peeled herself from him and cajoled, tossing first one boot, then the other, until, in her hallway, she was performing a homespun striptease. She removed her coat, her lemon A-line dress and her stockings. David watched, delighted at her clowning and the emergence of her skin. Lassoing her warm stockings, she entangled him in their silken strands and tugged. And he was in.

Facing him on her bed, she felt a measure of calm until she saw an extra blaze of intensity in his red-brown eyes. She held her breath as he ruffled her hair, the way she ruffled it herself, so that it stood on end.

'So,' he said lightly, 'what changed your mind?'

Though she preferred to be honest, she was reluctant to reveal so much: that he was, at every turn, disarming. 'I have a weakness for beautiful men,' she said, 'much like my weakness for sugar.'

David laughed. 'I thought you were smarter than that.'

At 5 a.m., she stirred to see the bed beside her empty. Stretching, she touched cool linen and remnant dampness. Some of it was massage oil but most wasn't. At least this time she'd been prepared. And they'd coped. Laughed, even. He was taking pride in the deluges and encouraging her to feel the same. It *was* a feat of sorts, not something to be embarrassed about. And she could see David was determined to interpret it as a good sign. To him, her downpours were heralding what was happening between them: their unlikely union. Perhaps he was right. She'd never had sex like it: his skin on hers was sublimely velvety; his body moved hers in ways she didn't recognise. Naked and with relief, she'd shed all inhibitions, again. Sitting up dreamily, little by little, she took stock. David's clothes remained scattered on the carpet alongside damp towels. But her ensuite was unoccupied. She roused herself. Wrapping a cashmere blanket around her shoulders, she tiptoed from her room. At the end of the hallway, light spilled. Puzzled, she crept towards her study. Naked and reclining at her desk, David was chuckling quietly, her new script in his lap. With alarm, she saw that he was almost finished.

Her voice, stripped of sleep, was loud in the stillness. 'What are you doing?'

'Hey,' he said. 'I love that she's a music biographer and he's been hired to adapt her biography into film. And I love her name, Freddie. This definitely reminds me of something Howard Hawks would've made.' His gaze was steady on hers.

'Does it now.' While her tone was dry, how she felt was less clear – miffed yet exhilarated, perhaps. She coiled the blanket around her.

'*Limerence* is an intriguing title but you never define it. What does it mean?'

She hesitated, surprised. He was right.

He sat up. 'Elle?'

'It's a term coined by psychologist Dorothy Tennov in the seventies to describe that heady, in-love state felt typically in the early days of a relationship, those all-consuming and intense feelings that inevitably pass.'

'Ah. But do they have to?' The force of his gaze belied his playful tone.

'According to Tennov,' she said, her voice cooling, 'for most people, yes.'

'But what about for you?'

'Oh . . .' A frown flickered across her face and she tried to catch it.

That first morning he'd teased her that, as a creator of romantic comedies, she trafficked in false hope. Well, there'd been nothing false about hers. She'd wanted a flesh-and-blood lover, who moved her. But, over the years, she had come to fear her problem lay not in false hope but in her makeup. Prior to meeting David, she had never felt anything like limerent. Now, feeling herself teetering, she was in new territory. She tried to duck his gaze.

'I can't say,' she said.

'You can't or you won't?'

In her chair, at her desk, he looked so damn appealing and cocksure. 'Can't,' she said, squaring her shoulders. 'It's never happened.'

'Really?' His eyes held a fresh gleam.

She had expected a glimmer of amusement or perhaps concern – for himself or maybe for her. But his reaction was more thoughtful. It seemed he could see the cogs whirling inside her, and was savouring the show. Unsettled, she turned from him. She leaned an arm against the doorframe as if to steady herself. She had not expected to share that revelation tonight. She glared at the script in his lap.

'It's not finished, you know,' she said, 'not even as a draft.'

He put the script down carefully. He hadn't intended to read it, he explained, but he couldn't sleep and it was 3 a.m. And he'd wanted, among other things, the night to last. 'But I see that I should've asked.'

'Yes.' She took in his wide-eyed innocence, his bated breath and underlying composure. On balance, she felt it as a small yet flattering theft.

'I like all these squiggly notes you've written,' he said, gesturing to her annotations. But when she didn't smile, he went on. 'I also like the way it's self-referential.' His words gained speed. 'Like Wes Craven's *Scream* movies. You're lampooning those clichés of the genre that I'd never thought about. The contrived way the couple is always clamped together, the heroine's physical transformation, the way the leads' internal conflicts are neatly overcome, without even a shrink, and at the end, in the race to her packed-up apartment, he's running in the street. You've even nailed the girlie soundtrack.'

'I'm glad.'

She retrieved her script and hugged it. A flare of excitement shooting through her. Despite his methods, he was impressive, insightful. Not everyone could read a script. And he wanted to say more. She wanted to hear it too, but equally she didn't. Her only hiccup at film school had been a devastating script assessment by a revered if jaundiced script editor; it had taught her the importance of keeping her own counsel, handpicking her early readers. Basically, she had one: her ex-sister-in-law and best friend, script editor and producer, Mira Raison. Above Elle's desk was the sunny poster for *Daisy*, capturing the rapturous mood of her protagonist, a female dancer. But even that phenomenally successful film had had its moments. *The Australian*'s Michael Schaeffer had called her aspirant characters 'overblown in the tradition of Australian comedies' and put her success down to 'dumb beginner's luck and the film industry's need for a new (female) face'. The Nasty Bastard's stinging attack had felt personal and it had taken her weeks to recover.

David watched her warily. Pale and naked, he slipped from the chair and sank to his knees. He took her hand in his. His grip was tight and warm. Her anxiety dispersed. She found herself awed by his ease with himself, with his graceful if untoned body, and his swinging penis. She was tempted to kneel with him.

'Though I'm not one for romantic comedies,' he said, 'the more I'm with you, the more I fear I will be.' He winked. 'And I reckon you're spot-on. The genre is ripe for an intelligent parody.' He pulled her hand to his lips and kissed her knuckles. 'And that script is the one to do next. No question. It has your stamp on it. Even as an early draft, it's all there. It's funny and fresh and true.'

He fixed his red-brown eyes upon her like a full stop and his face sprang into a smile. A brief silence ensued. Though he had caught her off-guard, he'd told her the one thing that she needed to hear. She gave herself a moment to digest what he'd said and done, and how she felt. In the morning quiet, she was aware that something was transpiring between them, something pivotal and profound. But she didn't know what. All she understood was that, held in his firm grip, she felt his belief in her. It was like the greatest compliment that had ever been bestowed upon her. And it felt, wholeheartedly, like love.

Snippets of memories play around her now, like a montage sequence in one of her films. She was writing at her desk when he appeared at her window, one Thursday lunchtime, with a tray of boardroom sandwiches. Her whole body recognised him: heart, gut and vulva. She was atingle. A week passed. Two. Humming, she snipped a small bunch of star jasmine from her vine and scattered petals through his briefcase. Naked, she sat on him, kneading his shoulders, her breasts tickling his back. The days were glorious and growing longer, the light brighter. At dusk, they were on a rug at the Royal Botanic Gardens. It was all so extraordinary and so enchanting.

At the gardens' moonlight cinema, *Adam's Rib* and *Woman of the Year* were playing. She had him there early, in the lawn's centre. In front of them, the screen was flanked by fruit trees. As they waited, hundreds of movie-goers and a colony of bats joined them. In the growing crowd she became nervous. In almost four months, everything she'd seen suggested that David was a fit for her: from his love of Alice Munro and Mark Rothko to his fondness for hot baths and organic chocolate. And she was not tiring of him – quite the opposite. She'd discovered that in essence he was more artist (or at least aesthete) than lawyer. And she'd been delighted, of course. But did he actually like these films? Films over fifty years old and black and white?

As *Woman of the Year* began, she cleared their picnic dishes. He'd enjoyed her leafy salad, smoked trout and watermelon. All that remained were grapes and half a bottle of white wine. He wasn't much of a drinker, which was good as neither was she. On his tartan rug, she sat between his legs, within the warm cave of his embrace. And waited, her fingers crossed.

The truth was she had always seen herself in Katharine Hepburn. She preferred trousers and was all elbows and knees. She too could be bossy. And she was misunderstood, deemed haughty and aloof at high school and university. As she'd begun the great Kate's autobiography, she'd realised their commonalities ran deeper: she also stood apart from her university peers, when her father died during a gall stone operation, just as Kate had when she found her elder brother, dead at sixteen, tethered to a sheet from his bed. Their independence, forged in the heat of tragedy. And, as she was coming to know David, she could see something of Spencer Tracy in him too. A man's man, with a rich vein of humour running through him; he didn't suffer fools but kept his closest friends for life, apparently. Men like Alex Carras, David's oldest friend (and biggest client), a man Elle was eager to know. During dinner, she'd raced through KH and ST's history as if they were grandparents he was about to meet. She told him that *Woman of the Year* was Katharine and Spencer's first film together. After it they would go on to make another eight. And she told him, blushing inexplicably, that KH had known 'right away' when they started: Spencer was 'irresistible'.

David had kissed her nose and said, 'Yeah, I've read it.'

And she'd laughed, embarrassed. Elated.

When the film began, she felt invested in it, almost as if she had written it herself. As the characters watched a baseball match and sparred, she imagined she could see the first sparks of the love that would come to last nearly three decades. Glancing at David, she hoped that he could see it too. But his handsome face, at rest, was inscrutable. And she felt eight again, bubbling with stories of hopscotch while her mother folded T-shirts without eye contact or comment.

Then he whispered, 'I can see shades of you in old Ginger up there.'

And she felt sated.

A moment later they laughed, together. She floated in relief, until Katharine and Spencer leaned into their first embrace. Around her, the crowd fell silent, enjoying the starry night. She leaned against David and he leaned into her, and a quiet conversation was had by their bodies. Hard to soft, fine-boned to thick. As

Spencer and Katharine broke from their clinch, scattered shrieks and laughter rose from the crowd. Elle could hear loud ticking and clicking. The sounds were familiar but somehow distant, the stuff of memories. They seemed to fill the entire Botanic Gardens. After that, it happened quickly. Water was spraying from a dozen sources across the grassy area. Sprinklers. Their many hidden heads had popped up from the turf in an orchestrated, fine, cool outpouring.

The big screen crackled; Katharine and Spencer dripped then disappeared. The crowd, a sea of contented bodies only moments before, broke up as if a storm was breaking. But among the chaos, the laughter and squeals continued as people ran for the trees and the flower beds out of reach of arcing water. Bats flapped from trees to eclipse the stars.

Elle clambered to her feet, followed by David. To their right, a sprinkler head was whirling. Everything within its reach was soaking: napkins, grapes, blanket, cushions, and them. She took in the joyous pandemonium. Young families, older couples and groups of youths scurried, arms stuffed with cushions and baskets and shoes. She felt the water on her skin and let it linger. She felt the cool seep into her clothes, her skin rise into electrified bumps. She grinned wetly up at David. His eyes were shining and his face was alight; she imagined she could see the beautiful boy he'd once been. Yes, she loved that boy and that man in a way she'd not loved before. This love came from her gut and throbbed. It was as palpable as the sheen on her skin. Delighted by this dawning, she flung her arms around his neck and whispered her love into his ear. His answer was a tightening of his bear hug and she was satisfied.

—

The next morning, they lay side by side in her bed. He passed her sections of her script as he read them. In his hand was a lead pencil; every page or two he scribbled on the pristine margins. She watched him as if he were a human, naked miracle. *Read the newspaper*, she told herself, *or Kate's life story*. But she couldn't. She couldn't look away.

The second time he chuckled she said, 'Where are you up to?'

'Where Freddie meets Mike at the Corner gig.' He smiled softly. 'You've tightened it. It's more fun.'

'And you still like her?'

'Yeah, she's sassy, trouble. Just my type.'

Elle sat back. 'Keep going.'

An hour later, her bedroom was filled with sunlight and he was done. He passed the last page to her with a deferential bow. 'It's good, really good.'

'And?'

'And . . .'

He leaned against the pillow and held her tender gaze. His hair and whiskers were richly brown against the white. She raised her fingers to touch his cheek but stopped herself. *Concentrate.*

'Well, it flags around page forty; I marked the spot. That only lasts a few scenes, maybe fifteen pages. Then it springs back.'

'Okay . . . Yes, I know where you mean.' She nipped her bottom lip. 'What do you make of its theme?'

Watching him think, she was torn between kissing him and prioritising her next thousand questions. He rolled onto his stomach, his face close to hers. Perhaps the real question was: Could he actually articulate it? She held her breath.

'Now, that's spot-on,' he said. With his finger he traced the curve of her jaw. 'Because love is the most transformative thing on the planet.'

Yes, she thought. *Yes*. Her blood was infused with joy. He brushed his lips on her wide smile. 'And I'm your first.'

'Okay, smartie, no need to gloat,' she laughed. 'But what about —'

'How about I let it percolate,' he kissed her again, 'and jot down some thoughts later?'

'Okay,' she whispered, her toes tingling. 'Deal.'

That afternoon, he made her breakfast. She watched him cha-cha with goats' cheese, mushrooms and tomatoes from fridge to bench to stove. The music was his and unfamiliar; pared back yet energetic, Latin. She watched as he moved consistently, un-self-consciously, off the beat.

'Is that for real?' she said.

'What?'

She gave her best imitation of his dubious footwork. He grinned and kept at it, channelling Peter Sellers.

'I auditioned for a Coke ad once,' he said. 'I was seventeen; there were about eight of us. We had to flirt and dance around a kitchen. I gave it my best shot. Then some guy called out, "We'll take all of them but that one." His hairy arm pointed to me.'

She could picture him then at seventeen – fresh, bristling with energy, uncoordinated. She tried to smother her chortle. 'And it's not something you've grown into.'

'Ah, no.'

Her laughter burst into the kitchen. His shortcomings were as adorable as the rest of him. And their existence, a relief. After that, he gave his best hip-swinging, shoulder-jiggling performance. She didn't let him stop until the mushrooms had set and the tomatoes evaporated.

A rumba is playing within her house. In her memory, she'd attributed their beginnings to David's enthusiasm for her. But that, she sees now, is not the whole story. You cannot, she realises, be a passive player in your own seduction.

From the ceiling, she takes in her galley kitchen with its petite, pearly tiles, the gleaming jarrah floorboards, the adjacent shelves of alphabetised films. Setting up her home, she'd thought of herself as successful, independent and happy. And she was. But equally, that year she'd been susceptible. Reckless. In a matter of months, she'd been undone by heightened sex, raw beauty and the first blush of love.

An incredible thing, she thinks, *for an intelligent woman to allow.*

3

Dave staggers from the toilet block. His ageing Merc is as he left it, lights on, door ajar. His briefcase and telephone, his dictaphone and wallet are all there, on the front seat. This on a Friday night and less than a kilometre from Footscray, Melbourne's drug-dealing centre! Nothing about this evening is making sense. Around him, the street's almost deserted. He turns off his lights and slumps against his bonnet. He closes his eyes and sighs, drawing in the night air roughly. His ears, he realises, are ringing. He slides a cigarette from his packet and inserts it between dry lips. *This is going to hurt*, he thinks, *but it'll be worth it.* Nothing like tobacco to sharpen the mind. And it works, by the third long exhalation.

Time to punctuate his story with logic and facts. Principles.

The cases that come to him are inked into his brain, courtesy of his brief and broke stint practising criminal law, long ago.

'See *The Queen v. Keogh*,' he says into his small black box, 'a 1989 decision of the Victorian Supreme Court.' *Provocation is possible with mere words* . . . He's never forgotten it. Keogh killed Cleary, his 25-year-old ex-girlfriend, outside the Coburg kindergarten where she worked. Keogh claimed he stabbed her to death because, when Cleary saw him approaching, she told him to piss off or get fucked. Keogh was found guilty of manslaughter rather than murder and was sentenced to eight years with a minimum of six. He spent less than four in jail.

Dave exhales in one long, slow breath. It seems impossible that he's in the same category as a criminal like Keogh. But if he is . . . He could be out before he's forty-eight. And more than a year clear of the fateful age of forty-nine, when his old man keeled over. Other cases come then too: *The Queen v. Moffa; The Queen v. Schembri*. Moffa, he recalls, killed his wife because she called him a black bastard, threw a telephone at him, and was apparently sleeping with other men. He was found guilty of manslaughter, sentenced to nine, served seven. Schembri strangled his ex-wife when she came to collect their daughter for an access visit. He pled guilty to manslaughter, and was given eight with a minimum of five and a half. *Yeah*, thinks Dave, *there's hope for me yet.* He tries to recall similar, more recent cases but the details elude him. Smoke curls from his cigarette. They will come.

Some people have a head for numbers, some for faces. With him, usually, it's names. Citations. It doesn't make you a good lawyer but it helps with the spin. Elle often said: 'Once a lawyer, always a lawyer.' And she was right. He's mulling over case law on the worst night of his life. The *defining* night of his life. He pictures next year's Victorian Reports and the pithy head note for his case: *Husband strangles new wife in kitchen . . .*

Shadows reach across the bonnet of his car. When they separate, he's back in her kitchen and sipping red wine. It is 6 p.m. Dinner, a pungent marinara, is in a pot. Sunlight spills across the floorboards, capturing her in a golden cloud. 'Look at you,' he says. At the stove, she stirs the cooling cauldron. Rests the wooden spoon on the pot's rim. He waits, not believing what he's seeing. When it finally comes, what she finally says . . . He still can't take it in. What she said and what she made him do. It's like a blind spot in his mind. A pall across his memory: dense and thick.

He stirs. Definitely time for the legal firepower.

Telephone in hand, he searches his contacts. He's relieved to see the number's survived. With a shaky *tap-tap*, he dials. Inhales, waits. It rings. It rings so long it's obvious an answering machine won't be picking up. As he waits, he scans his contacts. They're pathetic; so much for the legal fraternity. The telephone's in his palm when an elderly voice squeaks out of it.

'Hello?'

Dave's right eyelid tremors.

'Hello?'

Reginald Jeffrey Priestly QC had been his dad's closest friend. Dave last spoke with his godfather before Christmas, after he and Elle were married. The two men had talked about Dave's plans for children and dogs and a house at Apollo Bay. He can remember the pride in Reg's voice, and the surprise.

'Hello?' The voice breaks as it rises. 'Who's there?' The phone thuds as if dropped. 'What a pest.'

Dave has seen this man in full flight in court: sure-footed and direct, his cross-examinations pure grace. He can't connect tonight's quavering voice with the booming, black-gowned figure. Ageing is decline in one thousand humiliations. Some, perhaps recently, more dramatic than others. Thank God he was spared the process with his father, dead so young. Some men crumble into old age, some collapse. His faith in his firepower falters.

He fingers his dictaphone. The voice on the telephone snaps: 'Speak up. I can hear you breathing. You're a smoker.'

It's one thing admitting this stuff onto a tape, another thing altogether face to face with a Queen's Counsel. He imagines how Reg's face will become thoughtful as he listens. How Reg will weigh each word, holding it to the light like a jeweller with a gemstone. How, eventually, he'll take a magnifying glass and shine a bright light into that blind spot.

Dave's thumb hovers over the end-call button.

He hears his father's voice: 'Reg likes getting his hands dirty in other people's lives. Me, I prefer their cars.' And it was true; Reg's passion was other people's vices. The grimy and base: gloves off.

'Reg,' he says, his voice a croak, 'it's David Forrester.'

'What a night to be calling. You see that fire?'

Dave frowns. 'No. I don't know.' Over the ringing in his ears, he can make out the wail of sirens. 'Look, I need to see you.'

The old man doesn't ask a question. Maybe he's recognised the breathless tone.

'Give me an hour,' says Reg, 'to feed myself. The wife's at her kid's.'

An hour, thinks Dave. *Too much can screw up in one hour.*

—

Dave parks beneath a tree in a side street. This time, starting the tape, he addresses it to Reg. Nudging the tap, his memories stream. Vivid and bewitching. He tells himself to apply the principles of interviewing – focus on the facts in issue and their precursors. Nothing else.

'It was bliss,' he says, 'for a good three months.'

It was early December, a Tuesday, about 3 p.m. and they were in her bedroom. Late for a meeting in Collins Street, he was towelling himself dry. Only twice had they been to his Middle Brighton house and he hadn't let her out of the car. 'What is the big secret?' she'd taken to teasing, and, 'Who have you got hiding in there?' He'd sacked his cleaner and his gardener in the weeks before they met. And, though he'd lived in the five-bedroom house for six years, his oven trays were still plastic-wrapped. She said she didn't care – 'Let me see.' But he cared. From his circular driveway she'd studied his house, finally declaring his 'mansion' fit for an architectural spread. 'It's stunning,' she'd said, 'but I didn't picture you as a man with turrets.' He'd played along with her banter, knowing she was biding her time. Sooner rather than later he'd have to let her in.

During those early months, he saw that their time was spent wisely – at the cinema, eating out, in her bed. Her time was even more precious than his and she divvied it up accordingly; he was allocated, at best, only two nights each week. She was always having meetings or working on her script and knocking back other people's. She, like everyone else, had high hopes for her second feature. 'Otherwise,' she told him, 'they'll think the first one was a fluke.' Getting the script right was crucial. Without prompting, she showed him her script editor's notes. It appeared Mira wasn't a believer in love's absolute power to transform. ('That's a bald lie sold by too many romantic comedies,' wrote Mira, 'even the ones we like! Aren't we wanting to play with this convention?') Elle had warmed to her premise and he could see she was thrown. 'She's a ball-breaker,' he told her. 'But you can rejig it. It's all there, sweetheart, story-wise. Just adjust the levels again: a little more violin, a little lighter on the cymbal.' He didn't know what he enjoyed more – being her de facto script editor or her relish for his input. Apparently he had the knack. Appeased, she'd rewritten for days.

That Tuesday afternoon, he tugged up his trousers as she watched from her bed. His Italian suit was new, for summer, and she noticed. That morning, she'd commented on his newly matching socks. It was unreal, how much she took in. His suit had fine blue and red lines in the grey cloth, and he matched it with a mauve shirt. She said she liked how his ginger highlights picked up the blues, was reminded again of fire. A contained fire: a gas fire. His star sign was fire and his sign in Chinese astrology was the fire horse, but he didn't believe in that baloney. He didn't tell her about it, not even when she mentioned that she was watery: the fish. He liked the suit too, liked the blues and reds toning together. Beneath her gaze, he matched his tie, his cufflinks, his belt. He tucked in his belly, puffed out the crinkly shirt, and raked his hair. But by the time he was scrubbing his teeth in her ensuite, he was almost angry, drawing specks of blood from his gums.

'Mr Forrester, why do you keep going back?'

When he returned to the bedroom, she shone up at him, with eyes so white he still wondered what she did to them. He sighed. He'd been dreading this conversation. Happy people were sometimes a lot like God-botherers.

He sank onto the bed and she wrapped herself around him. 'It's clear your heart isn't with the law,' she said. 'And misery doesn't become you.'

'I don't know anything else.'

She gave his excuse air, as if it were new to her. 'You can't need the money,' she said. 'Why don't you paint? Or draw? See where it takes you.'

He coloured; did she miss anything? 'I loved to draw as a kid,' he said. 'But since then it's never crossed my mind.' He kissed her forehead and rose.

'Well, think about it.' She flung her sheets and stood with him, perfectly naked beside his suit. 'I'll support you, whatever you choose.'

Looking into her shining eyes, he believed her.

Driving to Freeman & Milne, he tried. He tried to find an answer to his gloominess as if he saw the world as she did. He knew if he came up with something, she'd expect him to move towards it. Drawing or painting. Rising above himself. If only it were that easy. Self-actualisation. Swiping his key at the lift well, he couldn't fathom the first step. He wasn't like her: gifted and brave.

That evening, he lay alone in his bed. It was only a matter of time, he realised, before he disappointed her. He'd guessed, months ago, that his persona jarred with hers: corporate versus creative. Maybe this was the beginning of her push. For change. For his sake or hers, he couldn't tell. His head began to pound.

The pain, throbbing and familiar, was behind his brow. It got worse around sunrise, when he was almost asleep. It shut his eyes and honed his hearing. He could hear everything in his street: the old man spitting en route to his dawn dip, some kid on a mechanised scooter, his neighbours' slamming doors and the crunch of their heels. The smells seeped in after that: the exhaust, the aftershave, the dog shit, and a cigarette smoked two backyards away. His nose became a magnet, his ears antennae, his eyes inoperative.

The pain itself didn't alarm him so much. But its return did. Almost a decade ago, when his headaches first began, he'd attributed them to his ex, her crazy ways. When they persisted after she'd left, he figured it was age. Over the years, he'd told himself that if people could beat cancer or survive an avalanche, he could outrun a headache. It'd become a question of competency, character. But over time he'd lost the battle. Tablets expired in his bathroom and books on the psychology of illness gathered dust on his shelves. Then he met Elle. And the headaches stopped. Or at least, they had.

A week later, he arrived at Elle's house after a tedious day in court. He'd decided midway into his walk back to the office that it was time to let her in a pinch more. He tiptoed into her bedroom to find her reclined, reading the autobiography. He kissed her ear and she kept reading.

They'd spoken only briefly about their families and friends. Fortunately, her headmistress mother was on long service leave in the Northern Territory. And Elle wasn't speaking with her younger, actor brother. A falling-out that had begun when Jude was overlooked for a part in *Daisy* – not because he was untalented; no, he was chronically unreliable. And a drinker . . . Sitting on the bed, Dave dropped his shoes and listened to the thuds.

He had managed to duck her friends as well, crying 'too busy' or 'too tired'. Likewise he'd kept his mates away, forestalling the culture clash. But sooner or later it would happen. He slid his tie from its collar with a cool hiss. He'd have to meet the would-be mother-in-law, the best-friend producer, maybe even the naughty brother. And she would meet Alex. One day, before too long, their sweet relationship would be exposed to the outside world, and their outing would incite expectations. Worse, strangers would try to know him and appraise him. To date, he'd kept his boorish ways in check but that, he feared, could change.

'Everything okay?' She was watching him, of course, from behind her book.

'Yeah.'

He sat then, naked and cross-legged, beside her. He told her about his parents: Bart, the workaholic grease monkey; Lillian, the fussy typist; how they looked like siblings, flaxen-haired and hazel-eyed; and how they loved and fought as viciously. He told her how their love was tangible in their small, picture-perfect house. Photos of them were everywhere – on a motorbike, at the footy, the races. How, when he was five and six, he spent teatime under the table, where he drew their toes or pretended to be a dog. He glanced at Elle and she put her book aside.

'Keep going,' she whispered.

He told her how, one Saturday night when he was seven, they went to a hotel in Port Melbourne. His parents were in high spirits, dressed up. St Kilda had won. Kids weren't allowed at the pub, so the plan was that he'd stay under the table. 'It'll be like our usual game,' said his mum. Dave had his tin of pencils and notepad. If he was quiet they'd give him hot chips and lemonade, and he was always quiet. But as his parents smuggled him towards their booth, he spotted an oil painting. He stopped. In the foreground was a white archway in partial shadow, and beyond it a cobalt sea. Dave had never seen anything so beautiful. Mouth open, he stared. In the busy dining room, his mother became agitated. 'Sit down,' she hissed. But he was spellbound. 'How did the artist make those shadows?' he asked, 'and that creamy light?' His mum shoved him then, hard and low. Her face was so ugly, and as he fell he dropped his pencils. Horribly self-conscious, he watched them scatter. He heard his father curse. If this was a game, he realised, he and his parents were on different teams.

'The waiter helped me pick everything up. My parents screamed at him but he still kicked us out, the prick,' he said. 'After that, Saturday nights, they left me with a neighbour; most other nights I ate in front of the TV.' Seven again, he felt that hurt and his abrupt aloneness. 'My dad died twenty-odd years ago; he was forty-nine. Mum was forty-seven. She's never remarried. I don't see her much.'

Aware now of Elle sitting up, he felt embarrassed and was no longer sure of his point. But it seemed to work. In the silence she touched his cheek with the back of her fingers. It felt to him as if she was making a decision, though it probably happened instinctively. A piece of her dislodged and floated to him; it stretched and wrapped itself around him.

He didn't realise how powerful his revelations would be for her. His pain matched hers in ways he couldn't have foreseen. After his purge they lay together, then to his surprise she opened up. She told him about the wet winter's afternoon she'd returned home from netball, aged ten, to discover her father catatonic on the couch, her brother crying in a cupboard. 'Mum? Where are you?' she'd sung out as she searched their baggy old house. 'Mum?!' It took her brother half an hour to come out of his cupboard. 'She's gone,' he'd screamed, 'and she's not coming back!'

'I felt as though I'd been punched in the kidneys,' she said. After that, she explained, their mother wasn't discussed, though in recent years Isla Nolan had tried to make amends. 'She told me last year that "maternal instinct" was a myth. Like lifelong romantic love. And that her leaving wasn't personal.' Elle's lip was quivering as she added, 'The sad thing was, Dad adored her until the day he died and he never divorced her.' To Dave's stunned silence, she added: 'Perhaps our lineage isn't so great.' She gave him a lingering kiss, 'But we can get this right.'

Dave was struck by their parallel stories and their binding effect. For once, dropping his guard had paid off. He lay with his eyes closed and she stroked his forehead. He slept until dawn.

4

The week before Christmas, Dave had a burst of energy. He tidied his house as if he was putting it on the market. He even bought a vacuum cleaner – his cleaner and his ex must have each had their own. That his ex had taken hers was unsurprising. He was still finding new things missing: his *Great Gatsby*, his Everest photographs. Only last week his favourite Fred Williams had walked. Elle suggested he write a list. And change the locks. But they both knew he wouldn't. He didn't have time for life's admin. In her home, Elle teased him about it as she restocked his toiletries, fed him fruit and poured him water.

But there were moments when he was more than capable. Tonight each living room was a burst of colour – white, orange, yellow – thanks to the tulips he'd purchased for their four-month anniversary. The fridge was stocked with Asian vegetables and salmon fillets for their dinner. He'd bought a wok and the plastic had been unwrapped from his oven trays. The garden paths were swept and the closets tidy – at least on the ground floor. Even his favourite music was playing, courtesy of a group of joyous old Cubans. Chuffed by his efforts, he felt like a fully functioning middle-aged man.

He heard the knock and spied Mr Sheen on the foyer's windowsill at the same time. It was 8 p.m. exactly, of course. She'd been waiting four months for this invitation. He hid the cleaning agent behind a shutter and double-checked the central foyer and its surrounding spaces. The white curtains were open and the sinking sun was pouring its apricot light into the main living room. Beyond the glass, the summery sea was lively. Two large, curved cream sofas faced the window, and a dozen orange cushions sat up expectantly. The glass coffee table reflected the sun without any hint of fingerprints. Across from the main living room, a red-gum staircase beckoned to the upper levels, and ahead was the kitchen. The cigarette butts, empty glasses and dirty laundry were gone and the space looked clean, but empty – only a lounge setting and an enormous flat-screen television graced the nearby family room. At least the walls were dressed. His art was mostly contemporary; his new favourite was a large Tim Storrier that dominated the furthest wall – 'Blaze Line at Williams Creek'. He hoped she liked its contained, fiery beauty, because he loved it.

You couldn't see the mid-renovation flux upstairs from the ground floor, but he'd swept the bare floorboards and rolled the smelly carpet. He'd dusted the bedrooms and tossed throw-rugs over the red divan and two empty bookshelves in the adjacent television room. He'd closed the doors to the two towers. But tidiness could only go so far. Wires jutted from the walls like bones, holes winked in the plaster, and broken tiles were scattered about the third ensuite like lost teeth. *It looks like we ran out of money*, he thought. He'd sacked the architect and the builder and burned the drawings. Whether work would start again depended, pretty much, on the woman at the door.

He would show the view from upstairs last, he decided. And maybe skip the turrets.

Nervous now, he slid the bolts, turned the handle and gasped. On his mat was his ex. Dressed in a purple singlet, blue jeans and thongs, Natasha looked as though she'd just ducked out for milk. 'Aren't you going to let us in?' she said.

Dazed, Dave took in her crimson toenails, long, loose hair and startling green eyes against dusky skin. Eight years ago, when they'd met, she was gorgeous. But lately, she'd turned into a taller, sassier version of her well-fed mother. Next to Nat was her kid, his twelve-year-old ex-stepdaughter. A rookie beauty herself, with her mother's eyes, dressed tonight in leotard and tights.

'Hey,' said Amelia, twirling inside. 'Have you got a new cleaner?'

Dave couldn't move, couldn't speak. He waited for the blow, for Elle to appear and his world to topple. He tried to breathe, to gather his wits. He and Elle had spoken briefly about his marriage. She'd known before he'd told her. He wasn't sure how she knew but he'd been relieved. He'd told her that Natasha was Elle's exact age: thirty-four. That they'd been married seven years when she'd left him, finally, for her dodgy French teacher. Nat, he'd told Elle, had liked to party and was inclined to lying. She was also an untalented sculptor. He'd made no mention of a stepdaughter. Maybe because it would've hurt.

Natasha craned into the house. Hearing the Cuban-Spanish,

she laughed. 'Coming over, is she? Things are getting serious.'

Dave tried to interpret her sharp eyebrows. Was she jealous or teasing? He could never tell. 'What do you want, Nat?'

Natasha smiled bravely as Amelia sprang onto the divan. 'Her dad's stopped paying again.'

Dave looked at his stepdaughter, her hair in its bun. It was a shock how much he missed her. From his pocket, he pulled a wad of fifties fixed with a silver clip. He gave her the lot.

'Ta.' Natasha's fingers brushed his and he took a step back.

'Amelia, sweetheart? Your mum's going now.'

Amelia's nervous frown echoed her mother's. 'Can't I watch some TV?'

'Nope, not tonight.' He eyed the clock again; it was four minutes past eight. His voice hardened: 'Natasha, I'll call you tomorrow.'

'I'd like to meet her.'

Dave understood his ex-wife better than he had for years. She didn't want him, but she didn't want him to move on either. He met her eye. 'Not tonight,' he said. 'Amelia, how about we see a movie next week?'

Amelia, seeing her mother's surprise and guarded irritation, nodded. 'Okay,' she said. 'We're having sushi anyways.' Skipping past him, she kissed his cheek and whispered, 'I hope she's pretty.'

Dave watched Amelia lead her dawdling mother from the house, beyond the gate and onto the street. Love and pain were like laces yanked in his chest. Next time, as much as he adored his stepdaughter, he had a mind to refuse his ex.

He'd straightened one cushion before the second knock. He paused, hearing Ibrahim Ferrer's lilting vocals. If those gifted Cubans could become international hot shots in their seventies, anything was possible. He could find love again, at forty-two. Humming, he strode to the door; for a moment, he feared it might be Natasha, but no, there she was. In an indigo sundress and black sandals, elegant and willowy: Elle. He wanted to coil himself around her. Her eyes were startling against her vivid dress and pink cheeks and huge grin. He could see every one of her teeth. Buoyed by her excitement, he spun her in his arms. 'Hello, you,' she said.

'Welcome,' he said. They both laughed, giddy and close.

'Thank you for finally having me.'

He kissed her nose and reluctantly put her down.

'Is my bicycle okay out there?' she said, ruffling her helmet-hair.

He recalled then that she'd caught the train from Seddon to Middle Brighton and peddled over. Having taken the bike path, she'd entered his property through a beach-side gate.

'Allow me.' He propped her bike in his foyer and grinned. Natasha, no doubt, was hiding behind a tree on the street.

He bolted the door and returned to Elle. With big eyes, she took in his house – the white walls, the Storrier, the sea. He waited for her reaction.

'Mr Forrester, what a beauty . . .'

He smiled as she saw beyond his home's grand bones.

'You, ah . . .' He could see she was tiptoeing. 'You could do with some furniture.'

'Yeah.' To his surprise, he felt disappointment – his and maybe hers.

'You have . . .' she stepped into the space, 'three living rooms?'

'Yeah, and a fourth upstairs.' Her eyes searched his, and they both knew he hardly used even one.

'I like the music,' she said. 'Who is it?'

'The Buena Vista Social Club,' he said. 'You remember them, in the nineties?'

'Ah, no.' She tried for a smile.

'Oh.' He frowned; he'd forgotten their eight-year age gap. She slid her hand into his and squeezed. Too tight. 'So, here we are.'

He led her further into his house. He could see her eyeing the kitchen: the stainless-steel fittings, German oven, marbled bench-top. Fancy taps. The things women noticed. He wondered if she knew how much that unused room had cost. Her brow was crinkled, but not in calculation, with worry.

At the rear of the family room, windows opened to the tennis court and garden, they paused. A path wove around roses, lavender and grevilleas, which were surviving – just. An outdoor setting and umbrella built into the garden were dotted with leaves and cobwebbed. Next to the house a rectangular pool was covered with blue plastic. Sparkling water would have helped the view but it'd been beyond him. Under the cover the blue tiles were most likely green. Though summer was well underway, he hoped he could get away with it. Seeing the faraway look in her eyes, maybe he had.

He waited: a negotiator's trick.

'That's a fine yard,' she said.

His smile was quick and hungry.

'I bet those liquidambars are spectacular in autumn.'

'Yeah,' he said, unable to picture his garden in fall. Maybe, as Nat had liked to moan, he did work too hard. 'Wait and see.'

Spying a stubby beneath a shrub, he steered her back to the kitchen. Pouring the champagne she'd brought, he thought to toast her but couldn't trust himself. He touched his glass to hers and sipped. He saw his house with her in it, and was heartened. Even her bike and backpack looked good in the foyer. This week he was seeing her for a third night. She was, he guessed, making allowances for their anniversary. Or for Christmas. Though her backpack was barely half full.

Beneath his quiet stare, she seemed distracted.

'This place doesn't feel like you,' she said. 'It feels like you're house-minding or squatting.'

'Squatting?' He smiled, unsure how to respond.

'It's not what I expected inside.' She was looking at him closely. 'It feels like an enormous, beautiful carapace.'

He frowned, taken aback. Her directness was a taste he thought he'd acquired. She spoke into her champagne flute. 'How did you end up here again?'

'Natasha was a water baby,' he said, glancing at the street, 'and this was the closest place to the bay we could find.'

'Okay.' Her small nod made him nervous.

'We were going to bowl the house over, but then she decided she liked the architecture. The turrets, as you call them.' He stopped himself. Who the hell cared what his ex had liked?

'It does have a lot of . . . potential.'

She didn't sound convinced. He felt a twinge in his gut as she eyed his house again. The yellow tulips were already drooping on the coffee table. Maybe she could see streaks of Mr Sheen. He held his breath. This house, its view and location: it was the best he had to offer. As it was.

'Ever thought of moving?'

'Well, no. I've worked hard for this house.'

Though it was too big and mostly empty, some of its memories were good.

'So . . . you work in a job you don't like, to own a house you don't seem to live in?'

That one he didn't know how to answer. The mood threatened to dip – his and maybe hers. Abruptly, the CD ended. In the silence, he could smell disinfectant. As the pause grew, he feared the size of the gulf between them.

He reached out to tousle her hair but stroked air. Before he could speak, she was across the kitchen.

'Is that your study?' She was making her voice light.

At the archway, he caught up with her. Within, three walls of bookshelves and a fourth crammed with photographs, pencil sketches and water colours faced them. Seeing the mess, her eyes teased. But, wary now, he said nothing. She stepped over a box of cassettes and frowned. She studied a photograph of a young Muhammad Ali in the ring. Then a photograph of Amelia, aged four, her face painted black and white, a silver All Blacks fern on her cheek. He waited for that question too but, happily, it didn't come. Instead, her eye went to a display of empty wooden frames, hand-crafted. She glanced at him as if to say, 'You did this?' When he nodded, her face softened. She looked then at the other striking thing on the wall. Long and narrow, a life drawing of a woman. She had full breasts, a narrow waist and hip-length, curling hair. She was sitting with her arms behind her and out of sight. Her legs were tucked away and her head turned to the left, taking her face from the viewer. The handful of black lines were crisp and sure.

'Wow.'

He felt her recede as she focused on it. When she read the dedication and signature, he knew he had to speak first.

'She was rather fond of mirrors.'

Was she pale, or was it just the light?

'You've captured her in six strokes.' He couldn't tell whether she was still impressed, or horrified.

'When she left, she begged me for it. And she's stolen it twice. She doesn't like her right leg there.'

Elle followed his hand to the curve of his ex-wife's thigh. 'Looks okay to me.' And then, 'Why didn't you tell me that you still drew?'

'I don't. At least, not any more.'

After a beat she said, 'You must take it up again.'

'No.'

His 'No' echoed in the silence. When she retreated to his books, he felt a squeeze in his chest. Her gaze lingered on his misery memoirs. What would she make of them? Why *did* he like tales of miraculous survival? Or was it the tragedy and hardship? He watched her slide *A Child Called 'It'* from his shelf. Saw her study the little boy's face on the cover. Saw her eyes change as she read the blurb.

'Let's go upstairs,' he said. 'You should see the view from the northern turret.'

'Okay.' Her smile trembled. Maybe she was out of her depth too.

At the front of the house, the sun had almost gone. He hoped the sky would hold its colour until they made it up the tower. Purple and pink fanned out from the horizon. He glanced at her but her face was downcast. The stairs weren't steep but he'd caught himself once, in socks, so he didn't interrupt. Natural light was fading rapidly and he'd forgotten to turn on the lamps. At the landing, the sun disappeared, making the space seem dull and almost derelict. The gleam left the staircase and, as she hesitated, the floorboards creaked. With her back to the windows, she surveyed the bare bedrooms and gutted ensuites, the shrouded television room and half-removed carpet. She put her hand to her mouth.

'I'd forgotten . . . the renovation . . . How long's it been like this?' Her voice seemed tight.

'About a year. When my wife moved out, work stopped . . . I mean ex-wife.'

'A year? But you separated over four years ago.'

'Yeah, we did, but then she came back. And she left again. And came back.'

Her frown was making her features harsh. 'When exactly did you get divorced?'

'Officially? Ah, around a month ago . . .' He'd meant to tell her that night, but they were watching his favourite film, *My Life as a Dog*. She'd been hopping into chocolate mousse.

'A month . . .' The rest of her sentence abandoned her. 'At least that explains the Fred Williams.' She hugged herself.

He tried to hold her eye but she wouldn't look at him, as if the sun were still behind him.

This conversation had caught him off-guard. Perhaps that was the theme of the night. He should've filled her in, from the get-go. Had her over in week one. He sat on the top step. Was this the time? He'd planned to do it over dinner, but dinner was in the fridge. When she didn't sit beside him, he sensed it wasn't. He took a swig of champagne.

'I love you,' he said, 'and I'd like you to move in with me.'

'Oh, David.'

She yanked open the closest cupboard. Washing tumbled out. He recognised long-lost socks. He prayed they were clean.

'Elle, I love you,' he said, more loudly. 'Move in with me?'

This time, her eyes darted to her feet. He'd expected surprise, even hesitation, but not worry. Or was that panic? He laughed, to jolly her along. But she stepped over the washing and opened another cupboard. This time she stood very still. He half expected her to step inside and shut the door.

In the cupboard was a child's clothes hanger with a teeny Hawaiian shirt. His last impulse-buy at a garage sale.

She slammed the door. 'Okay, I have to go.'

He stood up. 'What's wrong with you?' Seeing the fright in her face, he made his voice soften. 'What is it? Is it the house?'

She was shaking her head.

'Don't let it put you off. You could put your stamp on it.'

She chortled, then, and seemed unhinged.

'Elle, we can't keep sleeping over twice a week, like teenagers!' She wasn't looking at him. 'It's not as if we can live in Seddon.'

She looked at him then, squarely. He had a bad feeling he was sneering.

Her head shook again. Her lips were shut but her eyes were full.

'What's the matter with you?' he said again. 'You're like a flighty horse!'

'There's nothing wrong with me!' she yelled. 'You're the one living in this. And you want *me* to put it back together! It feels like she's just walked out – and the bed's still warm!' As she gestured to the bedroom, she knocked a lamp. Its ceramic shade cracked like an egg on the wooden boards. Startled, she shrank from the mess. 'I've got to go,' she mumbled. 'I've got to go.'

She fled, taking the stairs two at a time. He swore at her back and her steps quickened. He picked his way over the lamp. His anxiety and frustration had melded into anger. Over the top. But he didn't care. What was she on about? His divorce? Or his renovation? Or the house? He didn't get it. This was the Golden Mile – home to some of the most expensive real estate in Victoria. With direct access to the goddamned sea.

What did the woman want?

She was out of sight for a second but that was all it took. At the foot of the staircase he heard the thud. Then he saw her. Her long legs were twisted, a foot tangled in her backpack. One arm was wrong, very wrong, at the elbow. Her head was turned, as if she couldn't bear to look. Seeing her on his rug, he froze. The sense of deja vu was so strong. For seconds he stood, caught between a bad dream and the present. Memory and prophecy.

'David?' Her voice was small. 'Take me home.'

He cursed and bent to her.

5

The night is cold and densely dark. The leaden clouds overhead remind Mira Raison of the smoke from melting plastic; they are oppressive, threatening, though not with rain. She forces herself to turn away, as if from an eclipse, and thumps on Elle's front door. Her pyjama-clad boys, aged four and five, sit watching in her car idling at the kerb. Their eyes are big and their little mouths shut. She gives them a tight smile, as she adjusts her trench coat. Beneath the coat, she's in pyjamas too, and braless.

Somehow the highly unlikely has happened.

Twenty minutes earlier, thanks to a random spark and the leaking cargo from an oil tanker named *Eburna*, her cosy house was quaking. The series of blasts at Mobil's Holden Dock rocked her boys' superheroes on their shelves. *It can't be*, she'd thought. Though, of course, she knew it could. She lived opposite Melbourne's largest fuel storage and distribution terminal, where incidents have ranged from escaping gas-like odours to the leaching of fuel into neighbouring Newport's groundwater. Where grassfires have lapped at its boundary. The emergency siren was actually wailing the day she moved into her house, a mercifully affordable house, in her unlovely, wonderful suburb. But, despite the leaks and the near-misses, over the years she'd told herself the likelihood of catastrophe was extremely low. Which is why tonight, with the sound of that siren fresh in her ears, she's rattled.

A risk may be small, she thinks now, *but it still exists. It's real.*

She stops banging, her fist hurting. After the grassfires, Elle had suggested she and the kids consider relocating, permanently. When Mira scoffed at that idea, Elle had, only half-facetiously, devised their personal evacuation strategy. At the first sign of trouble, they were to meet here at Tennyson Street and, together, make a run for it. But back then, Elle didn't lock her doors. Back then, Elle and David had just met. Today, they've finally split and the locked door is one of his legacies. Frustrating. Double-edged.

Mira looks to her grubby white Saab for inspiration. In its recirculating air, her boys are being uncharacteristically quiet. Max, the older one, is still watching her. He's waiting, she knows, for the safe appearance of his favourite aunt. And he's doubly uneasy, adult-less in the running car. She fumbles for her phone. Hopefully Elle is inside, tapping on her battery-run laptop, oblivious to the nightly news and fading light. When the call rings out, Mira gives Max an encouraging wave, then holds her breath and dashes down the side of the house.

As she expects, the rear of the property is also dark. Few if any of the homes she has passed are lit up; the blackout is extensive.

Footscray, Yarraville, Port Melbourne, Spotswood and Newport are out; and the Williamstown and Werribee train lines are at a standstill. The car radio is bleating every few minutes: what to do, what not to do. Starting with, thanks to that ungodly cloud, pull down the hatches and stay in.

Creeping alongside Elle's house, Mira feels the eyes of neighbours at their windows. It's an eerie feeling being out when everyone else is in. Her instinct is to dart back to her children and drive for the Surf Coast. But she won't. Though their half-cocked plan harks back to days when they were closer, she intends to honour it. She won't leave Elle, to be holed up and alone, waiting on the whim of clouds.

She bangs on Elle's side door. 'Hello?' she yells. 'It's me. Elle!'

The sky is holding but it wants to descend; she can feel it. She looks to her phone: any minute now it will beep or ring with information from emergency services. She thinks of the dusty safety brochures on her fridge. Perhaps she was ought to have stayed put.

A flurry at an adjacent, lacy window distracts her. Elle's neighbour, Doris Tippet, is eighty-one and deaf without her hearing aids. She has a dowager's hump, remarkable violet eyes and fine, yellowing hair that is permed once a month, thanks to Elle's chauffeur service. Mira ducks her head but it's too late. Doris waves an arthritic hand at her.

'I'll come out!' she shouts.

Mira considers hiding, with no time for politeness tonight. Then she pictures the reprimand on Elle's heart-shaped face. In Doris's hand-me-down Valiant, Elle helps Doris buy her groceries and do her banking. Even at Elle's most heartbroken and distracted, Mira suspects that she was managing these things.

Doris appears at the lowest section of the grey paling fence and

Mira walks over to her. She feels remarkably tall. Doris is wearing her standard dress: white and covered in purple flowers. Her limbs are mottled a matching colour thanks to large bruises reminiscent of land masses on a map. These bruises are drawn from the edge of the sofa, or a book or the fridge. To Mira's mind, Doris ought to be tended to by professionals in a home, not left to roam with a buzzer around her neck. Once, after a fall, rather than push the button, Doris crawled to her telephone to cancel her hair appointment. Elle and the hairdresser had to break in to scrape her from the carpet.

'You ought to be inside, Doris.'

'I'm not afraid of a puff of smoke,' says Doris.

'I won't keep you, though. Have you seen Elle?'

'Well, no —' says Doris.

Mira feels a fresh nip of worry. 'I thought she was having a night in.'

'Could be she was,' says Doris. 'But he visited earlier. Must've parked around the corner.'

Had Doris been forty years younger, Mira would have sworn. She manages an 'Oh.'

'I considered going over but I didn't have the heart.'

'No.' Mira wonders what she would have done. Facing David was unpleasant but facing Elle after him was worse: Elle's reactions ranged from delirium to indignation to misery. Tough to watch. Badly, Mira wants to kick the paling fence. She scans the encroaching sky. *They could be anywhere now*, she thinks. *Worse, they could be in bed.*

'Thanks for letting me know,' she says as calmly as she can. Then she pivots.

'I didn't see them leave,' says Doris. 'To begin with I was in the sleep-out, folding washing. Then I heard a bit of commotion and it was quiet.'

With a sigh, Mira notes the time on her phone: 6.45. The drive to Troy's at Jan Juc takes an hour and a quarter. 'I need to get going,' she says.

'I couldn't be certain over the music but I thought I heard raised voices.'

Discreetly, Mira eyes the devices perched behind Doris's ears.

'The music is still on,' says Doris. 'If you come down the back you can make it out.'

Mira frowns. It is unlike Elle to leave music playing and go out. But she's had enough of lurking tonight.

'My boys —' says Mira.

'Oh, no you don't.'

Doris grips Mira's arm with gnarled fingers and shuffles towards the rear of the modest Victorian properties. They pass Doris's weatherboard sleep-out, which is adjacent to Elle's glassy kitchen, and there, from behind drawn blinds, is his unmistakable music. Energetic and distinct. Another thunderclap of anger rumbles inside Mira. All those late-night calls, the debriefings around her table when they should've been working, the lectures she delivered when the boys were asleep. This time the break had lasted two months and Elle had made headway. Or so Mira thought.

'You could fit in there, couldn't you?' says Doris, jabbing her hand at six levered windows high in the wall. 'You can slide them out, I understand.'

Mira blinks her surprise. 'I don't think that's necessary.'

Doris trains startling violet eyes on her. 'I wouldn't be so sure about that.'

Mira hesitates and the flesh on her arms goose-pimples. What she saw in David in thirty seconds, it took Elle the better part of two years to see. Much of what she saw she didn't like. But had she somehow underestimated him? Her fingers worry her right eyebrow. She doesn't doubt the intimate, unwitting knowledge of neighbours.

When Doris nods, like a patient schoolteacher, Mira's disquiet grows.

Briefly, Mira revisits the gist of what she knows: the bust-ups and stalemates. Then her mind latches on to an image of old: Elle, wide-eyed and hopeful, yearning to feel what Mira had once felt for Jude. Charming, irresponsible Jude. As if being swept away by love's madness was an appealing proposition. *Did Elle completely outgrow that naivety?* she wonders. Equally, what risk does David pose today? The two uncertainties seem to cancel each other out. She becomes aware of a moment's silence before the male singer resumes his crooning. No other noise is coming from within. And no answers come to her.

Unnerved, she turns from Doris's assessing gaze to the window above her own head. She'd have to climb onto the paling fence, tease the glass from the rusted lever clips, and propel herself headfirst into the gap. At best, if she removes all six pieces of glass, she estimates that the space is barely bigger than a pricey shoebox.

'I've got a step ladder in my shed,' says Doris.

A horn toots from the roadside, and Mira startles. 'That'll be the kids.' She takes Doris's hand in both of hers. 'Doris, the sky has got to us. Enough of this nonsense. No one's going climbing. Now get back inside until the wind picks up.'

With a wave, Mira runs from the crooning old man and the curious old woman.

At the gate, her bitterness surprises her.

Elle, you're on your own.

6

From the rear of her home, airborne and adjacent to her laundry, Elle watches Mira trot to the dusty Saab. She hears the car door snap open and the finality of the slam. She watches as Doris retreats into her sleep-out and hears the latch click. *Come back*, she thinks, *please*.

Mira and her darling sons are poised in the idling car, where Mira is on the phone. Time is unmoving and Elle is heartened; perhaps they won't leave, after all. To Mira, especially, there is much she would like to say.

Abruptly, the old Saab glides away, and Elle tries to glimpse her nephews. She longs to kiss the boys' soft necks, to breathe their angelic breath – one last time. But, to her surprise, she can't move any further from her body. Too quickly, the road is empty.

Mira, she thinks, *I am so sorry*.

—

The day Mira met David was the day after Elle's mishap in his mansion. The day she came home from the Alfred Hospital. A script meeting and a chat with an actor had been scheduled for that weekend, both of which she'd refused to cancel. It was a warm, cloudless and unpleasant December Saturday. Unpleasant because an odour pervaded all of Seddon. Blowing from the southeast, the wind had brought to the small suburb the fumes from the Spotswood and Yarraville Mobil storage terminals. When Elle and David drove up to her sweet little house, refined fuel particles were saturating the air. Invisible and almost imperceptible, the particles were clinging to her rose bushes and the petals of her magnolias, the stained glass above her door and the pickets of her fence. The odour greeted her as she rose, awkwardly, from the car. The bite at the back of her throat was unambiguous: industrial, petroleum-based, foul. Weary from her night in hospital, she felt frustration seed within her. How could this happen, today, in a capital city in a first-world country? Seddon, seven kilometres from the centre of Melbourne, was hardly a remote backwater. But, beside David, she bit her tongue.

In the emergency department her right elbow had been popped into its joint. Now, with her swollen arm in a sling and a directive to rest, she felt foolish for her clumsiness. According to Dr Singh, dislocating an elbow was quite a difficult thing to do. She feared she had dislocated much more.

David had been quiet since her fall. Courteous with staff, he'd fetched her extra pillows and said little. According to the nurses, he'd refused to go home or sleep on a rare spare bed; instead, he lay on the floor beside her like a loyal pup. By the time he escorted Elle out of the ward, he had two of the nurses cooing and clucking.

Although befuddled by the night's events, she'd felt a pang of pride.

'Your place, I take it?' he said, exiting the hospital. His hand was hovering over the indicator, his eyes on the intersection.

'Yes, please.'

She rested her head against the leather seatback and closed her eyes. That she'd been so unnerved the night before had surprised her. But, that morning, she could understand it. The truth was that he had ambushed her. In that graceful, neglected house he was living half a life. And then, the freshness of his divorce. She had felt both sad for him and exposed herself. Which was why, she supposed, she became critical. It was an old habit begun in primary school. (What had her mother called her? A 'hard little girl'.) And lastly, compounding matters, his poorly timed proposal. How she'd yearned to step into a cupboard and disappear. It had felt so flattering and good and so, so bad.

As they wove their way onto St Kilda Road, she thought of his sneer, his need and anger. So foreign and so inflamed. She tried to let the car take her, without thinking. She managed it for six seconds. While gaps in her understanding of him had emerged, so too had gaps in his understanding of her. He knew she had slipped joyfully from the law's golden handcuffs. But he was mistaken if he thought she'd share his overly large cage. He was driving intently now, manoeuvring his classic old car fluidly from lane to lane. Aggressively. She stroked her lip. As stately as his house was, or could be, it was also not what she aspired to – or needed. It was as if he thought, by sharing his career's spoils, she might validate his wealth and overlook his unhappiness. *That*, she had thought, glimpsing his concentrated stare, *would be impossible.*

—

Mira was curled on Elle's decrepit loveseat when they pulled up. She was nursing a casserole, a loaf of sourdough and a roll of film magazines. The magazines, Elle guessed, would be covered in flour and well-thumbed. The casserole would be pumpkin and red lentil. And out of sight in Mira's shoulder bag would be Elle's marked-up script. Raising her left arm to wave, Elle felt her eyes well. With her mother in a remote outback community and her brother busily failing as an actor, this small, wide-smiling, dark-eyed woman was her family. All thanks to the lobster scene in Woody Allen's *Annie Hall*, which they'd both cited as an all-time favourite in the first week of film school. And it had been three days; Elle had missed that sunny face with its blunt fringe and near-black mane.

Seeing Mira's puzzled expression, Elle felt a stab of guilt. She should have insisted that David meet Mira weeks ago. He was always 'in a late meeting' or 'wanting a quiet night', but she should have pushed. Especially as she'd met Mira's Troy Hosking months ago, and their relationship was as fresh. Troy Hosking was their age, a painter of some standing; someone's children were friends with his. Mira had seen his new SUV at kindergarten pick-ups, had liked the wild colours of his scarves, the way he dressed his girls. Prosperity was a relatively new prerequisite for Mira, a legacy of Elle's brother, who had left her with two toddlers. The bastard. Elle couldn't argue with Mira's pragmatism; she still felt guilty and mildly ashamed about her role in that pairing. But Troy Hosking had sounded just like what Mira deserved after two years of punishing single parenting.

When Elle had met him, a week into his relationship with Mira, she was wrong-footed. Perhaps because Mira was so taken by Troy, Elle had conjured an idealised version of the man – tall, intellectual yet earthy, good-looking. In reality, he was a petite, cheery fellow with scruffy, mousey hair. More like an ageing, tradie surfer than a successful inner-city painter. (And nothing like Jude!) Elle had marvelled that there wasn't anything extraordinary about him, except perhaps his wildly colourful beanies and scarves. After a moment, conscious of her critical eye, she'd chastened herself. Because, equally plain, he loved his twin girls and adored Mira. And his goodwill extended naturally to Elle.

Hesitating at her gate, too warm in her sling, Elle observed the shifts in Mira's face. Silently, her best friend and boyfriend each took in the other. David's grey suit pants, striped blue shirt, polished lace-ups. Mira's polka-dot yellow pinafore, well-loved sandals, daisy toe-ring. Their tribal colours.

David was first to the porch. He thrust out his hand: 'You must be Mira.'

Mira smiled politely but her hands were full. 'Hi.' She turned to Elle, her curvaceous mouth stretching to its limit. 'You klutz.'

The women kissed, a touch of lips. With a nod, David unlocked the door and entered. Elle followed, mildly aflutter. These two had to find something in each other to like. In the cool kitchen, Mira made coffee while David answered a work call. A moment later he returned and unravelled the morning's newspaper. To Elle's surprise, he inserted himself at the table between the two women and walled himself behind the *Financial Review*.

'David,' said Mira, to the newspaper, 'I hear you're a lawyer in town?'

'Yeah.'

'What's your area?'

His shrug was noncommittal. 'Banking litigation.'

'Okay, are you for the banks or the little guys?'

'The banks.'

'Oh.' Mira glanced at Elle in mock reproach. 'You must be busy.' Mira's grin was infectious and Elle caught it.

'That's the way we like it,' said David. He squinted at the share prices. Seconds passed. Mira considered him then, as if he were encoded. Elle's grin vanished. Mira's glance swung from David to Elle's arm, like a pendulum. Elle realised her text message had been too vague. 'So, guys,' said Mira, 'tell me the story. What happened here?'

Elle glanced at David.

'She fell,' he said.

'Okay . . .'

The silence deepened. Elle was getting hot. 'I was dancing,' she said loudly, 'and I tripped on my backpack.' She kept her gaze on David, who was puzzling over the fine print.

Mira frowned before lobbing another question. 'And where were you,' she said to David, 'when all this *dancing* was going on?'

'Don't worry,' he said, dipping the newspaper. 'I was there.'

Mira's large mouth stilled, then curved, almost comically, downward. Confused and increasingly embarrassed, Elle glanced to David. But he was obscured again by blocks of black print.

Mira sipped her black coffee. 'What sort of dancer are you anyway?'

Elle shot a smile at David.

'Not so good, it'd seem,' he said, as he turned the page.

Mira looked to Elle, this time, as if to a translator. Elle sat up, crossing her legs. They waited. Yes, Mira was being cheeky but she was harmless. Surely he had to give her something?

David inched his chair from the table, presumably to better

read. At a loss, Elle rubbed her arm in its sling. Mira's lips remained steadfastly closed. After a moment, David crashed the newspaper into a folded mass.

'Excuse me, that's my phone again.'

As he left the kitchen, the women heard his friendly greeting. Elle laughed nervously. 'He's not one for small talk.'

'You can say that again.'

'I'll have to, ah, train him up.'

'Oh, yeah.'

When Mira rose to clear the table of its two mugs, Elle's smile was rueful. 'I'm sorry for not introducing you two earlier. I . . . I wanted to be sure.'

Mira nursed Elle's empty mug. 'And now you are?'

Elle stood, smiled. Her voice came out too loud again: 'Yes.'

Mira's already husky voice dropped an octave. 'You're actually *in love*?'

Heat rebounded in Elle's cheeks.

'He's not what I'd expected,' Mira said.

'No.' Elle wondered if she could see disappointment in Mira's shapely lips. 'But we have a wonderful time. We're quite different, but we fit.'

After a pause, Mira put the crockery into the dishwasher. 'I can see one thing you like about him.'

'You can?'

'He's certainly easy on the eye – if you like that sort of thing.'

Elle waved, feigning indifference.

'Bring him over next week for paella,' said Mira. 'Troy'll get a conversation out of him.'

'Sure.' A stone plunged into the well of Elle's stomach.

When Mira's smile was a tighter version of her own, Elle made a decision: etiquette mattered. She would tell David she expected nothing less.

She rolled her right shoulder in its socket. 'Can we chat about the script tomorrow?'

'Yeah, you duffer.' Mira took the draft and her notes from her bag. David returned then to top up his coffee, with work to do.

On the porch, the women's hug was long. But, once Mira was gone, Elle felt herself relax. The scrutiny was over.

After a fitful afternoon sleep, she rose to find him in the kitchen where he was dancing among bags of groceries. She saw nothing funny then in his hammy cha-cha. Bemused, she watched as he unpacked full-cream milk, wholemeal bread, potato chips, chocolate ice-cream, recycled toilet paper and vegemite. Plastic bags flew in the air around him like bubbles. She opened her mouth to speak but he kissed her moving lips and headed out. When he returned from the car again, he had his laptop and three bunches of tulips – yellow, orange, white. Recognising the flowers as those from Middle Brighton, she smiled. A cautious smile.

He grinned. 'Well, I'm glad you at least like these.' His face sobered. 'You don't look so good. You hungry?'

'I could be.'

He pulled out a stool. 'Here.'

She sat at her bench while he chopped vegetables. The knife moved up and down unsteadily in his hand, and irregular chunks of carrot, mushroom, onion, broccoli, asparagus emerged. Elle watched, assembling her thoughts. She didn't comment when he forgot to wash the broccoli, or the carrots, not even when he dropped a handful of sliced onion on the floor, picked it up and tossed it in the wok. Finally, she said, 'Your behaviour's been rather odd, Mr Forrester, don't you think?'

'It has?'

'Yes, both last night and then this morning.'

'Ah, last night.' He shot a sideways look at her. 'Clearly neither of us was at our best.'

She pursed her lips. 'Perhaps not.'

'I guess,' he said, 'that was because I jumped the gun.'

'Yes, in part.'

Unsure of him, unsure of herself, she had nothing to add. What difference would words make to that hollow house? Silence fell between them, dense and bottomless as quicksand. She didn't dare move.

'And this morning with Mira, you mean?' he said. 'I wasn't in the mood to be sized up.' Onion sizzled and he tickled it with a wooden spoon. 'One look at me and she'd made up her mind.'

'Mira's not like that.' That was true: Mira was not so quick to judge. But Elle paused. She was reluctant to discuss his otherness. 'And she's my closest friend . . .' Her script was tucked beneath the toilet paper; she picked it up. 'The first reader of my scripts.'

'So?'

'So, you were rude. You have to at least make an effort with her,' she said. 'With all of my friends.'

David paused over the wok. 'I had things on my mind. Alex was in a spot and —'

'You were reading the paper.'

'I love you. I want to be with you,' he told her. 'I'm not that interested in your friends.'

Elle stared at him in silence. Again she was wrong-footed. If he loved her, wasn't that a reason to know everything about her, including her friends? Wasn't it a reason to behave well and impress them? She thought the real reason behind his reluctance to meet her friends was shyness or caution. And that would change. She sighed. What did love mean to him?

If only she had the vocabulary for these conversations. If love wasn't driving his behaviour, what was? His red-brown eyes were on her, his wooden spoon in mid-air. He was waiting for her to reciprocate. This alluring, wounded man. Perhaps he was like her: afraid. Her right arm felt heavy and her elbow throbbed faintly. Regardless of its origins, his recent behaviour was disturbing. She hoped she'd seen the last of it. She adjusted the sling across her shoulders.

'I don't think making an effort is unreasonable,' she said. She put steel in her voice. 'We'll have dinner with Mira and Troy next week.'

'Okay, if you insist.'

He kissed her cheek and began to whistle. He spun plates onto the table and juggled knives and forks. He opened a bag of potato chips and crunched. Wooden spoon in hand, he helped himself to white wine and filled her glass. In the small kitchen he was everywhere at once, like a benevolent octopus. Stirring, crunching, sipping, whistling, sizzling, pouring. As the minutes passed, he filled her space so completely, she found herself wondering how strange and quiet it would be without him. How empty and how wrong.

As the day's heat faded, he hired *Doctor Zhivago* and set her up on the couch. Amused by his ministrations, she requested extra cushions. When, midway through the epic, he called an intermission, offering to make iced chocolates, she laughed and took him up on it. Later, when he said, 'Take off your sling, I'll massage your shoulders,' she acquiesced again – milking his grand gestures for all they were worth. Long after the credits rolled, he kept at it. Until she was on the cusp of sleep. And all was indisputably forgiven. Then, unasked, he carried her to bed.

At two the next afternoon, Elle heard a toot and grabbed her bag. A moment later she was beside Mira in the old Saab. The day was hot again but the air was clean, the odour gone. With no air-con, they drove, windows down. They had twenty minutes to get into town. Perfect for an efficient meeting.

'Thanks for your notes,' Elle sang out above the airy thrum. 'I'm glad you think it's getting close.'

Mira dodged Sunday cyclists on Charles Street. 'Yeah, it is. Only thing is Freddie's expectations make her seem overly fickle now. But you can fix that.'

'Mm.' One-armed, Elle hugged herself.

'When Freddie asks, "What is true love?" at the midpoint, it gives the whole thing shape.' Mira eased the car behind an idling bus. 'I still think we can play with her transformation more.' Mira's glance Elle's way was stealthy. 'Show how hard it is to be vulnerable. Especially if you're damaged goods . . . Make it more realistic. Most people like Freddie, in real life, can't do it.'

Elle frowned. 'You want her to struggle more?'

'Yeah. But she can't be too broken. Just grappling to let her true self come out.'

Elle was holding her breath now until the bus moved off. True self, false self: she was uncomfortable with that terminology today. Or perhaps she was merely lost in semantics. After a moment, she drew a breath and nodded. Mira turned right into Buckley Street.

'If we go with Lucy now, everyone else will come on board. You give the script a quick tweak and I could make the next round of funding. If we get through, we could make a June shoot.' Mira braked hard at a red light.

'Why the rush?'

'It's Lucy's only window this year.'

Elle straightened her back, which was sticking to the seat. Before too long, she could see the industry of the port. Endless massive containers of goods needing homes. She let her breath seep out. Acclaimed London-based actor Lucy van den Berg was Mira's first choice for Freddie. But Elle had enjoyed *Daisy*'s low-key cast of unknowns. Launching stars seemed more appealing than accommodating them.

'What do you prefer again?' She was, she knew, deflecting her anxiety. '"Can men and women just be friends?", or "Why do men cheat?"'

'I prefer *Moonstruck*. Fear of death.'

'That's right, and I prefer *When Harry Met Sally*.'

She stroked her sling. A grin under-lit Mira's face. The wholesale produce markets passed them in a blur. Sunday-empty. Elle exhaled silently, feeling the heat.

Ten minutes later, Elle and Mira were cooling in the royal suite of the historic Hotel Windsor. And Lucy van den Berg was chatting happily: about the script, about *Daisy*, about being home in

Australia. Balancing tea and a scone, Elle studied the 24-year-old. In each of Lucy's films she was like a vision, straight out of the Golden Age of Hollywood. Fair skinned and black-haired, she had looked effortlessly beautiful, swanlike. Usually in corsets. But today Lucy was in cropped jeans and a black shirt. Her hair was messy and she'd had a fringe cut.

Elle tossed a look to Mira. She'd been uncertain whether Lucy's refined, historical beauty could be transposed into a contemporary, sexy comedy – albeit one with retro tones. But today, without a skerrick of makeup, Lucy was a fifties tomboy. Mira grinned back, and Lucy demolished a second scone. As they chatted, Elle focused on Lucy's navy blue eyes, her clear, rapid-fire delivery, her subtle, masculine gestures. Apparently, Lucy particularly loved Freddie's romantic idealism, her passionate independence. And she related to her quest for love. When Elle or Mira spoke, the young woman was all eyes: an active listener. An accomplished method actor . . . But was she Freddie?

Lucy licked jam from her fingers.

'A personal question,' said Elle, 'if you don't mind?'

Twin lines appeared in Lucy's creamy forehead. Above her nose, like minute parallel bars. 'Sure.'

'Have you ever actually been in love?' said Elle. 'I mean, completely besotted?'

Lucy hesitated, then her navy eyes became huge, erasing the lines. 'Yeah. Scared the fuck out of me.'

Mira laughed, Elle too. The answer: pure Freddie.

Lucy stood to retrieve a parcel from her bag. 'Here, I've laid down a few scenes for you. The one where Freddie meets Mike at the gig. And a later one, showing her softer side, where Freddie realises she's found her "big love".'

'Oh.' Lucy had pressed, agent to agent, for this 'chat'. Rarely these days did she need to audition. Flattered, Elle took the DVD. 'Thank you.'

Back in her Saab, Mira was driving like a delighted demon: tailgating, slamming on the brakes, accelerating in bursts. Talking nonstop. They were at Mira's in nine minutes. Pulling up in Hyde Street, Mira yanked the handbrake. 'What's your problem?'

'I'm not sure I have one,' said Elle. 'Except . . . she's a star.'

Mira considered Elle as if she were speaking Mandarin. 'Audiences love Lucy. Distributors, funding bodies – everyone loves Lucy.'

In the hot unmoving car, Elle ruffled her hair, at a loss.

'Not only is she a star,' said Mira, 'she was brilliant. And she looked exactly like Freddie.'

'Mm.' Elle tweaked her sling, which was digging. 'She had her clothes.' Truth was, with her mass of black hair and blunt fringe, Lucy looked like Mira: a taller, more beautiful, blue-eyed Mira.

'But she wouldn't be here for the auditions for Mike, didn't her agent say?'

'I'll follow up on the actor she was raving about. The one she met last year at Tribeca. Jay someone.'

'At least he's not a star, I suppose.'

'Okay, that's enough. We have to watch this, now.'

Back home, Elle was grateful for some peace and air-con. In her kitchen, she lured David from his laptop with a smuggled scone.

'I hate to agree with Mira,' said David with a quick grin, as he logged off, 'but Lucy van den Berg is a sensation. I saw her in the one last year, set in Paris.'

'Yeah. She was great in that. Pipped at the post for an Oscar.'

'Und zee vun about zee Russian Revolution.' His accent was so dreadful, Elle laughed.

'But,' she said, 'she's nothing like the Freddie I'd imagined. She's so . . . I don't know. Young and striking. I saw Freddie as, well, short with freckles.'

David swept Elle into his arms and waltzed her, gently if awkwardly, around the kitchen. 'No one says no to Lucy Lu,' he sang. 'Having her would be a coup.'

'I haven't said no! Not yet!'

'Gut, gut,' he said, dipping her, more or less.

Despite herself, she laughed. How did he do it? Get to be so incredibly silly *and* incredibly sexy?

That night, Elle watched the DVD again, with David. When the first scene finished, Elle could see that David, like Mira, was irretrievably smitten. Lucy had captured something of Freddie – her swagger and fragility. She had a deft comic touch. And she'd taken risks. Made the young biographer's flirtation almost rude. Lucy did it again in the second scene, this time revealing Freddie's excitement at finding love. Yet softening her. A dozen times, Lucy was dazzling. Preposterously. By the thirteenth viewing, Elle, like Mira, like David, was sold.

If only, Elle thinks now, she could put it in context. Back then, she had desired David more than she had ever desired any other man. Daily, he was enmeshed in her thoughts and nightly he was in her arms. Aged thirty-four and ripe for love, finally, she'd found it. He was her lover, her sounding-board and her new best friend. She reworked her script each day and, each night, he was beside her – reading, commenting – until the final draft was done. ('Freddie's pretty strident, Ginger,' he said, not long after Mira lodged their funding application. 'If you can, you might want to tone her down a bit. Got to avoid that overblown tag.') Quickly he became an integral part of her process, and her life.

But sharing her home was new too. And she was affected by every irksome change – the abandoned lace-ups mid-hallway, the endless washing of singlets, his nasty white bread. At times she panicked, confronted by his briefcase on her bed or his dictaphone by the bath. While she had craved intimacy and she loved it, it also terrified her. She had no idea how to do it. If only she'd been game to admit as much to Mira.

7

Dave is due at Reg's in nine minutes. It'll be tight, but he'll make it. The southerly drive from Yarraville to Williamstown is only five kays along Williamstown Road, which runs under the foot of the West Gate Bridge and turns into Melbourne Road through Newport. Driving, he feels better. Clearer. That noise in his head has gone. *Reasonable men kill sometimes*, he thinks. *When they're pushed.* It strikes him then: he didn't kill that glorious woman. He killed an imposter. He curses his steering wheel. It's fucking criminal – how she was when they began is so bloody unlike who she became. That shrew. She became so fundamentally other, she must've misrepresented herself from the get-go. There ought to be a law against misleading and deceptive conduct in love and romance. And a penalty: a big one.

The narrow backstreets are surprisingly bare. There's nothing but dim houses and parked cars. No chatting neighbours or home-bound Friday night commuters. He thinks of Reg's question about the fire. Tonight's stink is sharper and more bitter than usual. It could be coming from any dodgy factory or storage site. *It's time*, he thinks, *to be off the road*; he's far too conspicuous. He weaves his way over Somerville Road and onto Williamstown Road. He's putting his mind to his opener for Reg when he sees a car in his rear-view mirror. It's about 100 metres behind him and gaining ground. It's a Holden, late model, white.

He accelerates. Ahead blue and red flashing lights whirl at the Francis Street intersection. Stupidly, he speeds towards them. As he approaches, he can make out barriers blocking the city-bound lanes. Police cars forming a road party on the bitumen. Two pairs of cops hanging about.

Too late, he realises the lights are changing.

Oh fuck. He thinks to spin his steering wheel, do a burn-out, until he remembers that car in his rear-view mirror. He plants his foot to run the red. But, at the last minute, he changes his mind and brakes hard. His car skids. *Sweet Jesus*, he thinks, *what am I doing?*

Thankfully, the road-side cops scarcely consider him. They're deep in conversation, on the other side of the barriers. But that white car pulls up and its driver stares at him. He trains his eyes ahead and locks himself in. He finds a cigarette and smokes, Mr Casual. He doesn't look at the stains on his shirt or the scratches on his arms. But his gaze drops to the dictaphone on his dash. It's only half-done, his defence only half-baked.

He's not ready yet for the boys in blue.

He peeks at the driver and briefly his panic abates. It's a woman; alone, in uniform. She's in her mid-twenties, a ponytailed blonde.

Pretty for a cop. He waits. Her car seems to be floating next to his. In the long moment, his cigarette hurts his throat and he longs to toss it. He takes another drag and eyes the lights stuck on red. A fire engine zips through the intersection on the wrong side of the road, followed by two more cop cars. He studies the tip of his cigarette. All the while, the others – all men – talk heatedly while the woman gawks at his profile. His right eyelid jiggles.

His is the only normal car on the road.

When she looks across to the small uniformed group, he senses she's dithering. But what will tip her hand? His thoughts scurry until he has a good-enough idea. With his left hand, he finds his phone's earpiece and puts it on. He speaks. Chuckles. After a moment he glances at her openly and she's gawping again. He grins. *This one can talk*, say his eyes, or so he hopes. She frowns then, understanding, smiles. Seeing her wide, white teeth, he's encouraged by something he learned in Evidence 301, more than twenty years ago. The looks of an accused can be decisive. As if ending his call, he murmurs his goodbyes and taps his earpiece. Then he makes his smile to the girlie cop natural, genuine, interested. If he can count on one thing in his life, it's his ability to attract. At least, at first.

He waits, and she looks to the sky. He copies her. The sky is closer and heavier, more like smoke than cloud. That fire is nearby and nasty. She focuses ahead, and he sees then the whirling lights at the entrance to the bridge. And that's when it hits him: he's as good as stranded. Stuck in the west, with the bridge and who knows what other roads closed. Stranded, maybe permanently.

Thank God for Reg.

But he's not there yet. Abruptly, the men trot from the barriers to one of the two parked cop cars and further away from him.

The girlie cop watches them. What, he wonders, is she going to do? What if she follows him and pulls him over? Then what? He doesn't have a plan. That's been the story of his night, maybe his life. The lights turn to green and he waits. She glances his way. He gives her a salute. When she drives off, she has a teeny smile on her lips.

He shakes his head: for a moment, he actually had his doubts. But he's still got it. He drops his window, flicks his butt. *Silly bitch.*

Dave sits in a front room in Reg's renovated Edwardian. In centre place is a billiard table. A game is underway but God knows Reg isn't playing. Reg is not the man Dave remembers. This Reg Priestly is shrivelled and grey from the tip of his peanut-shaped head to his crumbling chin. A walking frame had greeted Dave in the foyer, dusty and derelict. At least there was nothing wrong with the Queen's Counsel's hearing. As the doorbell chimed, Reg had bellowed and Dave had snuck in.

'You need to brace yourself, Reggie,' he'd said.

'Pull up a pew and shock me.'

Dave had sidled into the well-lit sitting room and said, 'I've killed my wife.'

With the words uttered and heard, he'd felt more resolute. Reinforced. This much he'd rehearsed. He hadn't planned on much more. The old man had said, 'I'm sorry to hear that. I thought you were settled.' Then he'd gestured to an armchair, and offered tea. To Dave, it felt as if the burden he'd shed was threatening to boomerang. Was the QC's detachment merely professionalism? He couldn't tell. He'd never been good at detachment. At Freeman & Milne, his clients had soon learned that no matter how valuable their business, he wouldn't pussyfoot around them. He told them when their cases were screwed and their decisions idiotic. And they liked it. His unrestrained reactions, so unwelcome in his private life, were the makings of his legal career. For a time, at least. In that games room, Dave understood why his own irreverence had worked. Who didn't want their load shared?

'Intimacy is a dangerous thing,' says Reg, pouring tea from a pot. In the warm room, Dave stares at a steely piece of hair high on Reg's part. Badly, he wants to pat it into place.

'Well, obviously it was for us, we —'

'You should stop there,' says Reg. 'Now I'm retired, privilege probably won't annex this conversation from prying coppers' eyes. But I can give you a number —'

'I don't care about privilege. I want *you* to tell me where I stand.'

Bemusement fans from Reg's eyes. 'You do, eh? Very well, go on then.'

'In a nutshell, she pushed me past the point of no return. And I lost it.'

'Lost what?' Reg's tone is soft yet deft.

'What do you think?' Dave bounces his gaze at Reg. 'Control of myself.'

'Ah,' says Reg, his lips turned down. 'I gather you weren't in Sydney at the time?'

Dave feels a fresh wave of unease. 'No. Why's that?'

'Victoria gave away the partial defence of provocation back in November 2005,' says Reg. 'Tasmania did it first, in 2003. Gone in WA now too. It is, by the way, under review in NSW.'

Dave curses.

'You missed the Ramage case, I take it. That put the nails in the coffin of the partial defence in Victoria.'

'Fuck.'

Of course. Dave can remember the case now; the husband had looked familiar, like one of his clients. White, middle-class, moneyed. Only vaguely can he recall the wife, who had the nerve to leave him and find a new lover. But the manslaughter conviction he can recall; that and the furore.

The law reform, though – bugger it, he'd missed that.

'We live to higher standards today.' Reg focuses in tight on David. 'You cannot kill your wife because you have lost control *of her*.'

Beneath Reg's stare, Dave is conscious, all at once, of how he feels at his core: sour and ashamed. Head down, he walks to the fireplace.

'And we,' says Reg, 'cannot continue to blame women for their deaths.'

Dave wants to yell: *Why the fuck not?* He tries to focus on the mantelpiece and two rough-hewn picture frames. Familiar, old. Made by his dad, or maybe him. In a backyard shed, in companionable silence. Dave squints back at Reg. Beyond that shed, the silence was unremitting. *Why didn't you call the old bastard on his behaviour? Or doesn't intimacy have strings attached?*

As if sensing Dave's belligerence, Reg continues: 'But provocation is not entirely gone. It'll be taken into account in sentencing.' Reg tugs at his wayward lock. 'And, as old FW Maitland observed in 1909, "The forms of action we have buried, but they still rule us from their graves." The same may be true of your buried partial defence, regrettably.'

'What does that mean?' says Dave.

'That the flaws of the old substantive criminal law may yet be transferred into the law of sentencing. It is too early to say.' Reg shrugs again. 'But victim blaming is proving hard, extremely hard, to exorcise.'

Dave wonders how convincing he could be. His word against a dead woman's. Her silence is a boon and yet even in death . . . it's not absolute. 'And if the judge doesn't buy it?'

'Murder, and a sentence to fit the crime,' says Reg. 'Provided no other defence applies.'

'Fuck,' says Dave. 'Fuck, fuck.' He covers his face with his hands, a child trying to hide. 'What would I be looking at?'

'Difficult to say without all the facts. Around twenty years with non-parole of sixteen. Could be more, depending on who you get.'

When Dave curses again, Reg retrieves a miniature pink cushion from his chair and rubs it across his fingernails.

'I know this is upsetting. But let's take it slowly, shall we? What happened this evening, precisely?'

Dave glowers as Reg's right hand moves rhythmically across the fingernails of his left. Reg's nails are not too long, not too short. Dave has never noticed how womanly the old man is. Agitated, he walks tight circles around the billiard table. Tries to focus. Quickly, he's irritated by the over-furnished sitting room. The austere leather armchairs, fusty crystal decanters, and carpet of salt and pepper dog hair. His gaze snags on a photograph on the mantelpiece of Reg's third wife; she's at a party, with a tray of cocktails. June Cahill, a spritely, wide woman, was a magistrate, he remembers now, until she retired last year to look after Reg. Even the old man has someone.

'Now, she was my smartest decision.' Reg seems to be waiting for a response. Any response. 'David, she'd left you, I take it? When?'

Dave scowls at June. 'Does it matter? The fact was she'd promised she never would. She was my *wife*.'

Reg clicks his tongue. 'Two people can be so fused it's useless. Like a pair of melted candles.'

'You think?' Dave pivots the photo out of Reg's line of sight.

Reg moistens his lips. 'I gather you were hoping for a reconciliation and she was being *difficult*? What precisely did she do or say?'

Dave fishes in his pocket. 'Look, it's all on the tape.'

He skids the dictaphone across the oak coffee table. To Dave's surprise, Reg catches it. He considers it as if it were a gem in the rough, before putting it on a sideboard.

'I can't rot in jail until I'm sixty-odd.'

Dave turns his back to the old man's fresh concern.

'How it happened,' says Reg, 'what happened, who you are, who she was – it is all still vitally important. Judges are people too. That old defence is buried but it could do a dreadful haunting.'

Dave can hear that Reg is genuinely engaged. As if the Queen's Counsel still has something to offer. He wants to shove the old man back on his haunches. Reg resumes buffing his nails. 'In my experience, it is far preferable to face consequences than hide from them. Naturally, your garden-variety crook tends not to share that view.'

Dave focuses on the sliding pink cushion. He has an urge to grab it and dunk it in his tea. He resumes circling the room.

'Do sit down.'

Poor Reg. Isn't it obvious his case is fucking hopeless? But then, he has nowhere else to go.

'I can't help you if you don't tell me.'

Stymied, standing, Dave can see no way around it. He sighs.

'Okay, we broke up about two months ago. I hadn't seen her . . . until today.' He shakes his head. 'She looked like a dream, in this clingy navy dress. She'd been cooking spaghetti marinara. I was a bit shocked, I guess. She looked . . . fantastic.' He spits the word, and stops. 'We had a chat but pretty quickly it turned. She didn't want anything to do with me. She was icy. And sure.'

Reg's gaze travels from Dave's hands to his torn forearms and wet shirt. It lingers on his shirt and shoes – both damp and rinsed thanks to Reg's garden tap. Dave's face grows hot.

'Look, she told me to fuck off, then she threw her telephone at me, called me a coward —'

'Is that so?' Reg's brow is pinched but uncommitted.

'Yeah. So I shoved her, okay? To shut her up. She hit the floorboards, hard . . . I strangled her on the kitchen floor, okay?'

'Natasha was hospitalised once, wasn't she? A broken nose?'

'I don't remember!'

'Are you sure she is dead?'

Dave glares. The QC is like a veteran boxer, jabbing away, his technique impeccable. That blind spot threatens again. This time, his anger keeps it away.

'Yes, I'm sure.'

'And where is her body now?'

'At her place, in the laundry.'

'The laundry? What happened after you strangled her?'

Dave's eyes narrow. What has he done? He should never have forsaken his uncritical dictaphone for a QC. He has, he suspects, made a big mistake. 'I need a shower.'

Perhaps to mask his surprise, Reg studies the dictaphone as if he's just detected its teeny flaws.

Dave says, 'Listen to it for God's sake!'

'Yes, yes, very well,' says Reg. 'But I'll get you a number. Another silk: Sheila McCarthy. You should speak with her before you turn yourself in.'

'No.'

Reg's gaze is reassessing, but Dave's had enough. He's at the door when Reg sings out, 'Don't take too long, David. I won't be calling anyone, mind. But how you conduct yourself now is a factor to consider in your sentencing. Remember, every minute counts.'

In the unfamiliar house, Dave slams his way down the hall.

8

Elle hovers forlornly above her wall-hung dryer. Outside, the night is cooler and deserted. Nothing is moving, not even a possum. Despite the dozen small houses nudging against hers, no one besides Mira and Doris knows her intimate routine. No one else knows to rap and shout. No one else will be looking. But perhaps that's not so bad. She's not ready, she realises, to be found – to be publicly dead.

As if from a vast distance, she considers her body, flush against the washing machine. It's covered, torso to thigh, by a green towel. She sees the back of her head, the skirt of her navy, woollen dress and elliptical soles of her feet.

There is something about my body, she thinks. Something I'm not seeing.

—

The faint feeling of unease returns her to a Saturday, late in summer, at breakfast. They were sitting at her kitchen bench when, grinning, he skidded something to her. A small, blue box. Handling the velvet, she felt her stomach leap and plummet. The texture of the thing gave it away: soft, silken, almost antique. She barely glimpsed the pert sapphire flanked by three inset diamonds in an art deco setting before she set the box beside his bowl of cereal, casually, as if it were a glass of water. He was studying her, as if trying to see beneath her surface reactions. She let her eyes flick to his.

'We could have a long engagement.'

Her smile trembled. She loved him so she feared she might say yes. How she felt was frightening. It was so enormous. Daily, she was rising and falling on it like a raft on a tidal wave.

'I love you,' she said, 'but let's not have this conversation yet.'

David's eyes were trained on hers. 'I like being married, belonging to someone. And I want to belong, be married, to you. What we have is rare.'

Warmed by the embers of his waiting brown eyes, she thought, *Yes*. Then she remembered Tennov's wisdom on limerence: the way she felt was likely to last about two years. The way he felt too.

'I know,' she said. 'But I've never been fussed about marriage per se.'

Dave's telephone vibrated, announcing an incoming message, and he ignored it. He spun the ring's box, so that it became a blue blur. 'I'll inspire you then.'

'Okay.' She grinned. 'Let me know you, really know you, and we'll do it.'

He frowned for the first time. She felt the swell shift.

'Okay.' With businesslike polish, he put the ring in his pocket. Instantly, absurdly, she felt disappointed he was giving up. She watched as he checked his message and the animation left his face. 'I have to go in,' he said.

'So much for our walk.'

She gave him a neat smile as she cleared their cereal bowls but he did not move. Then he coughed. A formal, unnatural noise. That and the pained look on his face made her pause over the dishwasher.

'Before I go, there's one other thing . . .'

Elle felt instantly seasick. 'Oh?'

'I have a stepdaughter, Amelia. She's twelve.'

She hesitated, recalibrated. 'An ex-stepdaughter?'

'Yeah.'

The wave was taking Elle up again. An ex-stepdaughter? That wasn't so bad. She tried to remember how long he'd been married – seven years? So he'd raised the girl. She felt herself frowning, tried to stop. She shut the dishwasher.

His hand stroked the stone bench. 'She was the best part of that marriage. I see her sometimes. Not enough. I miss her like crazy.'

'Okay, wow.' Elle steadied herself, leaning against the sink. The existence of a child didn't, in itself, bother her. 'Why didn't you tell me about her earlier?'

David shrugged. 'I didn't know how you'd react.'

Elle didn't know either, as she wiped the bench around him. It had been an eventful morning and she was still in her pyjamas. The man she loved had asked her to marry him. And now he had an ex-stepdaughter. What did that mean? Anything? Rinsing the dishcloth, she glanced at David. Awaiting a response, he looked so tired, and in need. Despite an unsettled, excited feeling in her stomach, she had the urge to massage him. Stepping near, she slipped her wet hands under his T-shirt. She felt the tension ease in his shoulders. On balance, she felt closer to him than she had for days. Not only did he want to marry her, he had also shared his touching attachment to Amelia. No doubt that loss explained some of his lingering sadness. By telling her, he had done as she asked. Even though that closeness brought new questions, fresh doubts, she chose to ignore them.

That evening, naked in her bed, she savoured his proposal. Hopefully, before too long, he would ask again. Though she did not aspire to marriage particularly, she aspired to motherhood. And, for her, the two went hand in hand. At thirty-four, in the not too distant future, she saw children, brown-eyed, precocious children. She swept her lips across his shoulder.

'We don't have to . . . every night, do we?' he whispered. 'It's been a long week.'

A horn from the street gave her time to get her voice in check. 'No, of course not.'

But, curved around him, feeling the heat from his skin and the wondrous softness of him, it was more than she could bear. David twisted to kiss the tip of her nose then turned, stretched his arms across the mattress and was gone. Sighing, she took in his unruly hair, his shapely legs and manly arms reaching away from her – again. Since her elbow had healed, she'd become the initiator of their sexual intimacy. She was filling the space between them left by the absence of his desire. The desire that he seemed to have shed. She adopted it, adopted both their quotients. Previous lovers had been insatiable: throwing her over their shoulders, licking her every pore. Knowing only short-lived relationships, she was unfamiliar with the complications of libido. Or, perhaps, previously any imbalance was skewed in her favour. But that evening her desire was peaking and so was his apathy. She felt a twinge of concern. Fresh vulnerability.

Leaning over, she kissed his forehead – a lingering, wet kiss, as if to reassure herself, but he didn't stir. She ran her fingers over his undulating shoulders. She told herself that no, he wasn't an adolescent, aroused only by pursuit. More likely, he was *more* evolved – a man, not a boy. One day she may be thankful. But as she caressed, she intuited that somewhere within him was an intermittent fault, which was shutting down his circuitry. His moods, too. Lately he could be playful and attentive one day and silent and withdrawn the next. She was inclined to blame his intrusive clients. Studying him as he slept, she had the vaguest fear that, whatever its source, this intermittent fault could become systemic. Watching his warm chest rise and fall, she told herself she had better find it and repair it.

She slept fitfully until 4 a.m., when she stirred to see his vast silhouette above her, his lips kissing hers. She roused herself and resisted the urge to speak, lest she distract him. His eyes were half closed as he moved, his tongue preoccupied. She traced the lines of his shoulders with her fingertips, felt the cool texture of his skin. His hands were on her breasts and, as he buried himself into her, she surprised herself by feeling nothing. Though this was what she wanted, part of her was unconvinced. Perhaps because it was too late or uninvited. She wondered if he would notice.

He was expressionless as he moved over her, progressing from lips to belly. She longed for him to say something. Anything. They had scarcely spoken all evening, each retreating to work at their laptops. At bedtime, undressing, he'd looked so weary, his eyes tinged red, his breath bitter; she had decided not to insist on conversation. As she let his tongue work its way into her, she became aware of his absence. There wasn't any whispering, not even a groan. He wasn't listening to her or for her; rather, he was burrowing himself away.

For the first time, towels wouldn't be needed. The realisation was self-fulfilling. Muscles clenched as the tide of her body turned. But he didn't desist, didn't notice. She watched him – his arms disappearing into his shoulders into his head. Into her. She felt that she was having sex with a shell, a silken, all-embracing shell. She longed to knock on his breastbone and listen for the echo, or to roll him onto his back and shake him to see if there was a rattle. *Why aren't you here with me? Where have you gone?*

Though her unease grew, she didn't think to speak. Or stop him.

Once he'd fallen back to sleep, she slipped out of bed. And wrote.

The jaunty music ends, leaving her house in total silence. Outside, the shadows haven't moved. Reviewing their intimacy, she's struck by how telling it is. The pursuit and retreat played out in those scenes embarrasses her. *Our insecurities were so similar,* she thinks. If only she'd understood that then and acknowledged the shortfalls. Or the common knee-jerk need for distance . . . If only she had held on to herself.

But there's nothing to be gained now, she thinks, bemoaning her own lack of differentiation. *Or is there?*

9

The 67-kilometre drive to Geelong is flat and dull. Mira is trying not to speed, though perhaps it wouldn't matter. Normally on Friday evenings the Princes Highway is swamped with commuters and weekenders travelling to Geelong, the Bellarine Peninsula or Surf Coast. Tonight, it's as if an act of God has swept all traffic away except for her old Saab. Miraculously, both her boys are asleep, their heads folded forward like a pair of sunflowers. Glancing at them, Mira sees Elle in Jesse's overly long eyelashes. *Wherever you are*, she thinks, *resist.*

As the kilometres mount, she revisits what she knows. This man she thought was gone is back. And, though Elle hasn't mentioned any desire for reconciliation, they've been here before. What, three times? Mira winces. Despite her lay understanding of psychology, battered women and the vagaries of being *in love*, she's stumped. Her own experience of breaking up is so different. Once Jude Nolan's fledgling acting career became blatantly irredeemable, she knew things had to change. When he wouldn't return to computer programming, skill up or sober up, he was out. She had two small children and her own career; she couldn't afford an unemployed dreamer, no matter how lovable he could be when he was straight. To Elle's credit, she'd given him a serve as well. Not that it'd worked.

Travelling too fast at 120, Mira slows, sets the cruise control and tries to calm herself. Once, she'd asked Elle why she so loved David Forrester. Contrary to what Mira had expected, Elle didn't recite a list of attributes. Elle just knew, in her gut, they were a fit. Not because of his passion for film, his searing looks or his wry intellect. Not even because of his Cary Grant–like Mercedes Benz coupe. The man himself, the complex package of him, was simply *it*. A position, thinks Mira, with which it's hard to argue, avoiding as it does hard evidence. A chill makes her flesh tingle beneath her pyjamas and thin trench coat. Adjusting the heater, she takes heart: Elle went back to him, yes, but eventually she left.

It was the day after the first proposal. Relishing the sting of the sun, Elle was sitting on the patch of lawn in her backyard. Clad in a hat, Mira sat under the lemon tree. Hearing the news, she tried to suppress her relief. 'You don't see a future with him?' she said lightly.

'No, I do.' Elle closed her eyes to the sun.

Mira watched the dew forming on her friend's brow. 'What then?' she said.

'It's barely been six months . . .' Elle squinted across at her. 'I thought by now I'd be swept off my feet and it would just work.'

'How's it not working?' Mira's voice sounded remarkably neutral. 'Here.' She offered her fedora.

'Like all of us – ta,' said Elle, 'I suppose, he can be apathetic. Irritable.' In her left hand, she spun the hat. 'He's not exactly sociable either; he doesn't want to meet my friends.'

Heartened if spurned, Mira watched the blur of woven straw. 'That's his loss then, isn't it?'

Elle shrugged, embarrassed.

'Elle, it should be *easy*. You're in the honeymoon period. Look at Troy and me.'

'But Troy is permanently non-limerent,' said Elle, stopping her play. 'He says so himself. You can't compare.'

Mira laughed. 'Yes, I can. And it works. Because he listens, and he does what he says he will. He knows who he is, and he's good to us. We laugh.' She paused. 'You don't really want to be swept off your feet. You saw what happened, after Jude. I ended up marooned.'

Elle's tone was defensive. 'Not everyone ends up a single mother.' She tossed the hat across the yellowed grass.

'No.'

'Mira, I'm sorry.' Elle patted Mira's leg. 'But the thing is . . . I came *this* close to saying yes.'

Elle's forefinger and thumb were a millimetre apart. Her eyes were fervent and confused. In them, Mira saw the awful truth of Elle's words. She also saw an unfamiliar trace of self-doubt. Or fear.

'Well, I'm glad you didn't.'

—

Reviewing the empty highway in her mirror, Mira knows her disapproval was obvious. The instant she met David she could see that he was damaged, or at least inchoate. She'd met complex, controlling men like him before. And, at the six-month mark, his behaviour already indicated his affections were waning. For a man like him, that spelled trouble. His *irritability* was only going to worsen. The great frustration was that her beautiful, intelligent friend couldn't see it. Like Romeo, she was too in love with love.

Flicking off the warm air, Mira drives on. She approaches Werribee and its low-grade sewage stink. With another 75 kilometres to go, she knows, like it or not, she's going to relive this relationship all the way to the Surf Coast. That man took his toll on everything she held dear. Her friendship with Elle, her growing family, their film. Their glorious and fraught film.

It's become a habit of hers: mulling over the course of their second feature – from its script development to its post-production – and wondering what else she could've done. A frustrating habit and one she ought to give up. But there's a perverse pleasure, too, in tracing the downward trajectory. Perhaps because it dovetailed so neatly with his.

One morning, a few weeks after the proposal, Mira received the news she'd been waiting on. Instantly, she called Elle to say they'd got their funding. 'That's fantastic,' said Elle, quietly. A bubble of dread formed in Mira's gut. At the same stage with *Daisy*, she and Elle had raced to meet and break out the sparkles.

Half an hour after the call, they were sipping lattes in silence. On Ballarat Street, the Feedback Cafe, typical of the inner-west with its unpretentious, meticulous coffee, was busy. That morning, the crowd had spilled onto the footpath and they found themselves by the kerb. Alongside their table, on the other side of a canvas fence, cars waited to turn from Ballarat Street onto Anderson. In the Yarraville village the two intersecting main and slender roads forced the traffic to form informal queues. Sometimes, cars banked up across the railway line. Often, horns tooted. Usually the women enjoyed the village mayhem but that morning Elle was glaring at the traffic.

Mira retrieved a script from her bag and flashed a brave smile, 'What's this, then?'

Elle stirred. 'You don't like it?'

'"Do people *always* fall out of love?"' said Mira, with a pout.

'It seemed more fresh to me. And not so overstated.' Elle frowned, tugging at a piece of skin on her lip.

'But we don't need it.' Mira was afraid her words would sound rehearsed. 'Everyone loves the last draft we gave them.'

'But I prefer this. I think.'

'This draft is going backwards . . .' Mira paused, battling to contain her frustration, 'a long way.'

Elle was staring hard, like a lip-reader.

Mira smothered a sigh. She'd already put a huge effort into this film, liaising with everyone from the government funding bodies and local distributor to the international sales agent and other financiers to raise the budget. And what a budget – double that of modest *Daisy*. Thinking in millions was still surreal to Elle but not to Mira: she knew where every cent was going, and who had to be repaid what. And she intended to make it happen.

'We'd be back at square one,' said Mira. 'The investors won't accept this.' She tapped the script.

In that bustling cafe, Elle's face fell, muscle by muscle. Mira watched as Elle's gaze came to rest on a miniature, twisted image of herself in the stainless-steel napkin dispenser.

'Elle, what's happening here?'

Elle shrugged. 'All this redrafting is doing my head in.'

Mira thought of how Elle had written *Daisy*. It had taken three months. It seemed to come out well-formed, like a poem or song, in a sustained flourish, and it had only needed minor tweaks along the way, over the drafts. Almost all of Elle's other works at film school had been birthed as smoothly. This script had been written around the release of *Daisy* and its aftermath, and the advent of David.

Mira frowned. 'So stop doing it.' She sat up. 'There's no need.'

Elle seemed lost in the napkin dispenser. 'You don't think Freddie's too strident?' she said, softly.

'Oh, she could be slightly.' Mira braced herself. 'How about, when the time comes, we do the final pass for the shooting script together?'

When Elle lifted her gaze to Mira's, her eyes were awash with emotion. On the surface Mira could see her disappointment and disbelief; deeper, perhaps, she saw relief.

'And we have to change the title,' said Mira. 'People don't know what it means.'

Elle's mouth opened but nothing came. Mira knew Elle had complete faith in her instincts. Some of *Daisy*'s best lines had come in the script-development process – from Mira – and Mira could write. Before the kids, she'd written and produced a handful of well-received shorts.

Mira took Elle's hand. 'Elle?'

Elle smiled weakly. 'There's so much at stake, now, isn't there?

Last time, we didn't have careers. Now I can't stop thinking, is this better than *Daisy*? What would the critics think? What will you think? What will David?'

'David?'

A car tooted and Elle started. The car was so near, the driver was practically seated at their table. Mira gestured for the waiter. On Ballarat Street, two cars in opposite directions were vying for space. The car tooted again.

'Give it a rest,' Elle said through the car's open window.

The driver raised his middle finger and she raised hers. He was forty-odd, in a denim jacket, bald. They were angry statues, saluting each other.

'Elle?' whispered Mira. 'It's okay.'

A second driver tooted.

'Fuck off, why don't you?' shouted Elle. 'Just fuck off!'

Heads swivelled as Elle rose from the table. To Mira's relief, Elle strode beyond the cars, without a backward glance. Mira moved stealthily, collecting their handbags, leaving a tip. On the footpath, catching up, Mira slipped her arm through Elle's and tried to mask her worry.

10

A bitter odour is permeating the small laundry now; Elle can smell it, though technically she doesn't have a nose. Otherwise, physically, she feels nothing. Pain, fatigue, discomfort: all gone. Even her uneasy niggles about her body have been eclipsed by what she is remembering. She is energised, somehow, as she absorbs it all. The wistful decisions, the lust and hope. Not for years has she understood herself so well, or him. It is like fuel, like oxygen. Oh, the stories she could write now.

She sees herself, one memorable autumnal day. In the scheme of things, she feels proud. It was their first and only shopping trip.

That Saturday morning, plump clouds were gathering in the marbled sky. The night before, David had arrived home from the office at eleven and fielded calls past midnight. Something was up at Freeman & Milne. When he came to bed, around one, he didn't sleep. And neither did she. But she let him toss, too weary herself to muster interest in his legal skirmishes. Like a glum commuter, that morning he walked towards Seddon Station with his shoulders hunched and a light scowl on his face. Elle chatted at his side about the unseasonal humidity and a favourite, if gloomy, French film he'd chosen for their evening – Claude Sautet's *A Heart in Winter*. And he perked up. But by the time they re-emerged at Southern Cross Station in central Melbourne, clouds were nudging one another, threatening to burst. And his scowl had deepened.

He led her through the milling Melbourne crowds, his tower looming over them. Without slowing, he ignored it. He ignored the other office blocks too and the lure of big stores and split-level malls. He crossed Collins Street, tiered with trams and intrepid cyclists, and led her on, the gap between them growing to metres. He turned right at William Street, then left at Flinders Lane before slipping into a menswear shop.

Alone on the footpath, Elle took a moment to locate him in the boutique. Irritated, she stepped into the expensive quiet. Within, David was greeting the shop assistant warmly and asking for trousers: black, size 34, classic cut. Then he disappeared behind red velvet. Sitting on an overstuffed stool, bemused, Elle tried to deduce the source of this new mood. Was it something she'd done? Or had he seen Amelia? Sometimes she could tell when he had spoken to his ex, or seen her daughter: he was preoccupied, short. Perhaps sad. Lately, she'd learned not to ask. But no. Given their sleepless night, she guessed what it was. His work. His relentless, soulless work.

When he reappeared, he stood in front of a three-panelled mirror and looked fleetingly at his six black legs. He turned to the side, sucked in his belly and jiggled leg to leg as if he'd dropped something. The shop assistant was tending to another shopper, searching for jade silk ties.

Although he stood before the glass, David's gaze skirted from it. 'What do you think?'

She shrugged. 'They look fine.'

David eyed the approaching shop assistant. She was in her early fifties, with silver, oblong spectacles and discreet jewellery beneath her charcoal suit. Her hair was like a silver helmet and it shimmered when she walked. She carried an air of authority, as if she owned the shop. Elle smiled and felt foolish when the woman didn't respond. She became conscious of her own outfit: a cream shift dress, scuffed taupe ballet flats and bare, whiskery legs.

Gently, the shop assistant suggested to David that the fit was good, but perhaps a different style? With a nod, David retreated into the fitting room with two more variations on black.

When he returned to face the glass, he studied Elle and the shop assistant: lean and long, and short and silver. She tried to focus. This fit, she guessed, was also good. To her, black pants were like black T-shirts – a quick and easy buy. Besides, he clearly had a good eye himself.

Spinning from the mirror, David bent to her, so close that she inclined from him. 'What about these?'

'They look fine too,' she said, flustered. 'Black suits you.'

With a grunt, David stepped into the fitting room. Elle eyed a row of striped shirts beside her and tried to anchor herself. This man of hers would spend a lifetime in corporate stripes. To what effect? She peeked at the changing room and across the racks of shirts and jackets. The infinite variations of the corporate uniform.

When he called her name she jumped. He had an odd look in his eye.

'What do you like, the straight-leg or the tapered?'

She frowned at the ends of his legs. 'Which are you wearing now?'

David clicked his tongue and disappeared. He returned in yet another pair and avoided the mirror completely.

'What about these?'

Studying his legs, she tried to feign interest. The pants were black, not long, not short, not tight and possibly straight to the ankle. She tried to think of something to say that wouldn't betray her. His recent irritability had been persistent, but not like this. Abruptly, David's face changed: his forehead flattened and his wrinkles disappeared. He looked as if he was wearing a mudpack. A mudpack like the ones her mother liked to wear.

'Well?' he said.

Elle tried again to spot the difference between these black pants and the last. 'I don't like the crease down the front.'

'They've all got that,' he snapped.

She tried for a smile. 'Otherwise, they all look good.'

'But which type do you like?' David's small eyes shot out the question like a needle.

'To tell you the truth,' she said, tired of her pretence, 'I can't tell the difference.'

'These are stovepipe.' David glanced at the shop assistant as if at an ally. Stepping to Elle again, he put his face too close to hers. Elle felt the layer of heat that was pulsing from his body.

'Are you stupid, or what?'

She flinched, as if he had spat on her face. Blood rose like a burning tide to her throat, her cheeks and ears. She managed to mouth *no*, before averting her eyes from his. Stealthily, the shop assistant stood behind her. In a strong voice, the woman spoke over her head to David – not in a gesture of protection; more as if Elle had lost the right to exist.

They caught the next train to Seddon. At the end of a carriage, Elle found a seat by the window and, to her surprise, David sat next to her. Across from them, a group of baggy-trousered youths were bouncing off the walls. She ignored them. David turned his back to the youths and to Elle, facing the opposite window. The train slid in and out of darkness, slowed and accelerated, without enough space or regularity for Elle to find a rhythm. Her disgruntled silence was virtually unknown between them. The rope that ran between them had been pulled taut, and this time she had taken all the slack. It was for him to move to her. But he sat with his eyes skimming the landscape. His features were tight again, as though under that mudpack. As the tracks curved towards the west, she longed to be alone.

She tried to lose herself in the passing stacks of rusty red, blue and white transport containers at the Port of Melbourne. Her eyes skated over the skeletal, reaching cranes and huge trucks, the white, squat tanks of Coode Island, the state's central chemical storage facility. As the train slid along she pictured the frontier workers' cottages of Yarraville, those homes within a kilometre of the so-called island. She thought of that cloud over Coode Island in the heart of Melbourne in 1991; the day millions of litres of chemicals burned, ostensibly thanks to a lightning strike. Twenty-odd years later, that island and those rows of cottages were still the wrong bedfellows. Everything, everywhere, felt too close.

David's telephone rang. Turning it off, he muttered under his breath. She steeled herself for the remainder of the trip, conscious of how tired his company was making her and of how much effort she had put lately into deciphering or ignoring his moods. Effort best put, particularly given today's behaviour, elsewhere. A flash of anger roused her; in its heat, she made a decision.

As the train approached Footscray Station, she looked at him. Again, he muttered. This time she caught an expletive. Loudly, she said, 'What did you say?'

David levelled his eyes on hers. 'I said it fucking stinks in here. Are you stupid *and* deaf?'

She rose and turned on him. 'Are you a rude shit?'

The station's platform slid towards them and the train slowed. The moment of inertia was infinite. Around them, the baggy-panted youths fell silent, and exiting passengers, sensing the tension in the air, fled to the doors.

Abruptly, David laughed, like a kid caught out, as if she'd pulled a better trick than his. 'Yeah, I must be.'

The doors opened with a *whoosh* but her words were louder. 'Don't ever speak to me like that again.'

'Okay, okay.' He nodded, his gestures undersized; he was conscious now of their remaining, reluctant audience.

'I mean it,' she said, stepping away.

'Okay.' Surprised, he half rose. 'What're you doing?'

'I'm walking,' she said as she alighted. 'And by the time I get home I want you gone.'

An ugly look crossed David's features, so swiftly she wondered if she had imagined it. By the time the train pulled away, his eyes were wide and he was chuckling. She gleaned that this was new for him – wrong-footing, dizzying and almost appealing.

When she arrived in Tennyson Street, her house was empty; his clothes and car were gone. She felt only relief.

—

That afternoon, the storm broke. Shuddering thunder, snaps of lightning, pounding rain. The rain was driving into the ground, her garden beds and yellowing grass. She set herself up at her desk and watched the drenching. Wind lashed her row of magnolias and denuded them of their plump white flowers. Puddles formed across her courtyard, pooling beneath the timber table. Watching, she felt her skin enlivening. When it was over and the water had drained away, she felt cleansed. The world glistened, jubilant and clear. Returning to her script, she read each version with fresh eyes.

11

At Mira's to babysit that evening, Elle was midway through a fractured chat about David. The boys were in the bath. Cheerful anarchy reigned. She paced the lounge room as Mira darted from laundry to kitchen to bathroom. The seven o'clock news was on. A dead man had been found in Thomastown, another victim of the bikie war. She felt the usual relief: it'd been one of them, not one of us. A missing woman was found unconscious in a lover's car. And she felt the same thing. A Victorian father, convicted of murder for driving his three young sons into a dam, was back in court. She couldn't bear to look at him. That story still pierced her heart. She thought of the family's ongoing grief, the mother's impotence, the casualties of divorce . . . She poured herself a huge dry white and fetched her nephews' pyjamas in readiness for the post-bath frenzy. Afterwards, she hoped to finish her tale with Mira. And move on.

She closed the windows and settled back to wait. An item on IVF was underway now, something about its uptake by lesbian couples. Sipping her chilled wine, her mind wandered. She'd always feared infertility. She'd taken risks at university, uncharacteristic of her, and gotten away with it. More than a decade later, a question mark was looming over her uterus and turning neon as she aged. Perhaps now, without David, the question would unfortunately remain moot. When the news item concluded with a clipped reference to the 'socially infertile', she spluttered. Apparently, mid-thirties, childless and single, by default she was already there. Appalled, she thought about the connotations of that tag – the implied incompetence and its omission of all those boy-men her age or older, 'not ready' for children, or not equipped. Like David. The more she thought it over, the angrier she felt.

By the time Mira re-emerged, Elle was thinking about Jane Austen and the Brontë sisters lining up for donor sperm . . . Would they want it? Did she? And when? The truth was she wasn't sure she had the stamina for single motherhood. She was still mulling the question over when Mira dropped to her knees.

'We're seeing the latest Coen brothers' at the Sun; home around eleven. Have you seen my keys?' Mira was scouring the carpet, flinging shoes and picture books. A cockroach scurried.

The brief eclipse in Elle's mind passed. 'Mira, before you go, let me —'

'In the fridge, blue cup is Jesse's now; yellow is Max's. But Jesse mightn't want so much milk as he's coming down with a cold.'

'Yes, okay —'

'And three books, tops. Otherwise you set the bar too high.'

'Got it.' Finding Mira's keys wedged in the couch, she tossed them in the air. As Mira caught them, Elle said, 'Mira, listen, two things —'

Full of bluster, Jesse scrambled in, his face ruddy and gleaming, the tips of his bronze hair wet. Wrapping himself around Elle's legs, he grinned up at her with enormous blue eyes.

'Walk, walk,' he said.

Elle ruffled his hair, tickled his lily-white stomach. He crumpled like a piece of paper, giggling, but the giggles swiftly turned into a coughing spell and the crumpled body became tight. She rubbed his back and it abated.

Max appeared then, dripping, chanting, 'Auntie Elle, Auntie Elle.'

Before Elle knew it, Mira was in the hall and singing out thanks, goodbyes.

'Mira,' she called out, 'about the script . . .' Mira's footsteps halted, trotted closer to the lounge room again. 'I've read both drafts, *properly*, and you're right. Of course.' Elle gave a bashful smile. 'How about you do the final pass? And I'll shoot it.'

Mira's wide mouth curved. 'Brilliant.'

'On one condition: we keep the title.'

Mira gnashed her teeth.

'That's one small, one-word condition.' Elle rose to her full height. 'And no one knew what *Catch-22* meant, or *Generation X* . . .'

They were on either end of a silent tug of war.

'Our contract says something about the title, doesn't it?' said Elle, lightly.

'Our contract isn't exactly front of mind right now,' said Mira.

'No.'

Elle could see Mira wondering whether to pull harder or yield.

'Titles are important,' said Mira, giving a quick tug.

'Yeah, they are.'

'Okay,' said Mira.

Elle grinned. 'Before you go, one more thing: I left David, on the train. It's over.'

'Why didn't you say before? Hallelujah!' Laughing, Mira clapped three times before enfolding her. 'You're free! Fill me in tomorrow, okay?'

'Okay.'

Watching Mira scamper out, Elle felt a whiff of dissatisfaction. For some reason, she'd expected less fanfare and perhaps more commiserations. Her first and only love was gone.

Four books and a cushion fight later, the boys were in bed and the narrow cottage was peaceful again. Elle's certainty was replaced now by disappointment, vague and dangling. Switching off lights, picking up bath towels, she returned to her nephews' bedroom. In the warm, shadowy space, the boys were both asleep on their backs, arms thrown above their heads. She couldn't resist pausing over each child until she heard quiet breathing. Four-year-old Max's mouth was open and his front teeth protruded, large and gapped. They were her teeth, Jude's teeth: her father's teeth. The Nolan overbite. Uncanny how the genes echoed through the generations. Three-year-old Jesse, on the other hand, had even blocks of teeth, like tiles laid by an expert. Both boys, she decided, with absolutely no bias, were beauties. She lingered in their breathing stillness. Though she regretted the pain her brother had caused, without him these beautiful boys wouldn't exist.

And her world would be utterly childless. She had come to realise that her brother's loss had become her gain.

By the time she pulled the door to, she felt restored, if delicate. Soon, David's presence in her life would be as a footnote. Calm was descending. And she was back, unfettered.

Having brought an old friend with her, she slipped it into Mira's player. *A Heart in Winter* could wait for another time. Lately, David had tired of romantic comedies, especially black and whites, and she'd missed them. As *The Philadelphia Story* purred to life, she thought of a quote attributed to its female star: 'You don't choose who you love.' Tracy's bouts of drinking and darkness were renowned, and Hepburn had loved him anyway. *But*, thought Elle, *you could choose who you left.*

It was after eleven when Elle heard loud, harsh coughing from the boys' room. By the time she reached the hallway it had escalated, become insistent: distressed. By the time she was on her knees in the draughty bedroom, Jesse's face was pale and puckered, and dark rings had formed beneath his eyes, making him look like a pyjama-clad raccoon. His chest was heaving as he struggled, not to draw a breath but to exhale, crying between gasps.

Max was awake and watching with sleepy, worried eyes.

'Does he have an asthma inhaler now?'

Max shook his head. 'Nope. But Billy at kinder has asthma —'

Elle took another look at her distraught nephew. His mouth was moving but words were stuck in his throat. 'It's going to be all right, Jess,' she said. She sat him up. 'Try to breathe through your nose and out through your mouth. I'll call Mummy.'

Her sprint down that hallway was the fastest she'd run in twenty years.

Later, as Mira accompanied Jesse in the ambulance to the Western Hospital, Elle watched Max sleep and shed silent tears. She wasn't sure what had been worse, the look on Mira's face or Jesse's purpling lips before they'd fitted the nebuliser mask. As she watched the steady rise and fall of Max's chest, she consoled herself with the thought: Yarraville was close to virtually everywhere.

Returning home at 3 a.m., she felt as empty as her lifeless house. She thought to call Jude, knowing Mira wouldn't. Surely, despite his absence and silence, her brother cared about his sons? Dialling by memory, she found his number disconnected. The Nolan line, indisputably broken. She was fatherless and so were her nephews. At least they had Troy. She roamed from room to room, yearning to share her ordeal. She tried her mother, the equally absent grandmother. Left a message.

As Elle tumbled into bed, her mattress felt enormous. Her dreams flitted from sirens to wheezes. Troy's urgent question to Mira upon their arrival kept playing in her mind: 'What do you need me to do?' The care and concern in his face was indescribably moving.

The instant she awoke, she called Mira. Her youngest nephew was stable, his breathing normal. But his fragility stayed with her. As did her own, particularly now she intended to, again, live alone.

Unable to rest, she perched at her desk in her pyjamas and relived the night. If only they hadn't had that cushion fight. Or perhaps the tickling. She tried to distract herself online, researching asthma attacks. Skimming an article on the rise in single home-occupiers. Then she heard a knock. It was 8 a.m. Mira would, she knew, be cuddling her boys in bed and was unlikely to let them go for days. Doris would be dozing over crumpets. Stirring, she sighed. There was only one person it was likely to be. At least she'd had the foresight to double-lock the door. Steeling herself, she wished she'd eaten or showered or cleaned her teeth.

Through her peephole, she saw him on her porch in half-drenched running gear. She watched as he rapped again. Seeing his square shoulders and ginger-hued good looks, her conviction wavered; there on her mat was an alluring man, full-bodied, alive, for her. She unlocked the door but didn't open it. Her security chain gave them fifteen centimetres. She saw him noting her strip of blue flannel pyjama top and a portion of her pink stretchy-panted legs.

'What's this?' he said, tapping the chain. His long fingers lingered in the space between them. When she didn't respond, he added, 'Sweetheart, I've left my phone in the kitchen.'

She fetched the telephone and, through the gap, dropped it into his hand. They both stared at the blank screen.

'I'd love a glass of water,' he said, leaning into the frame.

She wiped sleep from her eyes. He was too close, his voice too tender; she was unprepared, her head full of Jesse.

David glanced down at himself. 'Jogging doesn't seem to become me either. Though I prefer it to misery.'

She managed to ignore his wry tone but not his physicality. What he said about jogging was only half true. He was dripping into his socks and his face was slick with sweat. But he looked better for the exertion. Against his pink skin, the whites of his eyes were bright and his irises were striking constellations of amber, red and brown. She unclasped the chain.

In the kitchen, he downed two glasses of rusty water from her tap. She didn't bother to remind him of the purifier in the fridge. But when he propped himself on her bench and looked at her, his attention poured into her like air, water, food. She wasn't prepared for the hit it gave her. Her blood seemed to fizz.

He brushed hair from his forehead with a shaking hand. 'I know I was bad yesterday, but was I that bad?'

'Yes.'

'I've always been a shocker at shopping,' he said. 'I've been going on my own since I was ten. Mum wouldn't come with me. But I do buy first-class presents – even my wife, ex-wife, told me so.' He gathered himself. 'I won't ask you to shop with me again.'

Elle hoped the silence was speaking for her. After a pause, she said, 'It's not only the shopping.'

David stood and pushed past her, as if too ashamed to look at her. Hesitating in her foyer, he saw the question on her face. 'I'm no good at this.' He tried for a smile but she checkmated it with a frown.

'Is that it?' she said.

'I'm done in,' he said. 'I'll come back later.'

Before she could refute him, he lifted his hand to the door. His fingers floated over the central lock. 'You know I've only had one long-term relationship before. And you, my young bolter, have only had flings . . .' He made a sad, snort-chuckle. 'We will get better at it.'

When he glanced at her, his red-brown eyes were glowing.

'No.' Her voice was trembling. 'I meant it; we're done here, David.'

'You can't be serious?' He stared again. Frank and open. Like sunlight. 'Sweetheart, it's early days.'

Despite herself, she tried on his words and married them with his stare. He seemed so earnest.

'Ginger, I've had a hellish week,' he said. 'One of my team didn't prepare for a hearing. The prick was punting on it settling. I should've told you. Not taken it out on you.'

Elle found a curl of dry skin on her lip and tugged. She considered his clients, his staff, their litigation. The pull of the law.

'I'm sick of your job,' she said. 'It leaches into everything, like poison.'

He blinked, as if her assault were too direct. Or perhaps he lacked the words to combat it.

'We've had a bad patch,' he said. 'I can do better; we can both do better. And you're making a rookie mistake, here, being way too hard.'

Elle frowned. Perhaps he was right. As troubling, she was hearing echoes of her mother. Hard was the last thing she wanted to be, and the last thing she felt.

When he opened the front door, the abrupt move startled her. She noticed the waterfall of dried sweat on his grey T-shirt, saw where his curling half-wet hair met his neck. Vaguely she could detect another odour; if she didn't know better she would have said it was recycled alcohol. Despite her misgivings, she longed to touch him. Be held by him.

'David?' The words escaped: 'Do you still love me?'

'Ginger, hey, more than you know.'

David smiled faintly. His eyes glistened, perhaps with tears. Feeling a pain in her stomach, she imagined it was his pain. Seeing his rugged beauty worn with worry, she wondered at the haste and fairness of her decision. Watching him, feeling him, she was struck by the overwhelming truth of their love.

He whispered, 'I will get there.'

Although she hadn't cried in decades, she wanted to. She wasn't sure why. 'Okay,' she said. 'We can feel our way together. But it has to be easier.'

'It will be.' David glanced at her sideways. 'I'm usually pretty quick on the uptake, but I didn't see this coming. It must be age.'

'Okay, come on.' She sighed, mustering herself. 'Stay, I had an awful night. I could do with a chat.'

David considered her, his eyes gleaming.

'Are you hungry?' she added. 'I feel like eggs.'

'Who's cooking?'

'You are.'

David ran his hand along the edge of the open door. 'It'd be my pleasure.'

He pulled her close and their bodies shut the door. The relief she felt was a shock. It was so exquisite and absolute. She'd missed him as if he had been gone months.

Looking back, she wonders at his mastery. He'd said so little yet she had heard so much. That night, he returned with suits and novels, Latin jazz and wine, and didn't leave.

12

On the steps at Flinders Street Station, she was wearing a new frock: asymmetrical, electric blue. It was seventies couture, second-hand. After his call, she had dressed quickly: her pixie hair unbridled, her face devoid of makeup. Twenty minutes later, she'd skipped onto a city-bound train. Feeling remarkably *right*. Behind her was the station's row of ancient clocks showing the different times for the different lines. A reminder that time, like so much in life, was a choice. Forgiveness. Happiness. Seeing his brisk approach, his Italian suit, she couldn't rein in her smile. They were both perfectly on time. They kissed for a good three minutes.

In the four days since their fractious weekend, she had managed to convince herself: he wouldn't squander this, his second chance. Somehow, already, they were closer.

'Shall we?' he said.

Taking his hand, she said, 'Yes, lead on.'

This time, as he led her through jostling commuters and city-dwellers towards Flinders Lane, they chatted. They chatted past restaurants and ignored the boutiques. They chatted about her day spent driving around Melbourne, taking photos, with Julia, her director of photography.

'So you just drove around all day?' he said.

'Uh-huh.'

For now she was freed up, at least until the script came back. Not that she'd mentioned that altered status quo.

At the last bar on the strip, she hesitated. But with a gentle wink he led her on. His jitters were growing. Hers, too. She didn't want to squander this, their fresh start, either.

For months she'd been wanting to meet Alex Carras. His best friend. His oldest friend. 'He's rather indulged,' he'd warned her on the phone. 'And he likes to joust.' As if the financier was an ogre. Or an orca, prone to tossing seals. Sometimes David forgot she'd been a top-tier lawyer herself. Or that, in production, she was responsible for hordes of people and thousands of questions. Daily. But now she did feel a ping of apprehension about her night with the suits . . . And it was a risk, venturing out of their cocoon.

On Flinders Lane, they strolled to the foot of black marble stairs. Her eyes flared as she read the sign: Gallery 22.

He kissed her nape. 'He's in here somewhere.'

'He is?' In her other life as an office worker, she had rarely encountered the city's art galleries. Perhaps back then she was blinkered by her own discontent.

Inside, a waiter found them, arming them each with a flute. With his hand in hers, David escorted her through the gallery.

From the outset she'd been keen to meet his friends. And to see him in context. In situ. This place, she intuited, more than his mansion in Middle Brighton or his office tower in Collins Street, was probably it.

The simple four-room gallery was filling steadily. Three artists' abstract works were like magical windows on the white walls. Windows to infinite imaginings.

'Haven't been here for years,' David whispered, 'but the crowd hasn't changed.'

Elle took in the mix of suits and jeans, the artists' families and the avant-garde. David waved at disparate groups.

'You still know a lot of people,' she said.

'I only know a few,' he said, 'but lots wave back.'

Laughing, she eyed the art and the faces, as if they were clues to the puzzle of him.

'Look at this.' She paused to admire a massive blue moonscape. Mysterious, dark yet luminous. Abruptly, a figure blocked their view. He was around twenty-five, well built, with a chestnut afro. His arms outstretched. At her side, David squinted, then found himself bear-hugged.

'I heard you were allowed out again.'

'I love the 'fro,' said David, plunging his fingers into the reddish-brown.

The young man grinned, his hair floating like a helium balloon. When David introduced her, she was agog. With his wide-set eyes, he was like a beautiful extraterrestrial. David gestured to the moonscape. 'This's his.'

Elle smiled. 'It's extraordinary. Congratulations.'

Each of them seemed to inhale, reflect. When the men grinned, she felt as if she had cleared a hurdle.

After a moment, she asked, 'How do you two know each other?'

'I used to be a waiter at Dave's firm. One morning he caught me in a boardroom admiring an early Jeffrey Smart.'

'So we snuck out and had a smoke,' said David.

Impressed yet unsurprised, Elle glanced at David, but he was flagging down a passing waitress. They each took a refill.

'Then Dave introduced me to Alex. Next thing you know, I was having a show.'

This time, Elle cocked an eyebrow and David coloured. 'This is Alex's place – well, Fi and Alex's.'

Elle found herself catching up: so, both he and Alex had unexpected facets. It made sense, of course: people weren't only ever this or that. She took a nip of sparkling wine. But why keep these things a secret? What to make, she thought, of his tendency to withhold, to drip-feed her pieces of his life?

Beneath her stare, David's shrug was sheepish. 'Alex showed Nat too, early on. For a while, we were here a lot.'

'Mm.' The lovely ET gave a judicious eye-roll.

'I see.'

Perhaps his memories were not all so fond. Perhaps it was pain he was masking. On balance, she felt honoured to be given access to it. She made her grin to him brave. When he stroked her back, she felt as if she'd cleared another hurdle. Was becoming a steeplechaser.

Then three more homely others approached: an illustrator, a photographer and a crusty portraitist. Kisses scattered across cheeks. David's gentle questions laced the group as they discussed their practices, their recent shows. She stood, holding his hand, beaming. Amid the chatter of studios and commissions, she felt validated. In this world, her man made sense. And so did they.

Perhaps now he might return to his own art.

When the portraitist made her excuses, David gestured to the trestle-table bar. 'There he is.'

Across the gallery, Alex Carras waved. He was wearing a precise black suit and white shirt; beside him, his wife, Fi, towered in swathes of green silk. Elle had forgotten their hosts. She watched as Alex excused himself from his coterie. Without fuss, he glided through the crowd.

'Welcome back, buddy,' said Alex, arms wide.

David had told her the basics about Alex. That he hadn't changed – since university in the eighties or his wedding ten years ago. Then, as now, he was short but fit, his face tan. Then, David had been his best man. Today, Alex's Leonidas Finance Group made David the highest-billing partner at Freeman & Milne. That was firm lore. But, what, if anything, did Alex Carras know about her?

David withdrew from Alex's hug and, without ado, introduced her.

Elle embraced Alex. 'Wonderful to meet you,' she said, her voice loud above the rabble.

'And you.' Alex's head inclined to hers. If he was taken aback by her familiarity, he didn't show it. She pulled away first.

'By the way, I enjoyed *Daisy*,' he said. 'Synchronicity's always fascinated me.'

'Me too. I'm glad you liked it.'

'This country's notorious for making unprofitable movies.'

'Kind of you to say so,' said Dave, shooting a dart at Alex. But Elle slipped her hand back in his, squeezed.

'Did yours make a quid?'

'Yes, actually. We were lucky.'

Alex mimed surprise to ET. 'How about that!' Elle grinned, unfazed. 'I expect it's a tough business for a woman?'

David's mouth was open. 'Can be,' Elle said, 'but fortunately good stories don't discriminate.'

'Ha.' Alex scrunched his raisin-brown eyes as the young painter slipped a complicit smile to Elle. It was David's turn to beam.

'I gather you're a man of many passions?' said Elle.

'I wouldn't say passions. Passion's an overused word,' said Alex. 'Too emotional.'

'What word would you use, then?'

'I have interests,' said Alex. 'And I give them my all.'

'No one could ask for more than that,' said Elle. She leaned in. 'And something tells me they don't.'

'Hell, no.'

Elle and Alex laughed. Followed by the young painter. But David's laugh was biggest. Beneath the bright lights, beneath his adoring gaze, Elle felt glittery and triumphant. A runaway champion.

Four hours later, they fell into a taxi. Having mingled all night, they'd dined only on hors d'oeuvre. But that didn't matter. Within twenty minutes they were at her house, on a dining chair. The windows were open, the scent of star jasmine in the air. This time, as she rose up and his thighs glistened, she was ecstatic. It was back.

In her laundry, her pride is gone and she is incensed. How easily she was swept away. A second time! It's extraordinary: how eager she was to ignore her instincts and indulge her heart. How ready to forgive. Believe.

If only, that lonely Sunday morning, she hadn't let him in.

On average, women in relationships like hers attempt to leave seven times before they succeed. She has learned that since. But that isn't any consolation now. It would have helped, she thinks, had she admitted then to the true nature of their relationship. Or to the dark side of limerence: the semi-delusional world view, the irrationality. Instead, as the months passed, she became more attached and more determined. She cast them as strong people having their inevitable clashes. *Relationships aren't easy*, she told herself; *no one is perfect; the path of true love . . .*

Clichés and limerence, she realises, make a formidable combination.

13

Dave rips off his shirt, spraying buttons, as hot water surges into Reg's bath. His fingers drum the china. What a goddamn lame godfather! A childless dilettante who chose wives with their own kids or faulty bits and bobs. A man who'd been divorced twice! He only got the job because Dave's parents didn't know any other *professional.* What did Reg know about the younger generations? About women? About intimacy? Reg told him once: 'A parent's love is unparalleled.' This from a man who spent every Saturday at the Forresters' covertly raging household when Dave was a teenager. What a fucking joke!

Dave clambers into the bath and stands. His ankles sting; the water's surface is biting like angry socks. He pictures Reg in his sitting room: his wrinkly ears attuned to that rolling tape.

Dave splashes his legs and winces. *Damn it.* Maybe he should've explained himself better. Said more about the good stuff. That his form wasn't always as poor as tonight's. He did love her well and make her happy, sometimes. He *had* lived to a higher standard, once. *Fuck it.*

The air becomes steamy, the water nipping now at his shins. He sits. Overcome.

He remembers her standing at Flinders Street Station beneath the clocks. They met there before every festival he could think of: Spanish Film, Melbourne Jazz, Comedy. And every time, her face, her sweet face, telling him: 'Lead on.' And he did; he did his best.

He'd never felt so loved in his life.

It lasted almost three months. By May, every night he could sense her desire, as if she was emitting a scent. He closed his eyes and tried to sleep. She was closer to him than anyone had ever been. And that was what he wanted. Wasn't it? Together, they'd seen a dozen shows in Melbourne and hadn't missed an opening at Alex's. They'd hung their new blue painting above the bed. He'd even led her in and out of Melbourne's galleries, her very own guide; at home he was her private cook. And he'd loved it – for a while. This time, as he wooed her, she was busier. The writing stage done, she was fully in director mode, with a production office up in Footscray. He'd hoped her pre-production might take some of the heat off him. But it'd had the opposite effect. The sound of her phone, her talk of recces and endless meetings were getting to him. Apparently, she had to meet with everyone from her camerawoman to her designer and makeup people. And after, overstimulated, she had to yak about it, with him! Then fuck.

That windy evening, in her bed, his limbs felt full of lead. He rolled onto his back but couldn't find an easy spot. He could hear her sighing as she stared at the ceiling. He told himself to relax, to unclench his legs and to sleep. He tried inching from her so they weren't touching anywhere. But before too long, her hand found his thigh and planted itself. Feeling her warm fingers on his thigh, he disowned his legs, as if they were a tree's dead limbs.

Three months, he figured, was about his limit. After three months of getting on, his feelings for her . . . went away. Was it boredom or was it fear? Whatever it was, it was violent. He wanted to smash the thing to bits. As much as he tried, daily chitchat and nightly wrestling were beyond him. Everything she did – her questions, her massages, her tinkling laugh – was a turn-off. It took all his strength not to leap out of her bed and sprint back to his dormant house, which he couldn't bring himself to sell. There, in the dark, his head began to pound.

He shut his eyes and lay like a mummy.

The next night, on Collins Street, sinking in the elevator to his car, he realised he was now expected in Seddon every day, like the postie. Every night they were together and every morning they woke up entwined. And every day, she tried it on. If he caved in, they'd jostle through their positions: missionary, spooned, askew. Mostly in silence; lately without the waterworks. Again. The one thing that had elevated their sex life, giving it an intensity he'd never felt before – gone. Again. He swore out loud.

In the glary car park, the ground dipped and parked cars swirled. He stopped and squatted on the cement. He put his head between his legs. After a moment, he found his phone.

And that was when it started: the nights out, flying solo. The circuit-breakers.

Five hours later, he arrived at her house. He was scruffy then, and slightly stinky. Alcohol rose from him when he walked. Though he held his breath as he kissed her, he guessed she could taste his last ten cigarettes. He tried to tiptoe down her hall like a naughty, big mouse, but she blocked his way.

'Where have you been?' she said. 'I almost called a hospital.'

Long ago he'd learned the best excuses were brief. He explained that Alex needed him at a thing for homeless dogs in Albert Park, and he owed him one. Listening, she stood tall; they were almost eye to eye. How gorgeous she was, and so . . . upright. He badly wanted to giggle.

'I could've come.'

He'd heard that needy tone before, but not on her lips.

'Boys only,' he slurred. He let out a grin and it slid across his face. He slunk around her. Time for cheese on toast. He was walking very carefully.

'David, I hope you didn't drive.'

He snorted a laugh and turned around. He put his fingers on her shoulders. 'No, no,' he said, lying sincerely.

When she nodded, he felt forgiven.

See, he told himself, *you can be with her and be calm*. Separate. He'd worked that out, earlier, with Alex. Though she would've liked the views across Albert Park Lake and the snaps of happy dogs, his time away had done him wonders. The sushi had tasted fantastic. So had the tempura. By his seventh shot, he was flying and his head pain was gone. Thanks to Alex. His friend's words came to him again: 'It's normal to feel apprehensive, buddy, starting over.' The more he'd thought about it, the more relieved he'd felt. He wasn't that unusual, or inept. He was a divorced man. Wariness and unease were a part of the deal. 'You can have your space. But you don't want to screw this one up,' Alex had said in parting. 'Combat the nerves by looking forward.'

Taking the backstreets home, Dave had realised his friend was a genius. He had lost sight of what he wanted. The thing he'd been yearning for, all these years. And now he felt . . . sensational. But it was midnight – maybe not such a good time to discuss it? Recalling his earlier efforts to progress their relationship, he hesitated. Her gaze was gentle, puzzled. He looked from her to her study: her laptop and drafts. The sight stung him like a slingshot and he sobered. When she was working, she was lost to him. Gone. It was the nub of their underlying difference and his next hurdle. Making matters worse, he'd stopped being privy to her script months ago. He had no idea why. He sighed. He needed to think. He kissed her ear and headed for the kitchen. For once, he'd opt for prudence.

That night, maybe because he smelled or snored, she'd slept on her side. He'd slept on his, with no bridge of flesh between them. And he was happy. As the clock ticked on 1 a.m., he was pain-free and reminiscing about the man he'd been when he'd first had his dream. He was thirty-four and solo, living like an automaton. Women were a disappointment, friends were few and his mother was a cow. Shuttling from his apartment to his office, eighty-odd hours a week, his life was winding-up applications and foreclosure files, ham sandwiches at his desk and takeaway Indian curries on the carpet. While he had two friends, both in litigation, they worked longer and harder than he did; he hardly saw them out of hours. Then, one fresh morning, passing a cafe near North Brighton Station, he saw Natasha Larsen. She had red streaks in her black hair and almond-shaped green eyes. She served him a long black – too weak or too strong but he didn't mind – and went on about her upcoming exhibition, other artists and her daughter. Her passion was contagious. Within a month, he'd bought one of her ceramic pelican sculptures. Within two months, he'd met Amelia. For the first time since high school, he was thinking about art. He was playing with kids.

When he met Amelia, she was four. They were at the St Kilda Botanical Gardens. They were playing tag among the roses and he was 'it'. 'Look,' she'd said, halting suddenly, her huge green eyes directing him to her chest. Briefly, he was distracted by her petite, proportionate beauty – somehow her skin and dark hair were even more beautiful than her mother's. 'Look,' she'd said again. Her chest rising rapidly. So he did. On her yellow T-shirt was a white and unmoving butterfly. For maybe five minutes, as they caught their breath, they studied its translucent wings and tiny black head. When Natasha ducked over to a nearby cafe, Dave didn't notice; it was Amelia who led them towards the gate, and, all the while, the butterfly was like a badge on her chest. 'She likes me,' she said, her smile bright. 'Doesn't she, Dave?' Watching her, Dave felt his heart open. Three months later, he married her mother. A year later, his dream of more children exploded.

Half drunk, half sober now, he felt a tinge of fear. Yes, how he felt tonight was no doubt fuelled by his failed first marriage. Okay, maybe that was normal. But what if he'd picked another dud?

Amelia was in her first year at school when he saw what he'd done. Though they shared her with her artist father, Red, Dave spent hours clapping her jazz ballet and reading her fairy stories.

He made her porridge and taught her how to tie her laces, ride her bike, tango. His strategy was simple: he did the opposite of what his parents had done. Natasha was more slapdash; laundry was rarely done and school readers often lost. But Dave filled the gaps. It seemed to work. Amelia thrived; climbed on him, learned to read beside him and called for him at night. Quickly, it seemed, she loved him. The good times lasted roughly twelve months. A record, he thinks now, thanks probably to Amelia. Then, one chilly Thursday in June, the curtain lifted and he saw backstage.

It began around 5.45 p.m., when Natasha phoned his office. She'd been caught, she said, at her friend's studio in Preston; after-school care finished at six and she wasn't going to make it . . . Though Dave rarely finished work before seven, within ten minutes he'd shifted two meetings and was dodging traffic on St Kilda Road. When he arrived, a bit after six, at Wesley College, Amelia was writing her letters, stony-faced: the last child there. Seeing Dave, her eyes flashed with hurt. 'Mummy will meet us at home,' he said lamely. With a sigh, she fetched her schoolbag and took his hand. When they pulled into his driveway and saw the dark house, she didn't flinch. 'Mummy must still be shopping,' she said. 'Let's go upstairs.' In the kitchen, Dave found sprouting onions and warm beer. Irritated, he tried his wife's phone again.

'It's okay, Dave,' Amelia sang out. 'There's an apple in my lunch box. Come on.'

Half an hour later, he was on a titchy chair at Amelia's red table. Drawings of purple, orange and green butterflies covered the carpet. To his amusement, most were his. Drawing, he'd discovered by her side, was like riding a bike. He hadn't done either since he was seventeen. Leaving school, scraping into law at Monash University (and briefly satisfying his parents), he hadn't seen the point in continuing. And neither had anyone else. Over the years, he'd fallen out of the habit. He'd learned to live with the nagging restlessness, which he took for a by-product of adulthood. But, alongside Amelia, he felt unstoppered. *Permitted.* The tension that he carried was replaced by a curiously beautiful sense of spaciousness. Best of all, his stepdaughter adored everything he drew.

An hour later, Amelia's bedtime passed and their pictures were sticky-taped to the wall. He was still in his suit and she was still in her uniform when Nat arrived in a jumble of pizza and groceries. *We all run late sometimes,* he thought, feeling generous. But then he saw his new wife's enormous pupils and smelled her hair. Had it not been for that sense of spaciousness and Amelia's wary silence, he would've smashed something.

'Honey,' said Natasha, 'let's eat.'

With a furtive glance at Dave, Amelia nodded.

That night, he and Natasha brawled for two hours. What she took in his absence, who she was with or when she fed her daughter were none of his business, apparently. Around midnight, exhausted, he checked on Amelia to find her upside down on her pink bed. Tucking her in again, he'd felt sick at the thought of what she understood, and of his negligible rights as her stepfather.

But that was the past, he told himself, and he was free of it. Shut out of it. The digital clock clicked over to 2.44 a.m. He rested a hand on the sleeping woman beside him, as if to draw strength from her. She was, he told himself, everything he'd hoped Nat would have become with his help. Together, he and Elle could never be as dangerous as he and Nat became. He was sure of that. Healthy and high-functioning, Elle was *there* for *him*. Parenthood, he told himself, would be the making of them. Best of all, this time, the kids would be his.

14

Over breakfast the following Monday, Dave knew that he needed to act. One thing was clear: love for him was rare and Elle was his last chance at it. No matter how uncomfortable he felt, if he wanted a companion for life, he mustn't stuff this up. She was the only woman who'd taken the time to know him and love him. The only woman he'd ever admired: for her intelligence, passion and talent. But with her shoot about to begin, he could feel her heightened energy, her soaring adrenalin. Soon she'd be both further out of reach and more demanding than ever. Something major was needed before he smashed the lot.

He saw the coming weekend as his last opportunity before she was completely consumed by her film. Oh so casually, he suggested they go away. At first, she laughed. It was 'impossible', she said; Mira would kill her. But when he insisted that they needed quality, uninterrupted time together, at least once in the next seven weeks, she sobered. When he watered it down to one night on the Mornington Peninsula and promised that Saturday would be a much-needed day of rest, breakfast in bed, massage, he could see her weighing it up.

'Tell Mira you need some R&R before the shoot,' he said.

'Oh, David.'

'You'll feel better for it,' he said, 'and we need it.'

To his surprise and probably hers, she caved. On the conditions that she'd choose their Friday-night accommodation, they'd be back by noon Saturday, and the budget was hers, not his. Within a day, he'd read up on Red Hill and booked masseuses. By the Wednesday, she'd managed to find a cottage. By Thursday, he was nervous, and wondering whether he could do it.

At 6 a.m. Friday morning, he dropped three hundred dollars by her bedside table. 'Buy some wicked stuff we can cook for brekkie,' he wrote on a sticky note. Lord knew she was busy but they had to eat. When he returned that night, he saw she'd packed his favourite French cheeses and Turkish bread, and her orange chocolate, plus both their bags. He stuck his head into her study. A circle of light was falling across her laptop, script and torso.

'Your front door was wide open again.' He shook his head. 'What're you doing in here?'

She stood and trotted to him, kissed his lips. 'Some last-minute tinkering after today's final read-through.'

He took in the haloed script. It was like a sponge cake now, with blue, pink and yellow pages. 'For God's sake, if it's not working now, it never will. Let it go.' His tone, he realised, was resentful. And maybe hurt.

She slunk back to her seat. 'Actually, I'm happy. I was just finishing.'

Kicking off his lace-ups, he left them like a trip-hazard on the floorboards, then strode into the shadows.

'Is everything all right?' she said, following.

'Oh yeah, you've been chatting with actors and *tinkering*,' he said, 'while I've been jiving with bankers since breakfast.'

He'd learned a decade ago that Friday nights were not his best. The working week tended to erode his personality. He thought she would've recognised the signs, given her Freeman & Milne days, and let him be. But no. He peered along the hall to her lounge room. He felt like hiding in the television.

'I stink,' he said. 'I need a shower.'

In the ensuite, his skin felt hot and gritty. And it itched. He longed to shed the lot of it. She was still behind him when he stepped into the shower. She sat on the bath, with her left foot jiggling.

As the minutes passed, steam billowed. The tiles began to sweat.

'I'll pack the car,' she said, springing up. 'Let me know when you're ready.'

She was at the door when he yanked the shower screen open; scorching water sprayed. 'I'm not in the mood for much tonight.'

She blinked through the mushroom clouds of steam. 'This was your idea, you know. I'm happy to cancel.'

'Yeah, okay.' When her face fell, he was pleased. She seemed genuinely torn.

'Actually, Mira thinks Mum's here for the weekend. I've got an eighteen-hour leave pass. I could do with a massage.'

David scrubbed his hair with soap and froth flew. 'Okay, if you insist. But I don't want to drive.'

'Good, because I want to.' She paused. 'Did you meet with Alex for lunch?'

Despite her ridiculous schedule, she remembered his stuff better than he did. 'His board wants to shake things up. There's talk we might have to tender for Leonidas' business.'

'But that's a first, isn't it? What's behind that?' she said.

Through soapy water, he bared his teeth in a brief smile. 'They reckon we're too expensive. Don't worry, Alex's got my back. It probably won't happen.' He could see another question coming. 'I don't want to go into it.'

'Oh, okay.' She tried for a sunny smile. But there was confusion in her face now. Seeing it, he felt better.

Twenty minutes later he was more comfortable, dressed in a red windcheater, ugg boots and old blue jeans. He was walking, empty-handed, to the car when he felt her eyes upon his rump. Her desire never let up.

'That's so much better,' she said.

'Yeah, okay.'

She clambered into the driver's seat. He opened the boot then stopped. 'What've you done?'

'I was in a hurry.'

In a jumble were their bags, a car fridge, a picnic basket, her bloody DVDs, massage oil, candles, a box of Scrabble and groceries. Wedged to one side were her laptop and notepads. On top was a box of charcoals and a roll of paper.

She appeared beside him. 'Oh, that was meant to be a surprise.'

He glared at the mess, the stupid box of charcoals.

'What is it?' she asked.

'We're not going like this.'

He yanked things from the boot, like a dog digging a hole,

stacking them behind him on Tennyson Street. He took out a camera, her script and her storyboard roughs, and looked at her. She held his stare but said nothing. He took out her laptop and notepads and that box of charcoals, and put them inside the house. It took him twenty minutes to repack the car. All the while, he was double-handling the very things he'd wanted to leave behind.

The road was like a tunnel in the country dark. Eucalypts fenced both sides of the unmade surface and met overhead. They parted only to allow the crossing of other narrow tunnels. He kept his face to the window and his shoulder twisted from her. He'd been trying, unsuccessfully, to rest. But whenever he shut his eyes, he thought of what he planned to say, and how she might respond. He wondered how soon they could start a family. He felt like a bag of birds, and bloody cross.

Although she was driving carefully at 95 kilometres an hour, he could see red-brown dust pouring from his car like smoke. Red Hill should've been a seventy-minute drive from Melbourne but they'd been going for ninety minutes. They hadn't spoken, other than to quibble over their route. He was responsible for that, although they'd both realised fairly quickly she could read maps better than he could. Thanks to his last direction, they'd taken a short cut on an unmade road and were now backtracking.

His telephone rang, loud in the quiet, and he jerked it to his ear. 'What?'

Elle turned sharply towards him.

'No.' He hung up and tossed his phone to his feet. Seeing her concern, he regretted his asperity.

'Not work again?'

'No,' he said. 'Natasha.'

'What does she want?'

'The usual: money. And she's trashed.'

He could see her surprise and questions forming. Her desire to meet his ex-wife and stepdaughter was a pain, but she wouldn't raise it tonight. The two were like oil and water and neither of them needed to know it. He rubbed his forehead.

'Are you okay?'

'I've got a headache.'

'Again?'

'Yeah.'

Their uneasy silence returned. Ahead, a tin-shed hotel marked an intersection of tree-lined paddocks. Elle slowed, waiting for his direction until they were at a standstill by the gravel lot. In the car park, men were pouring out of the pub, like bull ants streaming from a nest. Utes roared to life, lights blinked on. In his car, Dave stared blankly at the map on his iPhone. Beside him, Elle was checking her mirror for rear traffic. When the nearest ute tooted, Dave jumped. Looking up, he saw that the Merc was blocking a queue of cars at the lot's exit. He also saw the first driver's large, angry fist.

'Settle down, mate,' said Dave.

The pink-faced driver tossed a can of beer at Dave's baby-blue coupe.

'Drive,' Dave said, slumping into his seat. 'Right.'

Bemused, Elle accelerated, made the turn. Unobstructed, the utes fishtailed from the car park and followed – every one of them. The darkness at the Merc's rear was broken now by a train of lights and tooting horns. Dave felt a clamp in his throat as he kicked off his ugg boots. Soon they were cruising at 95 again.

'It's all right,' she said. 'They're only boys.' She was staring into the tunnel of eucalypts ahead.

'It's not all right,' he snapped. 'We're in the middle of fucking nowhere.'

She laughed. Nerves, he supposed, but still he glared. She frowned and eyed her mirror. Each car held two or three men. They were so near, Dave could see the brand of their beer: XXXX. Even so, she maintained her infuriating, law-abiding speed. Abruptly, one car swerved to travel beside them.

'Fuck!' said Dave. Low in his seat, he tried to ignore the jeers. It seemed the hoons were pissed to see a woman at the wheel. 'Go on,' he barked to Elle. 'Go!' Dave felt the vintage Mercedes weave on the narrow road. Ahead of them was yet another hill. 'Elle!'

Elle was eyeing the speedo and, in her mirror, the four trailing cars. Then the needle on the speedo rose. *Thank God.* The car surged. The ute, caught off-guard, floundered as the road began to rise. It returned to its lane.

Dave could feel his pulse in his head. He looked from the car in the side mirror to the rising speedo. The leading ute was still tailgating, its occupants now imitating Elle's upright, ten-and-two driving posture. But she didn't slow. And his old car managed it. Soon they were cresting a hill at 140. Ahead, the darkness was cut by the headlights of an approaching sedan. The sedan, innocuous enough, broke the mood. Dave watched as the gap between the convoy and the Merc gradually grew. Elle kept her foot down as, one by one, the utilities turned off.

'Morons,' he muttered.

Sitting up with a squeak of leather, he adjusted his jeans. He checked his mirror a final time. The road in their wake was comfortingly dark. His headache ebbed. In the silence, Elle let the car slow and Dave felt his face colour. It was possible he'd overreacted. In the cabin, he felt Elle's eyes on his face. 'No,' she said, 'that was awful. I'm sorry I laughed.'

He looked at her then, closely, for perhaps the first time all night. His ways, foreign to so many, she took the time to understand and accept. He felt it and she felt it. For the first time in days, he felt like kissing her. He leaned across the chasm created by their seats but his belt locked and their lips couldn't touch. Abruptly, she pulled back as the road terminated at another T-intersection and a paddock. Their cottage was close. The eucalypts set off in perpendicular lines. Elle squinted at her notes, scribbled on an envelope.

It turned out that their weekender was only 400 metres to the south. Elle stopped at a wire gate, got out and, finding it padlocked, neatly scaled the fence. In the fuse box, she was to find a set of keys. From the car, Dave assessed the house. It was a 1960s rectangular brick-veneer, with the character of a rubber thong: a home reminiscent of his parents' in suburban Moorabbin. In the middle of a wine property four kilometres from the centre of Red Hill. With one glance, Dave knew that it was a mistake. Her aversion to luxury staggered him. While she had an eye for beauty, she had no interest in buying it. He had to drag himself out of the car.

Judging by a monstrous wall of curtains, large windows ran the length of the open-plan living–dining area. He peered behind the orange and brown stripes but couldn't see a thing: just a paddock in shadow and blowflies on the sill. The kitchen and lounge room looked to have been renovated in the eighties and forgotten. The beige laminate bench was scratched, the bar stools antique Ikea. It was both familiar and not as he'd hoped.

His fingers were shaking as he put his travel bag and one box onto the kitchen's black and white faux tiles. He wandered through the big, high-ceilinged rooms and tried to get his bearings. 'Not enough air in here,' he mumbled. 'Dodgy deadlock.' As she unpacked linen, wine, toiletries, he locked and re-locked all the doors: double glass sliding, flywire, masonite, security. Once the car was empty she prepared plates of antipasto which they ate quietly. Afterwards she made the king-sized bed; and he felt worse. He tried to ignore the flap of the linen as he jiggled the double locks, chains and bolts. Long after the bed was made, he was still at it. He heard her call to him once – not with insistence, more, probably, because normal couples spoke to each other. He heard her try again. When he answered, his voice was small. 'I'm reading on the couch.'

'Oh, okay. I'm going to bed.'

Dave sank into the brown velveteen couch. In an ugly house in the middle of a paddock, his courage was deserting him. Nothing, he realised, had changed.

He woke up on the sofa around six, disorientated and cold. He propped on his elbow as something nearby mooed at him. He scratched his hair. What a shocker of a trip. But it could've been worse, he supposed. They could've been forced to stop. He rubbed his face to get rid of the thought, but it was too late. He could see himself roadside, blindly throwing punches at those hoons.

He waited until seven before tiptoeing into the bedroom. In his hands was a glass bowl of raw eggs. He paused at the door. 'Up you get, sleepyhead.'

She was stretched across the bed on her stomach. Her hair was sticking up, her right arm reaching to his side of the mattress.

'It's all ready,' he said quickly. 'Hup, hup.'

Elle rolled over and yawned, her eyes closed. 'Where have you been?'

Though he knew she meant *overnight*, he said, 'Cooking.' Since six, he'd been hoping she'd come looking for him; that he could make up the ground he'd lost. When she hadn't, though his head hurt, he'd decided to get to work. For half an hour he'd been *tap-tap-tapping* in the kitchen, and feeling better for it. The fat blade of the knife had been moving smoothly. He'd chopped from the thickest end, as she'd taught him. He'd watched the mushrooms form semicircles; the spring onions, rings; the cherry tomatoes, cute little caps. He'd watched, heartened, until finally, he needed the last ingredient for his omelette.

He knew she enjoyed her rare sleep-in and he knew her thoughts on raw eggs. She couldn't stand the viscous white, the clear and stringy gunk. When she snuggled into the covers, he knew he had to act.

'Oh no, you don't!' he said.

He streaked towards her, his penis bouncing with his laughter, the bowl of eggs thrust out.

'These are waiting for you to beat them, sweetheart. Up you get.'

A smile parted her lips, opened her eyes. 'Take that thing away. You'll spill it.' The sound of her voice was a relief.

He sprang onto the bed and straddled her. He swayed from leg to leg, swirling the eggs. Under the doona, she watched, repulsed, as a yolk broke.

'Hop off, you,' she said.

Keeping the bowl high, he bent to tickle her. She crawled beneath the doona and through his legs to run, in her T-shirt, into the lounge room. He and his eggs chased her.

'Nothing to be scared of,' he called. 'There're only six. With one feather and two globs of blood.'

She was grinning, hiding behind the geriatric television. It swivelled on its stand as he crept towards her, and she went with it. He lunged, the eggs swirling, beating themselves. He was giggling like a kid. Spinning the TV, Elle made a run for it across the slate tiles. He sprang to block her. He was face to face with her now, the bowl above her head. A devilish gleam in her eyes.

She wrapped her arms around his waist. 'Don't make me do it,' she said.

Outside, black and white cows mowed the front paddock. The sun was bright. Elle's hand writhed down to his crotch and squeezed. He laughed, wriggling, snagged in her fingers. He had a speech ready for breakfast, but this had to be the moment.

'Careful,' he said, 'we need them.'

Her glance up at him was coy. 'We do?'

A firecracker exploded in his chest. 'We certainly do.'

She looked into his eyes and he made them serious.

'What do you mean?' she said, letting him go.

'Well, don't you think we ought to start trying? I want to buy a new house, with no turrets. In Albert Park or Hampton, and fill it with dogs and kids.'

He laughed out loud with relief: he'd said it.

Her face was blank. 'Right now?'

His chest held the last of its light then went black. 'Yeah. I'm forty-four next year.'

Elle hugged herself. 'Isn't it early in the day for talk of progeny?'

'No.' His tone was hard now, maybe too hard. She looked around, as if she'd just woken up. He tried again. 'You do want kids too, right, Ginger?'

He swirled the eggs in their bowl, slowly. She watched the orange whirlpool. After a moment, she snatched the bowl and put it on the TV. She eyed the cows, as if for moral support.

'Well, yes. But I'm confused. Half the time, it feels like you don't want me around. Like last night.'

'Ah. I can be . . . moody,' he said. 'Don't take it so personally.'

'It's hard not to,' she said. 'But I think you're depressed. And, at the very least, you should talk with somebody, not take it out on me.'

Here it was, he thought, that 'you're miserable' conversation again. Except this time she'd introduced a new move by making his problems pathological. Maybe she was right. But he preferred his solution.

'Having kids would make me very happy.'

Elle fluffed her bed hair. Watching her, he wondered how far ahead in this game she could see.

'Perhaps you haven't noticed, but I'm making a feature film. There's no room in my head right now for children.'

'Well, there should be! God, you lot are selfish! All so fucking self-absorbed!'

She gave that superior laugh of hers. 'What's that supposed to mean?'

He was sure loads of actors, painters and writers had forsaken their families. He just couldn't remember their names. Chaplin? Picasso? None of them were women. But that didn't matter: he was becoming pretty sure artists made lousy mums.

'Forget it.' He peered into the now empty paddock. 'I don't know how you can prioritise that film ahead of a family.'

Elle squared her shoulders, fully awake now. 'Forget about my film!' she said. 'We haven't been together a year! Three years would be more like it – three happy, *stable* years.'

'That's ridiculous! You're thirty-five!' He yanked the bowl from the TV set and stalked to the kitchen.

'This is not about my fertility or my film!' she called after him, her voice breaking. 'It's about you. You need to do something! Talk to someone. Draw a picture! Paint! Do anything but what you do now!'

'Listen up, I'm not like you!' he said. 'I'm not that *lucky*!'

'No,' she snapped, 'you're a coward!'

He turned on her, his face contorted. 'Fuck you!' he yelled. 'Fuck you!' He threw the bowl at her. It soared across the living room. To his surprise, she dodged it. It smashed on the slate into a hundred gooey pieces. When she looked to him, her skin was blotchy and red. Fear and disapproval shone in her big eyes.

'You think you've got all the fucking answers,' he hissed.

He grabbed his clothes from the couch, yanked on his sneakers and fled.

15

There is a bright red handprint on the laundry's white wall. Large, long-fingered. The print is near the doorway and mid-height; its thumb up. How did she miss that? She can also see a smeared path on the shadowy floor tiles. And blood leaching from beneath the green towel. This blood is not the bright red of the handprint; it looks black and oily in the darkness. The puddle is slick and unmoving. It unsettles her. Twice before, he has been violent. While it had shocked her, it was nothing like this.

What happened before she blacked out? What did he do? It bothers her, this missing information. It feels increasingly important.

—

The bathroom in the Red Hill farmhouse was cream and green, untouched since the sixties, and somehow familiar. In other circumstances, Elle would have relished the large, lime-coloured tiles and spotlit mirror. Alone, she tried to soak in its character, take solace. Beneath the wide jet, her head was down and water streamed from her hair. But her brain was jamming with what she had done; she'd wasted her time and, worse, risked her peace of mind so close to her shoot. She wasn't sure what shocked her more: the foolish decision to come away or all she had learned about David since the night before. His vulnerability and paranoia, his headaches and anxiety. While his unhappiness was plain, she hadn't realised its extent. Or how much it could hurt her. She pictured that hurtling bowl, meant for her, and shivered.

She understood, or so she'd thought, the roots of his unhappiness. They lay in the confusion of his childhood. A peculiar echo of her own. And in his hollow, lucrative career. So she knew his behaviour wasn't *personal*, not about *her*. But it was frightening. His reactions were so other and so huge. She adjusted the water, cooling it, as her thoughts pattered on. In one conversation, she'd gone from flattered to repelled to fearful. Yes, he was far more fragile than she'd thought. And far too volatile. Closing her eyes, she put her face beneath the jet. She wanted to go home. She needed to be home.

Three minutes later, she was about to turn off the taps, when the rickety shower screen eased open and David slipped in. She saw him and felt him at the same time. He was damp with sweat as if he'd been running. With her head bowed, he couldn't see her face and she was glad of it. In her eyes, he would have seen confusion. Wariness. But in the surrender of her shoulders, he correctly read acquiescence. Wordlessly he stood behind her, as though waiting for her to act. In that brief pause, she realised what it was she most wanted: the good version of him. She wanted the pieces of their relationship put back together, to start over. Recover. She inched back into him. He whispered her name, cupped her breasts. When he pressed gently against her, she murmured, and that was it. He twisted her face towards his and found her mouth. His eyes were closed and she was thankful. His lips were gentle, nibbling, teasing. His hands were busily finding her, arousing her. Briefly, she felt ambivalent and edged away, but he was working too hard, too well; and she relented. This connection, though fragile, was at least enduring.

Before long he entered her, thrusting deeply from behind. As he moved, she leaned her elbows against the opaque glass of the shower and willed herself to relax. She had been wanting him all week, though not, of course, like this. In his arms, in the steam, she tried to concentrate. On them; here, now. It could reset the mood and get them through; or buy her time to think. But then, with his next thrust, she clenched her fists and formed the word: *Stop*. Perhaps he didn't hear her over the racket of the shower because he kept on, working his way deeper to her favourite place. She decided to let him, knowing soon they could be breathing the same breath. But then he thrust deeper again and she gasped. Though she felt him hesitate, he didn't pull back.

'It feels weird.' She was speaking to the cloudy glass. When he didn't respond, she added, waveringly, 'But, okay, go on. Gently.'

Resuming, he moved tentatively and, closing her eyes, she moved with him. Each of them, it seemed, was cognisant now of the fragility of even this connection. He pushed deeper and she felt a stabbing pain. Her muscles clenched and her body straightened. He withdrew quickly. Clasping her hands across her abdomen, she stepped beneath the force of the shower. Cast out from the warm, he watched her, while his erection shrank like a reprimanding snail.

'What is it?'

She shrugged and tried to find the words. From the beginning, she'd gleaned he knew more about her body than she did, but now they were both in the dark. When she lifted her eyes to his, she saw confusion and something else: a new emotion she didn't understand. Was it shame? No words came. The more she floundered, the more she wondered what she was doing. She thought of their morning's clash. Her body. And his menacing attempt to claim it.

Trembling, she turned off the water.

With the jet and its noise gone, she folded her arms across her chest and nibbled her upper lip. The longer she remained silent, the more insistent his stare became. She was, she realised, waiting for an apology. Or at least an acknowledgement of his wrongs.

With a long sigh, she stepped from the cubicle and found her towel. She wrapped it around her shoulders, like a sodden child. It was as if they were in a foreign room, an utterly dissimilar place to where they'd been only two minutes earlier. David stepped onto the bath mat and dripped. He made no attempt to cover himself, and she didn't pass him a towel. His penis hung between them, now like an innocent bystander, and she ignored it. To her bemusement, he gestured in the air as if he had tried, and headed out.

The Red Hill countryside was green and velvety. On a droopy banana lounge, Dave took it in. Fir trees marked the boundaries between properties, and the sea twinkled in the distance. It was, he had to admit, a sensational view. He sighed. Great chunks of this part of the Mornington Peninsula were owned by his legal peers and others: surgeons and retail giants, developers and celebrities – old money and new. They all came here on the weekends, to ride their horses or surf with their kids. Why, of all places, had he chosen this damn spot? To magnify his lacking? To make a joke of his dreams?

It was time, he supposed, to give up on that score.

His favourite misery memoir, *Alive*, about the stranded rugby team in the Andes that resorted to cannibalism, was open on his lap. He tried to read its secrets of survival. But Elle, he guessed, was somewhere in the brown brick box, snivelling.

When his mother rang, he was genuinely pleased to hear her voice. For about three minutes. She told him all about Clarendon House (the pricey nursing home he'd found in Brighton Beach), and of her top ranking in the footy tipping. She reminded him of his father's birthday, which had just gone. Dave didn't say much and she asked no questions. Twenty minutes later, when she hung up, he felt more alone than ever.

Then Elle climbed down a nearby fir tree. She was holding a drawing pad. She had pine needles in her hair and bark on her jeans. All this time, she'd been propped on a branch, doodling. What sort of woman was she, for God's sake?

She approached with her eyes downcast. 'I have to get back,' she said. 'Now. The car's packed.'

He surveyed their grim homestead. He should've guessed she'd want to bolt.

'I'm hungry,' he said. 'Let's eat in town first.'

She opened her mouth, shut it.

On the drive, they didn't discuss the smashed bowl she'd cleaned up or their aborted shower. He navigated again, despite two wrong turns. As they drove into the village centre of Red Hill, she said, 'We've missed our massages.'

'No great loss.'

Her sigh was loud and melodramatic.

Searching for a car park, he kept his back turned and went over their morning. While the bowl thing had been a mistake, he'd done nothing else wrong. As they drove past families chatting on the footpath, he felt his anger flare again. What was so bad about what he wanted? There was no future for them without kids in it. What was the point, otherwise? Having his own kids offered him his best chance of happiness. Provided he didn't screw them up. But he couldn't be bothered putting his case again.

His hot silence seemed to have melted her desire to clear the air or defend herself. When she finally parked, she was looking at him as if a barometer was above his head. He made like a smouldering rock.

'I'm starving now myself,' she said.

He grunted. She'd have to do more than that.

On their way to a cafe, he ducked into a bric-a-brac store and hid behind a dressmaker's dummy. He watched as she turned on the footpath and saw it empty. Her face showed alarm and vulnerability. A flash of anger too, and that was new. He smiled. After a moment, he stepped into sight without acknowledging her. He was glad to see relief in her eyes, though she tried to hide it. She looked at her watch. In the musty shop, he slipped past old maps and teacups like a child playing peek-a-boo. He hid in a room the size of a cupboard and waited until she'd passed. He dawdled over silver candlesticks and mother-of-pearl vases and forgotten medals. All the while she waited, with growing irritation. She was distracted for a moment by an art deco figurine-cum-lamp. She waited until, eventually, she couldn't wait any longer.

'Let's go, *now*,' she said.

He made a point of examining an antique cigarette lighter.

And she didn't budge. He was amazed. He'd never known such doggedness.

He left the store and she tried again, with a toss of his car keys. As if she could surprise him, tickle him, back to life. A hand-holding, middle-aged couple nearby saw her attempt. They smiled, watching the keys bounce off him and fall to the footpath. They smiled, until they realised he wasn't going to acknowledge the keys, or her, or them.

When she bent to the keys, he heard her breath catch. He strolled into the closest cafe. He was seated and swapping smiles with the sassy waitress when he realised he was alone. Out of the corner of his eye, he saw his car pulling away. *The tricky bitch*, he thought, *she's done it again.*

Instantly, he felt more comfortable, as though the temperature had dropped from hot to mild. The sensation was bittersweet. And brief.

16

Elle drove as fast as she could without breaking the law. She drove, gorging herself on orange chocolate. The picturesque, tree-lined trip from Red Hill felt surprisingly short without him. Initially, she travelled with a cloud of guilt. But then, surrounded by space on the Mornington Peninsula Freeway, her guilt lifted. Twenty minutes later she was merging in traffic on EastLink and listening to her phone beep, when her regret manifested like a nasty mirage. She'd been insane to have a night away. As good as negligent. She should never have taken the risk. Mira would be furious if she ever found out the truth! And so much for rest and relaxation! Elle munched another two wedges of the chocolate orb. As she overtook family wagons, her regret turned into disappointment – it could have been so relaxing, so romantic! And then to anger. How dare he treat her like that! She was done with him.

On the Monash, passing through Chadstone, she drew two columns in her head and performed a cost-benefit analysis.

Pros	**Cons**
Chemistry	*Inconsistency*
Fantastic times (esp. re art)	*Rotten times: escalating? Diarise?*
Good heart	*Lousy at intimacy: does he actually love me?*
Honest (esp. re rotten childhood)	*Depressed/stuck; anxious/angry*
Wants children	*Is he father material?*
Is improving/wants to change	*Not enough; def. needs professional help*
I love him	*I have a film to make*

Closer to the city now, the traffic swelled. And the answer became increasingly clear-cut every time she analysed her data. Yes, she loved him. Because she knew him, *intuitively.* In a way she'd never known another man. She knew him even better now, having deduced that anxiety underscored his anger – was most likely his default position. But still she couldn't do it. Her responsibilities, her film, trumped their relationship. She did not have the time for this. He was simply too damaged. She couldn't afford to carry him, or manage his inconsistencies. She had no idea how to do either and she didn't want to learn.

Then, hurtling into the Burnley Tunnel, it struck her. The fault line in her pros and cons. Driving steeply underground, she had to acknowledge what he'd done. A speeding truck was in her blind spot and she slowed to let it pass. Watching it career downwards, she realised that while he *may* not have *actually* meant to hurt her, she didn't want to live with underlying fear. With the prospect of violence. As the road levelled out, she drew a thick red cross through her pros and cons. She travelled for kilometres underground, holding her breath. Another semitrailer thundered past, identical to the last one. She tried hard not to think of truck–car collisions, underground infernos . . . Without reception for the radio, she was forced to hum. Minutes later, emerging from the tunnel, she dropped her window and accelerated towards the sun and sky.

It was mid-afternoon by the time she left his beautiful car, crammed with books, suits and shoes, in his Middle Brighton driveway. Its keys were atop its right wheel, her note beneath his door mat: *It's not working. Don't call.*

She spent the rest of the weekend on the telephone, grappling with lost props and panicked assistants, double-checking her storyboards and shot lists. Over a quick coffee, she gave Mira an abridged version of her split with David. 'Good riddance to bad eggs!' became her best friend's catch-cry.

By Monday, arriving early on set, Elle felt weary, almost as if the shoot were due to end rather than begin. But it was Day One of her Follow-Up Film. A pivotal day, two years in the making. The script, thanks to Mira's final polish, was ready and about to be realised. The mood on set seemed heightened, no doubt thanks to Lucy. As the lighting was being fine-tuned people whirred around

Elle, asking last-minute questions. She answered, pretending calm. Everything about this shoot she had considered, from the shots to the lemon-coloured towels. In total, it would take a jam-packed thirty-five days. And it was all up to her, and her crew and actors. The decisions they made today. Tomorrow. Briefly on her own, she sneaked a deep, centring breath.

The first scene to be shot was a sex scene. She wanted to shoot it early lest, over time, her stars' chemistry waned. She observed the two receiving the finishing touches to their makeup. Built like a rugby player, with Islander good looks, Jay Morehu was joking with the makeup girl. For a second, Elle appreciated his fortunate genes. Near the bath, dressed in lemon terry-towelling, Lucy was subtly studying, perhaps also admiring, her co-star. The two leads, so different to each other, looked right: like a pair from the ark chosen to propagate the species.

Which was why, seeing them together during rehearsals, Elle had been thrilled. But as the days had passed she'd noticed a shift. Perhaps because Lucy's Freddie was proving, at times, spark-snuffing. The actor seemed to be playing the strident character Elle had penned, not Mira's slightly more nuanced version. Freddie was cutting slivers off poor Mike. While Lucy was wonderful with the banter, Elle had had to pull her star aside twice during rehearsals and ask her to pull back. Afterwards, she'd seen Lucy's performance lift and Jay respond, but . . . Surveying the Footscray warehouse, which was now Freddie's shabby-chic home – complete with Asiatic artwork, fifties furniture and wilting plants – Elle couldn't help wondering: could her leads deliver the requisite heat? Could they recreate what was so difficult to sustain in real life? Her nerves trampolined in her stomach. It didn't help that the first scene was set in a lime-green sixties-style bathroom. Peering at the clouded shower screen, her face puckered. Her art was reflecting her life these days and not the other way around. It didn't augur well.

Their first scene was to be a long one. The characters were to talk at length before their kiss in the bath. While the crew tweaked their equipment the actors ran through it at half speed, reminding themselves of its rhythm, and they both understood its beats. Everyone seemed to love this scene, including Elle. It was one of the few wholly written by Mira. And it was so hopeful. In it, idealistic Freddie comes to accept the transient nature of being in love and opts to commit to devoted, fallible Mike. After it, the characters progress to what psychologists call 'affectional bonding', a *stable*, caring union. A grown-ups' happy ending.

It was, though, probably the most challenging scene in the shoot – especially given Lucy's contractual stipulation of 'no nipples'.

Questions continued to be flung at Elle, and she chose the least wrong answers. 'How sweaty do you want them?' 'Subtly glossy, please.' All the while, Lucy was eyeing Jay as he kidded about. Approaching her actors, Elle couldn't decipher her female star's expression. She whispered into Lucy's ear, 'Remember – here, she makes a choice.'

Nodding, Lucy turned to Jay. He grinned at her and gave a thumbs up. The warmth in his face was so intimate that Lucy blushed. And Elle was heartened. That spark flaring again.

Back by the camera, Elle found the questions petering. She savoured the final notes of the orchestrated chaos of two dozen moving people: the hot lights and leaning microphones, the veins of cables and the omniscient camera. Julia Carter, her director of photography, was almost ready for the two-shot. A big-boned woman with auburn ringlets, Julia, like the rest of the largely female crew and a third of the cast, had worked on *Daisy*. Julia gave Elle's arm a sisterly punch and Elle felt a belated pop of excitement. Yes, this was what she knew, who she was. This was where time evaporated, days disappeared, where she could fly. She took another deep breath. They were good to go.

She scrolled through the scene's dialogue in her head. As it reached Freddie's epiphany, the words suddenly resonated in a new way. She heard David's insistent proposals and her own repeated refusals. Her reserve and his frustration . . . She tried to resist the inevitable question. Failed. Were their troubles her fault as much as his? Shocked back to life, the nerves in her stomach rebounded and took flight.

The call went out to close the set. Superfluous bodies exited, upping the air's charge. As the actors shed their robes and climbed into the bath, the slate in Elle's mind went blank. She could hear the assistant director making her calls for quiet, for sound, for camera. The clapperboard slapping. Seconds ticking, dollars burning . . . She felt a tap on her shoulder. But she was gone. Back in the shower cubicle, with David behind her, cupping her breasts. Her pulse dancing. Heat creeping up her throat.

'Elle?' Her first AD's face twisted with concern.

An hour-long second passed. Elle swallowed, her cheeks flaming. She managed a nod. Then she made herself sing out: 'Action.' And they were away. To her relief, she kept David at bay until lunch.

By Thursday, she couldn't feel any pain. Or nerves. She couldn't remember how long she'd been shooting. She couldn't remember doing anything but making this film. The week ended with all scheduled scenes finished, and with minimal overtime. The powers that be were happy. Mira was happy. And so was she. As the shoot had progressed, she'd gone on, she thought, to work well with the actors. Lucy pulled back and Jay was extraordinary: sensual, earthy, fun. Elle was cheered. It'd been more than three years since she'd directed *Daisy* but, at moments, she'd been that lucid director again. And, remembering, she'd drawn strength from that version of herself.

Then, at 10.20 on Friday night, as she lay in bed replaying the day in her head, he called. And they spoke. Twenty minutes later, she heard him enter her house and tiptoe across the floorboards. Her thoughts split between her work and him. While her working week had absorbed her, arriving home she'd felt his absence like a grinding ache. Her kitchen and her bed felt redundant without him. When he entered the semi-darkness of her bedroom, a part of her separated, like the yolk from the white. He was wearing a new winter suit and he'd cut his hair. These changes somehow made their separation tangible and aggrieved her.

'How was day five?' he said.

'It's going well.' She could hear her own wariness.

'Good for you,' he said softly.

Sitting up, she searched his face for evidence of suffering. In their week apart grey flecks at his temples had multiplied like weeds, and dark pockets hung beneath his eyes. Somehow his face was rendered more compelling by his anguish. He looked so handsome and harmless, so unlike the man she'd left in Red Hill. Despite herself she thought to massage his shoulders. She imagined his skin on hers. She wanted to tell him about her week, share everything.

'Here,' he said, 'I found this; I don't think you have it.'

From behind his back, he produced a book, time-browned

and soft. Alice Munro's *Hateship, Friendship, Courtship, Loveship, Marriage.*

Taking it from his tentative grip, she was reminded that he had truly erred. And that she had made a decision. Sombrely, she set the book on the floor.

'No. Thanks.'

After a moment, he kneeled at the edge of her bed, his face expectant. She said the only unequivocal thoughts she had.

'Last weekend was exactly not what I needed. But the worst of it was you actually scared me.'

She watched him absorb her words, like a body blow.

'Elle, I know. And I've seen a psychologist, twice this week already,' he said. 'A woman in Albert Park. She's smart.'

Shock and relief tugged at her features; she clasped her hand to her mouth.

'I don't want to be like this any more,' he said. 'Please don't give up on me.'

His eyes glazed.

Then with him kneeling beside her, she held their relationship in her hand – again. This time, she felt its weight: almost twelve months, perhaps two hundred nights and four hundred telephone calls. It was small but heavy. Weary but warm. A relationship barely out of infancy; it had been fed by shared experiences, good and bad; had developed limbs through travels taken; had learned its own language; and it had grown. Yes, there had been missteps, but there was life. And, for once, miraculously, it was hers.

Peering into his pained, gentle face, she could feel herself teetering.

'You make your film. Our kids can wait a bit,' he said. After that, it took only a tremble of her brow. David lifted the covers, as if lifting a piece of skin, and climbed into bed beside her. He lay still, like a splinter, and she clung on to him.

'Elle,' he whispered, 'you've seen my worst; let me show you my best.'

In the dark, feeling his breath on her ear, his hip against her belly, she felt something give. The part of her that had separated fell away. And, with its falling, she shrank. Instinctively, she knew not to examine this development or her new shape. Otherwise, their slim chance would be lost.

One night the next week, around 11 p.m., she came home after hours of viewing the rushes in the edit suite. She was keen to sleep but he'd waited up. He'd been to see his psychologist, Marion. He poured her a red wine as she plonked onto the couch. Then, calmly, he revealed how her reaction, long ago, to his house had made him *feel*. Hurt, sad and frustrated. She managed to keep herself quiet, not interrupt, and stay awake. He went on to say that her reluctance to advance their relationship had left him demoralised. Confused and nervous. Gratified, she watched him. When he was done, she said, 'Thanks for telling me.' And, 'I didn't mean to hurt you.' After, they had sex for the first time in six days.

A week later, he cut back at work and signed up for life-drawing classes. He did their shopping and kept house while she helmed the runaway train that was her film. Their world was righting. Then, one Saturday morning, he proposed again and she didn't let herself hesitate. Yes, he was flawed, and his behaviour challenging, but he was hers. He was, in essence, a decent, intelligent person who could make her heart sing. And she wanted him close. Always. It wasn't, she knew, a rational decision.

David wanted them to marry as soon as her shoot wrapped. And they did, one dewy morning in September. Elle found it surprisingly easy. A few forms, an appointment here or there. A venue booked. And, in a low-key way, it was done. Easier than buying a house and far easier than making a feature. Harder had been breaking the news to Mira, but she had managed – largely because shock had rendered Mira speechless. Telling her brother had been difficult too, once she'd tracked him down at an IT company. Their call was beaded with silence, but, eventually, Jude had agreed to come.

On the day, Mira was rather subdued as her witness, but that didn't matter. The bride and groom were ecstatic and Jesse and Max were delightful flower boys, bearing jasmine. After the registry ceremony that Elle had stitched together, everyone picnicked at the Botanic Gardens beneath willow trees. Elle wore a baby-blue, sleeveless, knee-length frock circa 1954; something she found in a vintage store in Brunswick and swore she'd seen, by Givenchy, on Audrey Hepburn. And a cluster of jasmine in her hair. David wore wax to tame his kinks and an op-shop white dress shirt that she'd found for him in Coburg. And he'd surprised her with a gift: a lamp. An elegant, lithe woman clasping an orb above her head. Art deco. Elle had been stunned, thrilled. Thrilled too, for the day flushed out people from both their worlds: a cluster of his work colleagues, a handful of artists, and his impeccably dressed mother, Lillian Forrester. The young painter and his waif-like girlfriend, another extraterrestrial, were there too; along with, of course, the best man, the inimitable Alex Carras, with his charming wife, Fi. On Elle's side were her convivial composer, Jody Tan, and actor friend Kate Collins, and most of her cast and crew, including sweet-talking Jay Morehu, who had captivated the celebrant.

There were a few notable absentees. Lucy had declined graciously, as she was Frankfurt-bound. David's elderly godfather had double-booked himself. And Elle's mother had been grounded in Darwin by a sinus infection – a phone message her only presence. ('I'm proud of you, Elle,' it said, 'I didn't think you had it in you.') Her mother's absence was more disappointing than she might have expected, although it did neatly avoid the possible outing of her lie to Mira. Having a mother, it seemed, was becoming important to her again. And, hugely, she missed her father. But once the day was underway, she was pleased to see her younger brother making an effort as the ambassador of her family. A change had come over Jude in their three years apart; though his smile was still cheeky and his look vintage-scruffy, his auburn hair was shorter and he seemed calmer, plumper. 'Dad's given up beer,' said Max when Elle caught her older nephew peeing beneath the willow's canopy. 'And he wants to take me and Jess to see the dinosaurs.'

'Good for him,' she said, and meant it.

Jude emerged then beneath the willow. In the shadows, smiling with those big white teeth, he could have been her father. They faced each other.

'Please don't take this the wrong way,' he whispered, 'but the last time I saw you, Elle, you were as hard as tarmac . . .' His blue eyes misted. 'And now . . .' She nodded, the barb passing right through her: painless. 'Congratulations,' he said.

She hugged him, and it was as if something was restored. As if she was an expert now at forgiveness.

'You do put on a first-class show, sis,' he said later as he left.

On the whole, Elle thought their day enchanted. The finest part of it was seeing David in a wider social context; with everyone he was magnetic, courteous, lively. He introduced her around as though she was a rare discovery that he alone had made, and he scarcely left her side. Their friends mixed well and everyone suppressed their surprise at the speed of the event – everyone except Mira, who, perhaps wrong-footed by the shift in Jude, bickered with him and with Troy, and snapped at her children. The greatest surprise, though, was Elle's own copious, silent tears. Starting during the ceremony, they didn't abate until well after the kiss. Dabbing them away, she did her best to ignore them and so did the groom. When it was over, he pulled her close and she smelled his melon scent. 'Sweetheart, you won't regret it,' he said before kissing her tenderly again on the lips. And she believed him, wholeheartedly, as the small crowd clapped.

A week after the wedding, when Elle floated back to earth, she had a nasty shock. Her film, she realised, was intrinsically flawed. Early on Yvonne, her editor, had suggested there might have been a problem. But Elle had been confident of what they had, despite a tiny niggle of doubt. Initially, she hadn't quite surrendered her original idea of Freddie. But now, as if through new eyes, Elle saw the truth of it. Lucy's performance *was* uneven. At times she was actually unconvincing, specifically in the gentler scenes with Jay. And it was baffling. Baffling that it could have happened. Baffling that Elle did not see it clearly earlier, during the shoot or viewing the rushes. Others at the shoot and privy to the rushes had seemed buoyed by what they saw, including Mira. But that made her feel no better.

Sensing her mood, David suggested a drive one Saturday morning. The sea at Fairhaven was spearmint-green. Rugged-up retirees and knee-high children dotted the shore. During the journey he had tried to cheer her, though she alluded only vaguely to her problems. He liked the idea of her as an accomplished filmmaker. And so did she. By the time David parked, having left the Great Ocean Road to curl towards the west, he was singing and she felt better. Here was the good David. The man who had introduced her to love and who excited her, the man who wanted to share his life, have children with her. The man he was at his core and would become permanently, with Marion's help.

On the foreshore, wearing only jeans and a thin cardigan, she felt her skin rise into pale bumps. Impatient for the sun's remote kiss, her thoughts reverted to her film. Why was everything so difficult this time around? She tried to focus on the feel of the sand and the sound of the water. She stared at the faded, burnt-orange cliffs and distant sea spray. Further along the Great Ocean Road, surrounded by sea, were famous landmark rock formations, the Twelve Apostles and London Arch. As a girl she'd been captivated when part of the rocky outcrop that had been called the London Bridge fell. She'd spent hours toying with the notions of hard and soft, strong and yielding. Questioning the assumptions she'd made about rock. She'd thought of the thirty metres of layered rock as flesh, with its vulnerable under-side eaten away by the ravenous sea. But the most tantalising thing about the story was that for six hours a couple had been on the remaining stack of rock. A man and a woman: stranded and alone while the water lashed. As a romantic youngster, she'd been fascinated by how they got there, what they said to each other, how scared they felt. And then who'd seen them? Who'd helped? She glanced at David, locking his car, removing his shoes. What would he make of that story? Did he remember it? She thought to cite it but something stopped her: a vague wariness, perhaps, about his reaction to her whimsy.

Unsettled, she strode along the shore and he followed, walking on his heels across the sand like a tourist. Near the water, on an impulse, she shed her jeans and cardigan to reveal a black, forties-style one-piece. The mild spring air whisked around her, along with his gaze. She was thinner now than she had ever been.

'You coming in?' A hint of defensiveness crept into her tone.

'Are you mad?' he asked, incredulous.

She hadn't planned on a swim: the bathers more a reminder of summer against her skin. But now she felt compelled to have a dip. She watched the swell build as it approached the shoreline in sizeable, transparent sets. It was one of those days that surfers celebrated, when the conditions mysteriously came together – the breeze off-shore, the swell head-height, the temperature mild. The days that made up for the early mornings thwarted by too much wind or not enough swell. It was the sort of day that sustained and rewarded. And she felt it shift something within her. Grabbing his hand, she dragged him to the water's edge. To her relief, he allowed her coercion until they were standing at the outermost rim of the sea, where the foam met the dry.

Pulling up his trousers, he slipped her grip, gently. 'It's way too cold for me.'

A wave swept their feet and David peered about, as if expecting an eight-limbed creature to pull him under. Another wave came and she took a step away. She felt the icy water nip her ankles. Her father and his father before him had been men with bronze shoulders and effortless muscles, like the sunbaker in Max Dupain's famous photograph. After her mother left, her father had become an Iceberger at Brighton Baths, swimming every day at dawn, year-round. She was, she realised, unaccustomed to pale and shivery men hesitating at the water's edge. She turned to look at David, alone in the shallows. With his rolled-up blue jeans and his woolly red jumper he seemed so out of place, she wondered if he truly was that blue-flamed gas fire she'd first observed long ago in her kitchen. Her husband . . . And, despite herself, she laughed. He was so complex and so vulnerable and so beautiful.

Plunging into the ice-cold, she made a decision. No matter what he threw at her, she would cope. Because she was strong: stronger than him.

17

A cockroach slithers through a crack at the base of the laundry trough. It's dark brown, long and fat. In the pitch dark, it heads for the purplish-black puddle. Appalled, Elle watches as the roach skirts the wetness to climb nimbly up the damp towel.

The roach roams the length of her trunk, with its long antennae twitching. It is taking its time, disappearing into folds of cloth. Briefly, she fears it might venture inside her, into the wounds that she can't see or remember.

Watching, she feels horrified and protective, as if her body were sentient, inhabited.

—

I'm not a bad person, thinks Dave.

He's cramped in Reg's deep, short bath. The water is tepid now, his skin goosy and his mouth dry. He's very thirsty. Had he somewhere better to go, he'd be there. Any minute now, Reg will shuffle in, or call the police. The longer a jury takes, the less predictable the outcome. The same could be said, he supposes, for violent criminals the longer they are at large.

From the hall, Reg is calling. Something like: 'You've been half an hour, son!' But Dave is turning to mush. It must be the tub. He's only had half a dozen baths since he was a kid. And now he knows why. In the water there's nowhere to hide, nowhere to look but at yourself. His skin – crinkling, hairy and wan – is scratched, and angry pink bruises are forming on his shins, his thighs. Inside, the story's worse. Inside, it's foul. He lowers his mouth to the water, takes a gulp to clean himself out. It doesn't work.

I'm not a bad person, he thinks again. *I'm not.*

For the last half an hour, Dave's been arguing with himself. The voice in his head, though, is his dad's: 'What've you cocked up now?' the voice is saying. The old prick. It occurs to him he's glad his dad is dead. At least Dave will be spared Bart's fiery reaction to this. He pokes a leg out of the bath and pushes against the wall. For once, he's done something deserving of his dad's wrath. Something warranting the shame his parents bred in him. A sob bursts out of him. He was an unwelcome stray in their home, and tonight he's become that cliché. An old mongrel hurt one time too many. He takes his other leg out of the water, slides his body lower, and sinks his head under. His heart judders. He tries to stay under. Can't. When he comes up, he sees himself, grey and drawn, an older version of his dad, leaving jail, starting over. His self-pity is laced with panic now. Who'll wait for him? Who'll understand? Alex? Natasha? Amelia? No way.

They'll be disgusted. That blind spot threatens. He can almost see it. His breath is ragged. He's straddling Elle, his right arm in the air.

'Hello in there?' says Reg. 'That's long enough.'

Dave sits up. He eyes the bathroom; it's long and narrow, its amenities in a tight row. The far wall is half mirror, half ceiling-to-floor window, fixed shut. Ignoring his reflection, Dave considers the window, as Reg raps on the door.

'I'm coming in.'

The door slides and Dave scrambles to stand. Water runs the length of him. Everything is shivering. Judging by Reg's face, Dave doesn't look good. Worry bounces between them and grows. Grabbing a towel, Dave clambers out. In the tight space, he and Reg jostle to find a respectable distance. Dave's shocked by how titchy Reg is: barely up to his chest. Wavering, Reg puts a hand to the towel rail. Dave busies himself with drying.

'We need to have another talk,' says Reg. His voice is breathless – with worry or maybe exertion. 'But first,' he puffs, 'if you don't call Sheila in the next five minutes, I will.'

Dave shakes his head, muttering, and fastens his towel.

'You have to act, lad.'

'I have nothing to say.'

Reg raises his arm, as if to pat or hold Dave; but Dave deflects him with an open hand. Reg's face is pained, and also somehow complicit.

'I'm sorry,' he says. 'We failed you.'

Whatever he's feeling, it's thirty-odd years too late. Dave shoves him away. The shove, though not hard, skittles Reg across the tiles, fast. Dave sees everything, and then, a second later, hears it. It happens so neatly, like it's choreographed. The skittling, the skull-on-china thud, the splash.

—

Dave's head is pounding as he breathes into the old man's mouth. He pauses. Reg's brittle old chest won't rise on its own. *Damn it.* Too fast, Dave does another set of breaths and pumps. He stops again. How long's he been at it? He scans the bathroom for a clock but sees only the mirror and his large frame kneeling over Reg's wet body. He does another two rounds then stops. The old fellow's definitely still. Dave waits, mumbling, 'Fuck, fuck, fuck.' He waits about thirty seconds. Then another fifteen. He can't see what else to do. He lifts Reg up from the floor and repositions him in the water.

Fighting tears, he hunts for buttons on the tiles. He's gasping as he spies a robe on a towel hook and puts it on. Then, in a mad flap, he charges around the house. He does the dishes, grabs his dictaphone and Reg's notes, and runs. In his head is the picture of Reg, face-down and bobbing in his bath. He can't shake it. That grey hair moving in the water, one wrinkly foot sticking out of the tub. *Oh, Reg, you poor bugger*, he thinks. *I'm sorry too.*

Within minutes, he's speeding next to the mouth of the Yarra. He is scarcely aware of what he's doing, where he is. He tries to get his head around how he feels, and what this means. This stay of execution. He is taking the curve on Douglas Parade when he sees another roadblock in the distance. The only way back, he realises, is the way he went out. He spins his wheel and his car twists beneath the bridge. It skids to a halt beside the barrier. He's so close he can read the plaque about the thirty-five workers who died when the bridge fell. He climbs out of his car and runs to the edge of the marshy land. His chest is heaving and his headache is bursting his skull. Vomiting again is a real chance. He stops at the watery edge. Nothing happens.

Then he sees it. Across the Yarra, downriver, smoky and dramatic in the heart of the port: an inferno, thirty metres high. The flame is surrounded by an army of lights – red, yellow, blue. Breathless, he watches the brilliant orange, the volumes of grey pouring from it. The air is toxic. *Jesus.* Guilt overwhelms him then, as if it were his fault. Everything else has been, so this probably is too.

He watches for a long time. So long that his guilt fades and his body pulses in sympathy with the raging fire. He thinks about fault. And reactions. And disaster. Luck, too. What he's done tonight is criminal and reprehensible, he thinks, but it's not entirely his fault. And, relative to that inferno, it's minute. He's not proud of any of it, but he has been stupidly unlucky.

By the time he's back in his car, he has a plan. It goes something like this: over 35000 Australians go missing each year. She can be one of them. Unhappy since making her film and leaving her marriage, she's run away. That's plausible. All he needs, before he disposes of her – God knows where – is that knife and a bit of help.

Ten minutes later, he's staring at Nat's place. Her house is like her neighbours': ugly and double-fronted, a blonde-brick box, built in the fifties. Though the eras are different, for his money, Newport and Seddon are the same: too close to industry and the West Gate. That his ex-wife and his current wife live – lived – so close together has bugged him. Often when driving on the bridge, he'd imagined he could see both houses. He'd come to think of them as fixed reminders of his fuck-ups.

Though tonight, maybe that would change.

He jogs up the concrete path, the night air tickling his chest. He pulls Reg's terry-towelling dressing gown across himself. How to explain this outfit? Should he bother? He knows Nat still has some of his old clothes stuffed under her bed and plenty of odd socks. He knocks twice, pauses, then knocks twice more on the glass panel in the green wooden door. It's his knock and she will know it.

The hand that flicks the light switch is covered in red glittery nail polish. He sucks in his breath. *Amelia.* He's forgotten all about her. He fears her touch might just undo him. This gorgeous girl-child who was never his. But shouldn't she be in bed? It's well past nine. What a shame he can't tiptoe in and play tennis with her on the Wii.

'Hi, sweet pea,' he says through the door. 'It's me.'

The girl's face appears, squinting through the glass until she recognises him. Then her green eyes become like grapes. Her eyelids are dusted with glitter too; her dark hair is loose and long. She's taller than she was a fortnight ago. She's wearing orange pyjama shorts and a green T-shirt covered in guitars. She's less dancer these days, more fledging party-girl. Even so, seeing her, he craves the clutch of her thin arms around his neck. Skin-hunger. He'd never understood it until he'd inherited her, all too briefly.

'Hi, Dave. Where've you been? Did you remember my birthday present?'

Dave curses under his breath. She was fourteen in June; her first birthday missed, probably now one of many. Soon she'll be all grown up, and he'll have missed the final stage. He battles to keep his cool as the sparkling fingernails reach for the lock. Beneath the globe, he feels conspicuous and silly. An older woman appears on the other side of the pane. The tortured smile slides off his face.

'Is that you, David?' His ex-mother-in-law is short, darkly freckled and round. Her face is scrunched like a piece of newspaper. Her Kiwi accent is thicker than he remembers.

'Hello, Marjorie.' He steps from the door and speaks to his feet. 'I didn't know you were in Oz.'

She cranes to see him on the edge of the shadows. 'What do you want?'

'To have a word with Nat. Where is she?'

Marjorie takes in his outfit as he tries to see inside. He can make out the usual debris of Nat's life strewn across the purple carpet – dirty clothes, clumpy pelican sculptures, half-full mugs. Something numbing and addictive is playing on the TV: country girls becoming ladies. Nothing changes. Not the good and not the bad.

He can feel his anxiety rising, like a weir in flood.

'She's gone out.'

'But Gran, she's on the —'

Marjorie pulls the girl from the door as if he were a snarling dog. 'Leave her be, David. You're not welcome here.'

Dave hops onto the front step, in full light. 'That's not what Nat said last week. Come on, let me in.'

Marjorie frowns and shakes her head, as he knew she would. He knows, too, this news will rattle her. It'll undermine her faith in her daughter, and in their recovering relationship. As he glowers, she retreats and another face appears: coquettish but cautious. Marjorie glances up to her daughter and sighs. They've all been here before. Married or not, it doesn't change.

'I'll be right here, Natasha,' says Marjorie.

Barefoot in jeans and an orange jumper, Nat greets him and undoes locks. She has crimson toenails tonight. Her ears are dotted with a line of glassy green stones, which curl around her lobes like mirroring question marks. Unfortunately, he can remember tearing one of them. He can just make out the scar. He has his own scars too, though, like the one under his right eye. Thanks to a bottle of beer hurtling at him across a dance floor in Brisbane. And that night they weren't even fighting.

To his surprise, Nat barely opens the door – leaving him stranded on the mat. Her eyes are puffy. 'Hey, Dave, can you come back tomorrow? I'm in the middle of something.'

'No, I can't.' His hushed tone is more sinister than he intended. 'Let me in.'

'It's not the right time, honey,' she says, her tone placating. 'Amelia's on her way to bed.'

'I'm not here to see her,' he says and his voice breaks. 'I need to speak with you alone.'

'Why are you looking at me like that?'

'Let me in.'

She eyes the heavy night sky. 'I can't, Mum'll flip.'

'I'm in a fucking dressing gown.' Marjorie coughs from close by. 'You come out then, Jesus.'

'No. I mean, we're not meant to.' Nat peers into the blackness and touches her puffy face. 'Anyways, now's not a good time, Serge wrote off my car this afternoon . . .'

He badly wants to yell. How does she pick these Gallic losers? The bigger the arsehole, the better? He wants to shake her. He would, too, if her mother wasn't loitering in the hallway. He tries to calm himself down. But she always makes him feel like this, like he's had too much coffee.

'Nat, I'm in a spot.' He stops, inhales. One step at a time. 'I need . . . some clothes.'

Nat's smooth skin rumples. 'You've been back to Elle's, haven't you? And you've had a fight.'

Dave tightens his flimsy belt. 'Nat, please.'

Worried now, Nat tugs her ear, stretching the question mark of cheap stones. He doesn't look at the scar above the top dot of green.

His ex tosses her head towards the north-west. 'Just forget

about her, Dave. Go home and get some sleep.'

David blinks, disarmed. 'I can't.'

His stare turns inward and he can't hold her eye. His silence is tinged with guilt. She's not the brightest woman but she could always read him. Her emotions skate across her face – victory, surprise, fear. Her green eyes glitter with tears. 'Dave, what have you done?'

God, he hates the tears. 'She didn't give me a fucking choice!'

'Oh, no,' she whispers, 'oh, no.' She pulls back to shut the door, but he shoves it. She stares at his fury, as if seeing it for the first time. And he makes a decision: to escalate. When he speaks, it's an eruption.

'I was here tonight, Nat. I don't care what you say to your fucking mother. I was here from six, and I stayed all night. Now, let me in!'

He is leaning into the space between door and frame. The door crushes his shoulder as Nat leans against it with her mother's help. Together they push, until he yanks himself away.

'Fuck, Nat!' he yells, as he hears the bolts. 'Fuck, fuck!'

He kicks the green wood panelling and mangles his toes. No doubt Marjorie's on the telephone, calling the cops. He can't believe he's done it again. Royally screwed up.

18

Passing Corio and its oil refinery, Mira feels a sense of dread. *Please don't let it be like last time. We simply won't recover.* Giving sage advice, having it ignored, is tough.

Eyeing her stirring children in their booster seats, Mira promises to do better with them, to let them fail without judgement or recrimination. Briefly, she wonders whether she can pull that off. Then, speedo rising to 130, she remembers the shocking day when their friendship imploded.

It was early one Monday morning in October, when Elle pulled up outside Mira's house. Though it was barely daybreak, she was twenty minutes late. A long day lay ahead for Elle but she'd insisted on helping a car-less Mira. The boys were on the verandah, bags on their backs, a teddy in Jesse's arm, Spiderman in Max's, primed for their family day-care. Mira was behind them, squinting at Elle's headlights, her mouth already a thick, straight line.

'What took you so long?'

'I'm sorry,' said Elle. 'I got caught up.'

Elle's smile was instant and, in it, Mira could see a stencil of David strewn across her bed. The marital bed. Feeling the matching etchings of a frown on her own face, Mira turned away. Though she hadn't seen Elle since the wedding, a fortnight earlier, how she felt was still red-raw. Ever since Elle took the man back, Mira had developed a recurring fantasy: in broad daylight, outside the Sun Theatre, she was slapping sense into Elle, as if they were living in a 1940s screwball comedy. The slaps went on and on.

Mira had tried to calm herself by focusing on Yarraville through the car window. All along Francis Street grey semitrailers clogged the road, idling and unmoving, like massive, panting, prehistoric beasts. Inbound, the trucks were performing their morning ritual as they headed for the Port of Melbourne. Puffing, grumbling and poised. Elle's old Valiant, with its windows down, was like an ant surrounded by asthmatic dinosaurs. An oblivious ant.

'Can you close that?' Mira glanced back at Jesse. Quietly the window rose, and Elle set the air to recirculating. Fenced in by trucks, the car barely moved.

'Okay,' said Elle, her voice wavering.

In the sealed space, Mira could feel Elle's agitation. Perhaps this lift to the mechanics was more than a friendly gesture. 'How's it going with Yvonne?' Mira asked. 'Have you finished the rough cut?'

'Almost.'

'Good. You're on track.'

When Elle spoke it was to the steering wheel. A whisper. 'Mira, it's not as I'd hoped.'

'What?'

'We're doing what we can. But you need to be prepared.'

Max's gaze from the back seat swung between the women, worried and confused. He thrust a thumb into his mouth. Mira peered into an enormous stationary wheel alongside her. She should, she realised, have seen this coming. She shouldn't have left Elle alone to slog away with Yvonne. While that had worked beautifully for *Daisy*, this film was proving to be their difficult second child. 'What's wrong with it?'

'Well, Lucy, mainly.'

Mira snorted.

'Mira, Lucy is great with the banter. But the love scenes – she's not feeling it.'

'She looked great in the rushes.'

Elle sat up. 'The bath scene works, I think, but the tender scenes after that . . . I'm wondering if something happened with Jay.'

Mira battled to keep her tone even. 'Let me get this right: you missed it during the shoot, watching the rushes . . . but now you're sure.'

'I had a tiny hunch during the shoot but . . .' Elle paused. 'Mira, I'd love to be wrong. And I'm trying to make it work.'

Engulfed by anger, Mira kept her face to the window. She knew she shouldn't have accepted this lift. Especially not with the boys in tow. She couldn't trust herself to speak. In the silence, her anger multiplied exponentially.

'This isn't about the film, is it?' said Elle.

Mira shrugged. No, it wasn't. 'I don't understand what has happened to you.'

'Nothing. I'm happy.'

Mira's laugh was unkind but she couldn't restrain herself. 'These last four months, it's like you've taken up with a cult. The last time we spoke, properly spoke, you'd left him.'

'Then he came back and we worked things through. Can't you respect that?'

Mira turned in her seat as if to launch a verbal rocket. 'No.' She spoke to the shock on Elle's face. 'I'm not going to collude with you on this. Every time I see you, you look more shattered.'

'David loves me, and he's better now. You don't know him the way I do.'

Mira shook her head, as though further discussion was pointless.

'You know, we don't need your blessing.'

'Pull over, we're here.'

As Elle turned into a cramped car park in front of a private house, Mira sprang out.

'Quick, boys, Mummy's late.'

The children burst out of the car like slingshots, and Mira couldn't help herself. 'I want the old Elle back, because if this is love, you're better off without it.'

Elle's voice was raised as a line of semis rolled forward, exhaling. 'You're hardly a paragon of good judgement!'

Fuming, Mira glanced to Jesse's pale, wee face and grabbed his hand. She took a step, stopped. 'Do you even remember Hal Hartley?' she yelled. 'Love is respect, admiration and trust!'

Pricked by guilt at the memory, embarrassed too, Mira veers off the Princes Highway and into the gloom of a tea-treed rest area. As the car idles, Jesse grumbles in the back seat but she ignores him. After that, all communication with Elle ended, other than talk related to their film, and that became even testier once the investors saw the rough cut and gave their notes. Though Elle organised the occasional social event, which Mira attended grudgingly, Mira mostly left Elle to her *husband*. The cost of that course of action she still feels.

'Why are we stopping?' says Jesse, his voice croaky with sleep.

'We're having a rest.'

This last break has been by far the longest – two months. And Elle managed it on her own. Yes, Mira thinks now, the old Elle did come back, sadder and disillusioned, but restored. That muscle, the one that was so weak for so long, must be strong by now.

In the silence, gradually Mira's emotions clear like clouds to reveal the question she's been avoiding. If Elle refuses him, categorically, how will he take it? With a nod to Doris, she thinks: *What is he capable of?*

Reviewing Elle's behaviour through the prism of possible physical harm, Mira doesn't like what she sees. Didn't he throw a bowl at her once? The longer she considers it, the more the trajectory from Elle's unlikely elbow injury to her guilty backflips and waning looks worries Mira. Especially when it culminates, she can see now, in Elle's behaviour at their film's opening night, which was the last time that Mira saw Elle with David – the one night, even now, she's not ready to recall.

In that deserted rest area, Mira's car is cold by the time she dials Troy, blurts her concerns. Troy asks her to repeat herself. Three renditions of the story later, he agrees, reluctantly, to meet her at their favourite pancake place in Geelong, feed the boys and take them to Jan Juc.

'If it will make you feel better, I'll call him,' he says. 'But Mira, I think she's fine, wherever she is. He's a tosser but he's not a brute.'

Forty minutes later, Mira is alone, finally, and driving wildly in a north-east direction. Her telephone rings, weirdly upbeat in the cabin.

'Yes?'

'I got through.'

'And?'

'He hasn't seen her since June.'

'Shit.'

'I could hear the lie in his voice.'

'Fuck.' Mira accelerates.

Troy breathes, hesitating.

'What?'

'He told me how she's ruined him. He wanted to know whether Elle understood the damage she's done.'

'Ah.'

'I will never understand that relationship.'

'No,' says Mira. 'You won't.'

Troy clears his throat. 'Mira, ring me as soon as you find her.'

As the call ends, Mira's resolve is palpable. In another forty minutes she'll be back in Melbourne, and she will find Elle tonight if she has to stalk the coward herself, police in tow.

19

Desolate, Elle doesn't want to observe any more. She was so foolish, so impressionable and weak. She considers her body soberly in all its sordid detail. Viewed from above, from the back, it looks so narrow and slight. Her hair, that morning cut into a twenties bob, is fanned across her face, and beneath her head it is soaked in clumps. At least she can't see her eyes and any dead-fish stare. Even so, her body looks so frail and inconsequential. One hand is outstretched, above her head, in front of the washing machine. It is reaching as it does when she's asleep. But she doesn't look asleep, not with her legs twisted like pipe-cleaners and her fingers streaked with ribbons of black.

As a final insult, on her right foot, on the big toe, the cockroach is nibbling.

Perhaps, she thinks, *I deserved this.*

—

Too late, she identified the interplay between what she did or didn't do, and this tendency of his: to punish.

Married, they had hit several cherished high notes: picnicking at the Heide gallery, lunching with his mother at Brighton Beach, taking Alex's girls to the zoo. They even had two mildly torturous dinner parties with Troy and Mira. And David kept up the appointments with Marion, fortnightly. He'd begun to quote her like an oracle. 'I wish I had a dollar,' Marion had said, apparently, 'for every time a client longed for his relationship to be the way it was in the beginning.' And, 'Disappointment is an inevitable part of any long-term union.' And then, 'A secure, loving relationship can have positive long-term effects on both parties.' Elle listened, wondering what exactly they talked about. But she didn't dare ask lest she disturb the process.

During this time, David danced around the house, gave her pre-loved fiction and made chocolatey desserts. His anger abated; the jagged edges were shaved off his moods, and he continued to be civil to her friends. Perhaps because Mira and Troy were having troubles, with Troy pushing for their clans to move to his new Jan Juc house and Mira reluctant to hitch her wagon train to his so soon, David and Troy struck up an unlikely camaraderie. It transpired that David was familiar with Troy's florid paintings of seventies surf culture. A meeting with some buyers was mooted. He was, for a month or two, being good – good, that is, for David.

Marriage had seemed to agree with him: he was fit now, his body muscled; he ate well, slept at night.

Most importantly, she had seen fresh glimpses of who he could be if he let himself be happy. She'd caught him in unguarded moments singing as he dressed, or exhilarated after a jog, or laughing on the telephone. Cheeky, playful, boyish. The David she loved, the man she married. But, despite her efforts – schlepping on the domestic front, sharing none of her anguish in the edit suite, ignoring his farting and his naked television viewing, even feigning interest in his legal matters – the good David didn't last and the promised David didn't come.

Little by little, he began to snap at her again. 'Isn't it your class tonight?' she'd ask, or 'Can't someone else go into the office?' And he'd fire back: 'I don't care,' and 'No, they can't!' She found herself retracing their steps, questioning her memory. She began to ask less. To curb her chattiness to ward off his tetchiness. And then, for reasons she didn't quite understand, their art-centric social life collapsed.

One muggy evening, as he walked his fingers up the jutting staircase of her ribs, she felt apprehensive. Outside, rain was trying to fall. She told herself that if she acquiesced, perhaps it would go smoothly. It would be over in half an hour. It might dislodge her disappointing day, quiet her ever-rattling brain. Like going for a bike ride or eating fruit. And it might not hurt.

It had been hard to predict, that prodding pain born in Red Hill. One moment, when she was on top, or her legs were over his shoulders, it was there; yet the next time, there was nothing. He could slam into her and find no resistance. It was random, unpredictable. But its very unpredictability taxed her. Whether it hurt or not, she was thinking about it. Anticipating it, trying to avoid it. David found it irritating. Sometimes, when she asked, he tried to steer to the left, to pivot or rotate. But, more often, he forgot or stopped.

Oddly, though, while dulling her desire, it had the opposite effect on his. As soon as she laid her head on the pillow, she was overtaken. Overtaken by a determined army of tiptoeing fingers, ready to pilfer and thieve, as if her body was unguarded or without borders. While she wasn't looking for passports and visas, a salute, given eye to eye, would have done the trick. Or at least one line raising the question. It would have given her the chance to choose, to acknowledge their separate states. Or at least remind him of the pain.

David edged his body closer. She could feel his hands on the back of her neck, kneading the clammy flesh beneath her hair. His body curved around hers like a hot shadow. She could feel his penis nudging her thigh. It was at once enticing, menacing and infuriating. She wanted to grab it and snap it in half.

Turning towards him, she opted, for once, to decline. But as her mouth opened he kissed her so deeply she felt invaded anew. Listening to him groan, she wondered how they had travelled so completely from his nocturnal indifference to this – his plunging tongue and penis – when she felt that prod. As usual, the pain was hot and angry. She sucked in a breath.

'That was a definite stab.'

David pulled away from her. 'Again?'

She nodded. To her surprise, twin tears escaped.

David slumped onto his back.

'I'll see a doctor,' she said, 'once we finish the final cut.'

He made an indignant *humph*. And she curled away from him, an island again on the sea of mattress. Outside, the rain had been blown away. The wind had deferred to silence. And her foreboding grew.

It was early morning when she felt his touch again. She imagined she was floating on the sea, ebbing with the tide. Even in sleep, her shoulders were clenched and knotted. David worked away at her, rolling the folds of her in his hands. He sat on her backside and caressed her arms, her twiggy wrists and the bony tail of her spine. She murmured. Wordless. She was an undulating land without border control, its leader subterranean. He slid along her and sat on her thighs. He massaged her buttocks. He took his time. Like this she was separate from him yet surrendered.

Parting her cheeks, he entered her.

She awoke, completely, and propped on her elbows, her hands in fists. 'Get out.'

'Hey, it's okay.'

'No, it's not.'

David withdrew. 'I thought you might like it. Did it hurt?'

'I don't. And it did.'

David slid his hand along her leg, as if she was a flighty filly he'd ridden for the first time, and she stiffened. He gave her thigh a quick, hard slap. 'Okay, okay.'

Dazed, Elle lay flat on the mattress with her face in her pillow. Sleep had been torn from her, along with a kind of virginity.

That morning, she visited her GP then made scores of calls until she found a gynaecologist with a cancellation. Mr Hanna was younger than her and an enthusiast, both of which compounded her anxieties. He bounced like a recent graduate in his airy, cool office, decorated with bronze statuettes of naked women – bending, stretching, standing tall – and explained the workings of her body. She listened, rendered silent by the statistics and the deductions he made – based on her age, lack of pregnancy (ever) and one symptom.

'Ninety per cent likelihood,' he said, 'it's the wayward weeping of a disappointed uterus.'

Once, she would've laughed. But she'd come with fears of cancer – ovarian, uterine, even bowel – so this news brought relief, for a moment. Until she thought of her husband's reaction to this news.

It was the endometrium going outside the uterus, the wrong way, like a backwash of pool water. She studied Mr Hanna and his milky teeth as he went on. The backwash was like a normal menstruation, he said: it bled and wept. But then it healed like a sore. A lesion. It grew sticky, clear gunk. It attached itself to other organs. Caused sticky links. *Like glue*, she thought. Weeping and gluing. Weeping and gluing.

That evening, she dozed fitfully until daybreak. Her dreams were the colour of hibiscus. Blood poured from her, soiling the bed, the sheets, flowing across her thighs, down to her ankles. Amid it, she heard a man's voice, over and over, describing the uterus and menstruation: the weeping of a disappointed uterus. The wayward weeping. Then the blood swelled within her and she saw it floating in bubbles towards other organs – the ovaries, the bowel, the bladder. Even as she dreamed, she knew it was her body turning against itself. Rebelling in frustration. Binding her organs to one another. Filling spaces meant to be void. Shedding from a place meant, by now, to be occupied.

When she awoke, she was cradling her abdomen. Though her foreboding was acute, she knew she had to tell him.

On the city-bound train, she watched the houses pass like the slow images on an old film and tried not to think ahead to their impending conversation. Apprehension churned in her gut. But what, she wondered, was she so afraid of? He could hardly throw a bowl at her at Freeman & Milne.

Today, she was pretending that they were like proper couples – couples who popped into each other's work or who spoke on the phone, without concern about whether it was a good time, whether he was in the right mood, whether there would be silence or sarcasm or aggro. As if they were as her parents had been once, a couple who followed each other's concerns with genuine, impossible interest. She craved the highs and lows of daily intercourse seen through each other's eyes: shared, relived, split. She wanted to share herself with him, unreservedly, unguardedly. Specifically, she wanted him to know, somehow, her film had slipped away, and, married to his changeable behaviour, she was unhappy.

But outside his building, her ready words dissolved.

Since leaving, she hadn't been back to Freeman & Milne and she saw its tower as though for the first time. The whole fifty storeys were constructed of charcoal glass. Rain slid down the windows like oil. Inside, offices were alight and stacked like shelves. Figures were bent over desks, burrowing in filing cabinets, on the telephone. There was such busyness. Making her way to the elevators, she counted heads to steady herself. More people were in this foyer than she'd seen all year. Some sat on streamlined couches and sifted through briefcases while others carried coffee and paper bags from the cafe. There wasn't one person doing absolutely nothing. Even the security guards were animated. Suited men and women passed and she averted her eyes. She was reluctant to be recognised by her old colleagues, as if she couldn't trust her face. As if she had lost all memory of the language of this place.

When the lift doors opened she faced a vast, five-star reception area. Charcoal marble and crimson flowers greeted her. Beyond the entrance were panels of glass and a long drop to the street. A young woman was on reception, speaking into a mouthpiece; with her black hair coiled and her skin creamy gold, she was another spectacular ornament that Elle didn't recognise. She glimpsed her own reflection in the glass. Her hair was stiff, her jeans green with stains, her boots leaving a trail of mud on the marble. Ducking her head, she slid past the desk, heading for the southern tower.

As she pushed through an internal door, she spied beneath her fingernails remnants of her garden's basil. Briefly she was unsettled. How much she had forgotten herself. In the hall, a staff waitress passed, regarding her with something like pity.

Approaching his office in the south-eastern corner, her nerves grew. His unpredictability was, she realised, worse even than his bark.

She crept past glass boxes housing bent bodies. Stress emanated from the walls of densely packed shelves. One by one, she eyed the solicitors, associates, junior partners, but each ignored her. To her relief, not one of them was familiar. As she neared his corner, she felt eyes flicker in her wake, with the prospect of tearoom fodder. In his vast space, two walls of glass met. And there he sat, stooped over a thick document on his desk as an older, standing man stabbed a finger at the print. The man's voice was a low rumble, but his face was crimson. Out of sight, Elle stopped.

She loitered on the other side of the grey partition. She was facing now a cell of four women, who were typing and answering calls. Ignored, she felt even more conspicuous. Abruptly, the wall shuddered and the man exited. He passed her as if she were a pot plant. And she vacillated anew. Clearly, now was not the time.

Then David appeared. Fully suited, clean-shaven and in matching socks. But ashen. Seeing her, he started. He took in her work boots, her jeans and wayward hair. She was, patently, in the wrong uniform, the wrong barracks.

'Where's the fire?'

'Hi. I thought we could get some lunch, go to Treasury Gardens.'

He shook his head. 'Not today.' He gestured to the lift well. But she didn't move. She bit the inside of her lip. 'Everything okay?' she said.

'Everything's fine.' His brown eyes glinted.

'I needed a break from the edit suite . . . I need to talk to you.' Her words came out loud. 'Now.'

Frowning, he considered her. To her surprise, again, she felt vulnerable and wrong. An interloper. Her lips began to tremble. As if newly conscious of her fragility, or their hushed audience, he nodded.

In his office, Elle could see as far as the Dandenongs. She had forgotten how spectacular the views were. David closed the glass door. Though his office had a couch, he sat behind his desk and she sat in front of him. For seconds he sat, staring at the wall behind her. It, like the other wall, seemed to be constructed of black-labelled folders. Each folder bore a golden, round shield: Leonidas. The densely packed shelves and their folders reminded her of bars. Rows of black bars. She made herself look outside. Rain was pelting into the glass. The wind had changed. David's eyes sought his computer.

'This won't take long,' she said.

Sighing, he leaned across his desk and retrieved from a wooden box a packet of cigarettes. Though no longer an office worker she was familiar with certain developments in the law. Furtively, David lit up. She thought to speak but became aware of the bounce of noise beyond his office: telephones, talk, photocopying. Through his closed glass door, she could see the spectacled eyes of a middle-aged woman in the secretarial corral.

'Why don't you say what you have to say?'

His mood, she saw, was against her. She should have called ahead. Or at least gone to reception. David inhaled without looking at her.

'Okay,' she said.

David turned in his chair and exhaled onto the window. He watched the smoke spread and thin across the tinted glass. His body was squared, as if bracing itself against her.

'Yesterday I visited a specialist and he thinks I have a gynaecological condition called endometriosis. That's what's been affecting our sex life.' She paused. 'It's closely linked to infertility.'

David stared at his depleting veil of smoke. His lack of response astounded her. Fireworks she had anticipated, but silence? She found it dizzying, like she was suspended over a trapdoor. She stood, realising this was not the place for this conversation, not the time. Her lack of judgement, again, wrong-footed her.

From the orchestrated bedlam of ringing machines and purring copiers, the PA was watching openly. Elle ducked her head. The woman glanced at her colleagues, a stealthy invitation. More eyes turned to the theatre-screen of David's door. David didn't move, though he sighed. He opened a drawer and extinguished his cigarette into a clean ashtray.

She walked to his thick window and peered down at the human specks on the bitumen below.

'Spit it out.'

'Okay.' Her face felt hot. 'I need to have a procedure to confirm the diagnosis and if it's right, cut away what's there. He thinks

I should have it immediately, but . . .'

His eyes narrowed, and she saw twin pinpricks of anger.

Into the silence, her voice croaked. 'I don't like hospitals. I want to get a second opinion.' She wiped her mouth with a trembling hand.

'What's the point?'

Elle frowned, uncertain of his meaning. Watching his stillness, she realised that he was unsurprised. He jutted his lips into a Neanderthal pout but she could see guilt in those red-brown eyes. When he spoke, his face turned a deep, sour red.

'I've had enough of this.'

She sank into the couch. 'This? What do you mean?'

David slid the leaden document from his desk. Impassively, he crossed his legs and observed the sets of eyes on the other side of his door. He angled his chair so that he could see neither them nor Elle, and turned the first page. Amid scrawled annotations on the cover, she glimpsed the ubiquitous shield and the word: 'Tender.'

'You don't get it. I want to be a father, not with someone defective.'

His smile was a surprise: fat and thick, rich, like a poisoned dollop of cream. She hadn't known a smile could hurt so much. She rose from the couch gingerly, as if giddy with it. She rested her fingers on his desktop, like struts. His phenomenal selfishness struck her.

She found that she was struggling to breathe. As her chest rose and fell, he stared at the slab of paper in his hand, as if it was the most fascinating document in the building. As the seconds passed, it took all of her strength not to yank it from his fingers. She imagined climbing on top of his desk and tugging his face to hers. Tears sprung from her eyes and she crumpled as her fingers gave way on the desktop.

'I can't cope with this,' she said. 'I can't cope.' She said it over and over, as if the words were new in her mouth. The more she said them the more she shocked herself. The more she knew it was true.

'Don't do this,' she said. 'David, don't do this.'

The absence of his anger now was creating a vacuum into which she felt her emotions sucked and magnified. Her chest continued to heave while David continued to stare at the document. She found herself sobbing. It took her a minute to realise that he didn't intend to speak again.

With tears sliding off her cheeks she left stealthily, ignoring the startled faces of the administrative staff and the sudden hush. In the corridor, a familiar striding figure, leaner, more concave, stared through her; Andrew Milne's disinterest was the final paper cut. Back in the elevator, her chest was a cage of pain.

For five days, she didn't hear from him.

Tears, delicate and ephemeral as feathers, became a part of her days. It was as if a great stopper had been tugged from her and she trickled. She became accustomed to the unheralded wet sensation on her cheeks. In the edit suite, on the footpath, in the toilet. She tried to remember to stock tissues in her backpack and every pocket.

In the small hours of the night, she unpicked their relationship until she understood. They had been entwined, playing off each other for months, and the more she'd needed him the further away he had gone. But the insight didn't change a thing. She couldn't breathe without him, couldn't eat, couldn't concentrate. On day six, she called him and he hung up. On day seven she tried again. On day ten it seemed she'd paid her penance, and he came back with *The Old Man and the Sea* and tickets to Tasmania to visit the Museum of Old and New Art. They picked up where they'd left off.

As soon as the final edit was approved, the picture locked, she and David went to Hobart. And he doted on her. But not long after their weekend away, he started to yell.

One Friday, he yelled because she hadn't made an appointment for her laparoscopy. He called her irresponsible, short-sighted, selfish. And, by way of punishment, he took off for the weekend, without another word, only to return with a handcrafted picture frame for her. One Monday, he yelled again when she asked why he'd stopped seeing Marion. He called her a harridan and a hypocrite, and hurled his phone across the kitchen. After, spanking-new his-and-her smartphones appeared on their pillows. One Thursday, he hollered when she confessed that her film, now in the final stages of post, was a disappointment. 'What's all this been for?' he screeched. 'All my goddamned sacrifices!'

When he shouted, she told herself that she could take it. That she must be calm. Stronger. That it would pass. Mostly, late at night, she couldn't stop herself from shaking; even so, she made her voice firm and demanded he stop. He'd fall silent, and, while he didn't speak to her again for a day or two, afterwards he cooked and waited on her. Sometimes she mustered the courage to tell him she had no need for his gifts, and he'd nod, hangdog. Or, amazingly, he'd make her laugh. Vindicating her enduring faith in him. Sometimes, though, when he yelled and she pushed back, he yelled and swore and she felt more afraid. And, then, ashamed, she cried again. As the weeks wore on, it became a dance. The more he yelled, the more she cried, the more he yelled.

—

Late one night, he was strewn across the couch. That day, he and his team had presented their pitch to Leonidas. It had not, she gathered, gone so well. His hot scrutiny, his malaise, radiated from his nakedness. In the unlit room, cross-legged on the rug, she stared at the television. Watching it had become his leisure-time activity of choice.

'I'm trying here,' he said, out of the blue, 'but it's probably going to get worse.'

She felt him looking at her, awaiting her reaction. For months, as she withstood his moods, she'd been trying to will the good David into being, permanently. His warning was, she supposed, fresh evidence he still existed. Even if he was saying: *Go. If you can.*

'So you should see Marion,' she said, gently.

'She said I didn't need to come any more.'

Once she would have laughed or screamed. 'Well,' she said, 'she was wrong.'

She rose then for bed.

'You don't seem so good yourself,' he said. 'Maybe you ought to go see someone.'

She nodded, numbly; perhaps she should. Lately, managing him and spruiking her film seemed to be getting the better of her. Just that morning she'd mumbled her way inanely through a radio interview. He gave her a ruined smile. Dutifully, she walked to him and bent down. He kissed her cheek.

Brushing her teeth, she wasn't so lost as to deny the truth of her lot. Her marriage had become a type of hell. Undressing, she peered at the leaning tower of books on her bedside table. Why, she wondered, was she still there? And then, the baffling answer came.

Despite everything, she loved him. The decent, clever man he truly was beneath the murky hurt and rage. And the thought of her life without *him* filled her with grief.

20

On the evening of Thursday 5 June, she stood before her mirror, blinked mascara onto her lashes, dabbed rouge at her cheeks and grazed lipstick across her lips. Her hand moved half-heartedly, the faint tremor of her fingers more beguiling than the result created by the creams, dusts and gunk. Her hair was in a towel and she forgot it: the heaviness on her head, the dense, cold sensation around her ears. Only once the towel began to unravel did her focus shift from her fingers. It was then, as the towel tumbled, that she felt the inexplicable urge to gag.

Gagging was the latest in a litany of changes she was observing. Anxiety; she had never realised it worked in such peculiar, tangible ways. Her vagina smelled, her skin was scaly and her hair was coming out in clumps. Each week as she took stock of herself, to her horror, the list grew. Her body was shrinking, her cycles haywire, her sleep disturbed. Worse, observing these changes seemed only to magnify her anxiety; so on it went.

Her hair, wet and tangled, waited on her shoulders for the gagging to pass. With her throat still heaving, she glanced at it. A visit to the hairdresser had been booked but forgotten. She rubbed at the matted strands with a sandpaper-y towel until the bile in her stomach settled. Then, yanking and plugging in her hairdryer, she turned upside down. The hot air blasted onto the base of her skull and she left it there, like a punishment. She could smell hair singeing and heard the dryer groan. She shook her hair and dried it patchily. Right way up, she didn't look into the glass but merely flattened the tousled mess and exited.

For a night like this, she would never be ready.

Opened in the late 1920s, the Regent Theatre had been one of the first and most extravagant picture palaces in Melbourne. Once, she had thought its golden Rococo interior was fitting for the opening night of *Limerence*. Tonight, ascending the red-carpeted staircase, she regretted the theatre's size and opulence; its romance and grandeur. With a gritty smile she slid past the small crowd of onlookers. Posed for the photographers. In the foyer, briefly unobserved, she tarried. She tried to take heart from the resplendent velvet furnishings, the glowing candelabras. In its long life, the theatre had survived a fire, a flood, a twenty-year closure, and threats of demolition.

At ten past seven, already she was late.

Midway across the crowded foyer, she heard a voice. But it

wasn't possible. When she'd called, awaiting him in Seddon, he had been snared in a meeting in Richmond. Disappointed but pragmatic, she had called a cab and waited. Nothing about this film had gone as she had hoped and its opening night wasn't to be the exception. Listening for that voice again, she surveyed the faces, mostly youthful, some middle-aged, but all dressed similarly in black evening clothes, and many breathtakingly beautiful. She found it unsettling, the relentless tallness and beauty. Where did these people come from? Scanning heads, she couldn't see his distinctive wayward hair. But still she hesitated, confronted by so many faces; her momentum was lost, caught in a crosswind.

A waiter appeared alongside her, barely twenty and as beautiful as the rest of them. He recognised her. Plucking a water, she turned from his reverential bow and thought of hiding beneath the staircase. Then, once the lights dipped, she'd be able to slip in and watch her film alone in the back row – as she had at its test screening. Thanks to some disengaged murmurings from that audience, twelve minutes had been shed since then. At the eleventh hour, she'd come up with an introductory disclaimer: 'The relationships depicted herein are purely fictitious, and bear no resemblance to actual relationships, past, present or future. Please don't expect this at home.' As well as quirky intertitles, each a chapter heading beginning with 'Love is . . .' or 'Love is not . . .' Even with its retro soundtrack, featuring Blondie's 'In the Flesh', she still hadn't saved it. Not much she could do with an uncommitted lead or lack of sparkle. The investors' contradictory notes hadn't helped much either. Over time, some people had come to appreciate the film's irreparable problems. ('This is not the Lucy we paid for,' one investor had complained.) Others, even now, refused to see them. Like Mira: resolutely optimistic Mira. Perhaps, thought Elle, that was the enduring power of Lucy van den Berg.

A burst of laughter from the middle of the foyer turned heads. *It can't be,* she thought, craning, but it was: David. She blushed with unexpected emotion; given he'd arrived ahead of her, his presence felt like a betrayal. Few nights if any were hers. But it wasn't anger that pinked her cheeks; it was shame.

Weaving towards him, she saw him foxtrot away, holding a tray of champagne flutes. A spick-and-span David. Not the David in his homey clothes, not the David in his work suit. This David had wax in his hair and was wearing the op-shop dress shirt that she'd found for their wedding. This David was jiggling to the music, a middle-aged raver. Mesmerised, she watched as the purring, sparking David glided with his tray above his head through the crowd. She felt like a mother, stunned to see her child out of context and in his element. She was dressed like a time-poor parent, in black trousers and a black scooped-neck top – as good as in her pyjamas. Clothes had become a dull necessity, like water. Her interest in her appearance had fallen away months ago. She had been focusing exclusively on her film, her anxiety and her reproductive potential. But the months, she realised, had had the opposite effect on him; he had grown toned and tidier. In the crowd of younger, fresher faces, he was shining. As he sidled towards three brunettes, Elle observed the youngest of the set flutter and stretch like a young horse trying out its legs. She admired the girl's clinging halter dress and the way her shoulder blades jutted. She watched David bow as he served them. It was almost too much to watch: his gracious levity, his charm.

Conscious now of Mira, pinched and searching from the mezzanine – with a photographer in tow – Elle slid between bodies to better see. What had she done to deserve this? Or was he always like this when she wasn't around? Incredibly, perhaps, she had never wondered at his behaviour in her absence. She had simply assumed he'd be glowering and alone, at an empty cocktail bar. Or engaged benignly at Alex's gallery.

As she watched, David retrieved his wallet and gave his card to the girl, who pocketed it like a child receiving her first dollar. When he withdrew, he danced further into the foyer. He dusted himself around – laughing, inquiring, touching shoulders. This David was hers, though she hadn't fully formed the thought before. *His. Hers.* These weren't constructive words. But they were flaming above her head as she watched him spray himself onto smiling women as if fertilising flowers. Energy, she thought – it was so subtle. And her presence, her energy, was least relevant of all these people's to him tonight. The realisation cleared her head like a blast of cold air.

In her pursuit of him she had drawn closer to the staircase but she didn't acknowledge the friendly faces, the press and ascending acquaintances – all here for her film. Instead, she watched him. What was she doing? Was it grit or was it pride? Was it pride or was it hate? Whatever it was, she thought, it wasn't love.

The realisation brought with it a kind of panic.

She felt twin stabs of colour in her cheeks, as if she'd been slapped. She was startled as much by her clarity as its timing. She folded her arms, clenched her trembling fingers. Perhaps something shifted in her, or her energy altered, for David saw her then. When his face didn't respond, she busied herself with her handbag.

Nonchalantly, David extracted himself from a group. Approaching her, the light in his face dimmed. 'When did you materialise?'

'Oh, not long ago.'

'What are you wearing?' he said, his eyes flinty.

Elle glanced at herself, straightened her top, which had risen, revealing her belly. She felt conspicuous to herself now. Enervated yet knowing. David thrust his keys into her hand and she clenched them until the metal dug. As he scanned faces, Elle took in his new, old shirt again, his obedient hair and freshly shaven cheeks, his sweet melon scent and new shoes. He was humming – there was no denying it – and impossibly beautiful.

As David sipped champagne, they stood side by side, unspeaking. Around her, the din underlined their silence. She felt herself sinking into it. If she wasn't careful she would disappear into it again and they would go on as they always had. She wondered if she had the strength to act. She told herself that when the time was right, she would – decisively and with dignity. But not yet: not on her opening night.

In the grand, darkened cinema, watching Lucy's uneven performance, listening to the jokes misfire, Elle realised that sometimes, being right was worse than being wrong. If only she'd listened to herself, casting Freddie.

Within the silent crowd were the cast and crew, the investors and critics. She thought of Yvonne and Julia, Lucy (regal again and exquisite), and Jay, Mira and Troy, even Jude and her mother, somewhere. Surely now all seeing and sensing what she was. She longed to slip out. Though all too familiar with her film's shortcomings, she felt remarkably unprepared for sitting in that audience. Yes, there was the occasional chuckle or murmur. But every misstep was magnified, every dry kiss. She felt so patently inept. She vowed to avoid everyone she knew, when it was over.

As the lovely, guarded Lucy loomed from the screen, someone

began to cough. People behind her wriggled. Even David scratched his head, crossed his legs, again. Energy; even the collective energy was now turning against her. Her eyes filled. She nudged David, as if he was a normal person with a hand to hold or tissue to offer, but he didn't respond. Briefly, she doubted that he'd felt her touch, but with her cheeks dripping she peered again to see his profile set like rock. Never before had she been so well ignored.

For the first time, she hated him.

Looking past him to the rows of upturned, wan faces, she was bewildered, unable to recognise a single one. In the midst of so many, she felt herself crumbling, cast off and forsaken.

Elle is mortified. Bad enough that she publicly persisted with him, that she thought she needed him; tonight, she has become his *victim*. She imagines all those people watching her film, the fans of *Daisy*, her peers from high school, from university, from Freeman & Milne . . . All of them seeing her now – *on the tiles*. The arsehole.

In the space of a few hours, he has reduced her to a tabloid 'murdered wife'. To be read about on page one or three. To be, like the women murdered before her, held too briefly in the public eye. A tragic, if mundane, inevitability, like a road fatality. Fury engulfs her. No matter what she has done, or tolerated, her life was precious. And he must be caught. Punished.

Her rage is so intense, it ignites something within her. A need bigger than her own; a hunger for justice.

—

Outside Nat's place, Dave is gripped by new panic. He paces around his car like he's locked out. All he has now are questions: Where to? What now? And that biggie: What's he done? He sees her that day at Fairhaven, in her forties swimsuit. How happy she'd been in those freezing waves, with him. What the fuck's he done?

Earlier, on the phone with Troy, he'd tried to say as much, but it didn't come off. He could hear the guy's dislike. He glares into the low grey sky. He wants to bellow like a wounded bull. He feels a pain in his chest, his left shoulder: here comes the heart attack. He groans but the pain doesn't budge.

He should've picked he'd feel like this. Lately, seeing his ex has had a bizarre effect on him. It's made plain who Elle was and what he's lost, as if clarity is somehow relative. Elle was his top-shelf girl. A genuine one-off. She didn't want to be kept or saved or mollycoddled. She didn't rant at him or tie him down. All she wanted was for him to be happy too.

She was, he knows, his last chance.

After the screening, the applause was polite. For a full house at the Regent Theatre it was conspicuously modest and Dave knew why. The film was patchy and that made it average – not shocking, not terrific. It was, he guessed, the result not of Elle's efforts but of Mira's. Tonight's film lacked Elle's wit and had nothing of *Daisy*'s joy and optimism. It was pragmatic, unromantic. It shocked him too that Lucy's performance was so lacklustre. What should've been sexy was instead hard to watch, the leads like two dancers out of step. And what about the transformative power of love? There was none of that magic.

He walked beside her in the throng. How would she resurrect her career after this? 'You're only as good as your last . . .' Isn't that what they said? He sighed. She was so emotional these days; for sure, this would topple her. Her fingers dug into his and he tried to let go. But her grip was mighty. All around were post-mortems of her film. He tried to ignore the grumblings. He didn't have the stamina for her creative life. It taxed him and eclipsed him, and gave him back so little. Propping up a gifted artist was one thing, supporting a dud something else. He'd done his time with Nat; he had to live with himself. He didn't need more disappointment in his life.

What he needed was a beer.

Elle was tugging at him. Her face was pasty, despite her ghoulish makeup. She was so thin and frail now. He didn't get it – the ferocious drive of artists, where nothing else matters. And then, on completion, the soul bared to all. Whatever the cost. Yeah, he missed that spaciousness, that peace, but it wasn't a life he envied; not any more. And he was pretty sure now: it and motherhood were not compatible. Her dodgy plumbing had done them both a favour.

Yeah, he needed a drink. He squirmed out of her hand, mumbled then merged into the mass. Somewhere, Alex would be terrorising a waiter.

An hour later, the foyer was like a bar room, sticky underfoot, and people were beginning to leave, when he found her sitting behind a flower arrangement.

'Hi. I want to go home,' she said.

He peered at her red eyes and dry lips. Her hands were shaky. 'I'm not ready and you're drunk.'

'I've had one drink.'

He cursed; knowing her, it was true. 'Then it was spiked.'

She stood, turning her back to the foyer where Mira and Lucy were cloistered sullenly near the exit.

'What've you been doing? Where's your mother?'

'I don't know. I haven't seen her.'

To his surprise, her eyes welled. He shook his head; even now, she expected her mother to rise to the occasion!

'Go home,' he said.

When she didn't blanch, he was surprised.

'I want you to come with me, now.'

This was his final test, not that he knew it at the time. It'd take him weeks before he understood. She'd had lots of opportunities, lots of reasons, but she'd stayed. He'd almost come to believe the impossible: that her love was bottomless. Irrevocable.

'No.'

Someone shouted a goodbye. He smiled, waved, but she didn't move.

'This was meant to be my night,' she whispered. 'We're going home, together. You're drunk and I'm driving. Now, let's go.'

A hot wind of frustration gusted through him. She had his keys. She'd made this flaccid film. She'd hidden all night. But why had he given her his balls? She couldn't fucking use them. And he wanted them back.

'Give me my keys.'

She peered up at him, pleading, but defiant too. She twisted her right arm so that her handbag was behind her back. Without blinking, he grabbed her right elbow and squeezed. Her eyes shrank, the pupils becoming two fierce black points. He was mesmerised by the way he could do that to her, shrink her.

'Please,' she said, her voice rising. 'David?'

At that moment, Alex appeared, mildly drunk. 'There you are! What a film! Very . . . grown up.' He looked at Dave and then at Elle. 'What's going on, Dave?'

'I could do with another beer.' Dave kept his face neutral. 'Go on, mate.'

'Elle?' said Alex.

Dave held his breath.

'Elle? Are you okay?'

Her head nodded: a far too ambiguous gesture. Dave squeezed her elbow again.

'Fuck off and get me a beer,' he said.

Alex glowered. They'd been here before – he knew it, Alex knew it. With Nat, it'd been unspoken. But it'd been ugly. And there'd been a fall-out: four long years without art.

'Let go of her,' said Alex.

Dave dropped Elle's arm and raised his hands. Elle smiled weakly.

'Are you okay?' said Alex again.

'Yes.' Her voice was soft but her smile was brave.

'I admire your loyalty,' he said. 'But I can't stomach mine. Not any more.'

Dave drained his beer. Alex kissed Elle on the cheek and strode into the crowd. Dave knew he wouldn't see him again that night. What he didn't know was that Alex was taking a stand. A costly one. For keeps.

'Jesus,' Dave said, 'let's get out of here.'

He clamped her hand and led her through a fire exit. Quickly, they were in a cobblestone laneway in the company of rubbish bins. A dead end, without any of the city's nooky, hidden bars. The silence worsened his mood. All he wanted was his fucking keys! He grabbed her arm again. He felt her squirm, seeking out the brick wall. He watched her clinically. Did she have any idea what he could do? His fingers dug in her flesh. Her fear was growing. But he could see her grit.

'Please, David, let go. Let's just go home.'

He snorted. Jesus, why wasn't she giving up? He dug his fingers deeper. His nails were breaking the skin. He could feel the pressure in her knobbly joint. This moment, he knew, was important.

He upped the pressure. Her bones were so thin they could snap in his fingers. The pain must've been moving in hoops now, up her bicep to her shoulder. How much longer would she last? For a frail-looking woman, she was tough. He pushed her arm into the bricks, to let her know he wasn't stopping. She was asking too much. Sweat rimmed her hairline. He didn't blink. Within his grip, her elbow screamed. He could hear it. A high-pitched wail. Reading the pain in her eyes, he shoved her, hard, against the wall. Her handbag burst from her hand.

'Go home,' he said. He grabbed his keys.

She averted her eyes, and he thought he'd made his point. Then she started to cry. Pain he could handle, and her measly anger too. Even her defiance. But not those fucking tears.

'Why do you hate me?' she said.

He yelled then. He couldn't stop. She was whispering. Tenderness. He threw everything he had at her, to shut her up.

'All I've ever done is love you!' Her words hit him like stones.

'Shut up!'

She flinched as he lunged at her. His hand connected with her hot, wet flesh. Her jaw jolted as the slap drove her into the wall. The thud was dull. He watched her twist and fall, like a piece of spaghetti. Conscious but silent. When her blue eyes closed, finally, he did hate her: for taking so long to yield, for being so goddamned stubborn. For telling him he needed to see a frigging psychologist. For challenging him. For loving him. Most of all, he hated her for making him do what he'd promised himself he'd never do again.

Twenty minutes later, he was in his office tower. The building was holding its breath. He swayed in the lift, his eyes shut. On the fiftieth floor, he swiped his key at the doors and staggered in; if only the office had windows that opened. At least the place was empty. In his office, he pulled a pillow and a blanket out of a drawer. He rolled a joint as quickly as he could with sore knuckles and thumb. Lying on the carpet behind his desk, watching the smoke, he kicked out like a toddler. Why are the only women he's ever loved so goddamned unstable? It was only later, once the dope moved from his lungs into his blood and to his brain, he felt the chronic self-disgust.

He got up and urinated into the closest filing cabinet.

For an hour, he muttered into his dictaphone. Two tapes later, he was wondering when to stage his return. Facing her after a fight wasn't his strong suit. He couldn't bear to see the reproach in her doe eyes, the need quivering her chin. About five days was his limit; five days to breathe again, fill out and freefall, until the hunger came back. Until the tipping point when his fear of losing her was greater than his need to be free of her. At that point, that yearning returned, hot and urgen, and he wondered what he'd been doing. How on earth he'd let himself take the risk.

He mumbled into his black box until he saw things with new

eyes. Despite her film's faults, it did have something. A word to describe how he felt during that intense stage: limerent. Despite his meandering conversations with his therapist, he hadn't really understood it until tonight. But, watching, a bell had chimed inside his head. He laughed, miserably. He had to admit, he was like Freddie in the set-up – he far preferred head-over-heels pursuit or making up lost ground.

The real thing, standing still, was hard. How on earth did other people do it? Cope with the boredom, the uncertainty and that nasty urge to destroy? Or was that last bit only him? Maybe he should've mentioned that little impulse to old Marion. He paused his tape. This time, if Elle took him back, he'd resist that urge for good. If people could climb Everest and survive tsunamis, he – they – could have a real relationship. He could hold his ground. He could lay back on a dozen couches and dissect his life, until he got it . . . And he would – if she took him back.

The amazing thing was, she always did. After her elbow, after their shopping debacle, after Red Hill; she even pursued him after that scene in his office. It was remarkable and he'd never understood it.

Only now, as he sat beside the reeking filing cabinet, did he get it. His erratic behaviour kept her constantly limerent. And powerless somehow. Maybe this time, though, five days would be a stretch. Even her limerence must have its limits.

Sitting on the kerb in Newport, he can see that he'd waited too long, pushed her too far. Their pattern was smashed. Tonight, she's gone. His beautiful, top-shelf wife.

21

Arriving home from the Regent Theatre, shamefaced with the kindly cabbie, Elle went directly to her bathroom, where she spent long minutes prodding, cleaning and inspecting until she was unable to deny it. What he had done, what she had become. Not long after, she collapsed into bed and slept heavily.

At daybreak, in the seconds before wakefulness, the night's events echoed like a long and detailed dream. Upon waking, she was aghast that the startling images of failure plaguing her sleep accurately reflected her life. From her film's abysmal reception and her mother's absence to the violent denouement of her marriage in a laneway. As she lay, dazed, her fingers crept to the sheets beside her and found them cold.

She sat up but, again, the physical evidence was plain: he was gone. Hugging her knees, she tried to understand how she felt. In the mix now, distilled and potent, was real fear. Shame, too, that she'd let herself get here. Yet equally powerful was that yearning. It was still there. With an ache in her chest, she craved him. Restless suddenly, she propelled herself from the bed.

Dawn, and the day was already dissolving. The sky had folded back onto itself to drape its clouds on the unmoving river and erase the other bank. Elle walked through the clouds only to find more mist ahead. It was transporting, that mist: cocooning like a mild anaesthetic. There were few other walkers on the Maribyrnong's shore. Those who were out appeared on the path two metres ahead like time travellers, then disappeared behind her. The only sounds were the dull slap of her runners on the cement and the disembodied, floating voices.

Seeing her, one or two walkers nodded or smiled briefly. No one flinched or gasped. She found it strange. Wrong. Her eyelids were like pink sausages. Almost spent, they squeezed out another tear. It found its way to her unfamiliar upper lip and she brushed it aside, causing a prick of pain. Her mouth had taken the brunt of the impact from that slap; the swelling and the tenderness had collected in her lips and around her teeth. The top lip had torn; a jagged arrow pointed to her right nostril. There were two other hot spots. A hole had been dug in the side of her right cheek when her teeth crunched on impact. Her tongue fussed with the wound now, prodding, finding its shape, testing its depth. It tasted bitter and metallic, as it filled with saliva and drained. The third spot was under her right eye, a puffy cushion of flesh on her cheekbone nudging into her eyelid and threatening to shut her eye.

How she felt emotionally was complicated.

As a teenager, she'd come across a girl at school with a scraped cheek and a purple eye. She could remember the girl's downcast shame and the whispers that shadowed her. Her father was a widower and an engineer, the girl gifted at music. Beyond that, while Elle's own childhood was blemished by occasional hauntings from famous kidnapped children, like the Beaumont kids, thanks to her mother's stories, she knew nothing of the dangers that existed closer to home. She was raised to avoid the dark and lonely stretches outside, not the anger of loved ones up close. She was taught nothing of the risks posed by those who claim to love you, the risks that manifest at night in family kitchens or after the party. It would have helped, she thought, if someone had explained the warning signs: the moods and outbursts. And what they were: covert attempts to control. Then she could have had a language and a context for how she felt today. Better, she would have been forewarned.

On the misted path she had an overwhelming sense of him, as if he was beside her. Melon soap, starched shirt, damp hair. His giggle as he chased her with a bowl of eggs, his gapped grin as his long arms reached out for hers. In bed, his leg over hers, her body curled into his. A true fit: that's what she'd thought. She picked up her pace, began to sweat. That fit had not been in evidence last night. Not, she had to admit, for months. Yet she'd trundled on, believing in it.

A blast of heat rose, like a balloon, to her face. During their relationship, she had come to believe that love was as malleable as plasticine. That it could bend and warp and mutate so that it became something entirely unrecognisable from itself. She had insisted what they had was love, incontrovertible and true.

She had stayed because of these lofty feelings, even though their relationship became cramped and uninhabitable. She'd lived within that space, feeling entrapped, even though at times he flung the door open. She stayed because of their great love, even though what they had no longer even resembled care or like.

A final tear trickled down her cheek. She kicked a pebble, watched it ricochet from kerb to puddle. So that was it. So much for limerence, the smokescreen. In the end, she'd learned what love was by its absence. She felt like a fool – part writer-director, part con-artist, part dupe – and ill.

Why had she been so determined to make it work?

Fleetingly, she thought of Sidney Lumet. In his book *Making Movies*, the luminary director talked about the early days of kitchen-sink television, when a flashback would be inserted into a story to explain the psychological underpinnings of a character. Bald and unsatisfying, those scenes were avoided by Lumet – and by Elle too, as a filmmaker. But in life? In life, that morning, she was foraging desperately for answers. But none came pat.

A breeze picked up and cleared the mist, dried her cheeks. Soon she could see the other side of the river. On the eastern bank was the barren flatland of containers. In the river's brown midst she could make out the so-called island and its tanks of horrors. The island rose out of the water like an indisputable truth. A colony of toxicity: risk-managed. As she stared at the impervious, curved white walls, her emotions distilled. Humiliation, naivety and anger coalesced. Studying the beautiful, desolate landscape, she felt the magnitude of the compromise inherent in it as if it had been her own. Quite simply, it was too volatile and too close, as David had been, for too long.

As the last of the mist evaporated, she put her tissue in her pocket and turned around. She moved gingerly, as though the sediment in her blood had been stirred and was travelling through her system again – to unknown effect. But two things were certain: she was done with David and done with the inner-west.

It was barely 9 a.m. when she returned to Tennyson Street. Walking head down past Doris's house, she ignored the gentle, concerned face at the lacy window. Once inside her own home she downed her blinds and snibbed her locks, secured her chains and crept into bed. The telephone rang and she willed herself to ignore it. It rang another dozen times. Though a few calls at least would be Mira's, Doris's, her agent's, most – she knew – were his. Now that she'd seen his magnetic social persona, she didn't let herself speculate on where he was, what he was doing, or with whom. She didn't allow herself to wonder what he had to say. Every time her thoughts reverted to him, she changed the channel in her mind. The problem was her film, too, was now taboo, so her thoughts flitted from memories of her childhood to scenes from other people's films. Soon, the memories and the scenes began to merge. She saw her parents on a bench seat, like the old couples in *When Harry Met Sally*. Her father was young and beautiful, before the struts in his face collapsed. Smiling, he explained they'd been high-school sweethearts, married just in time before the first baby came. *But babies and love*, her mother said, her smile slipping, *pull you apart*.

'Cut,' called a voice, perhaps her own. 'Cut.'

Around dusk she heard a key in the lock, and the security chain straining. She heard him calling for her, heard him swear. And:

bang. Afraid, she burrowed deeper into her mattress and clamped her eyes shut.

She stayed like that for a fortnight. When hunger came, she ate water crackers. Even tea tasted foul and she avoided it. She dozed, stirring occasionally to watch the light creeping across her walls.

She felt guilty, of course – hiding from Mira, ignoring Doris, abandoning her film. But there was nothing she could do.

The world's first full-length, dramatic feature film was produced in Australia in 1906: *The Story of the Kelly Gang*. Once, she had relished her country's film history and had been awed by her place in it. That her name was linked with Gillian Armstrong and Jane Campion had humbled and delighted her. Not so long ago, she'd been touted as a significant part of a fresh renaissance in Australian filmmaking; the beginning, perhaps, of a new wave of commercially successful yet intelligent cinema that would one day reclaim the Australian film industry's mantel. To her regret, the Nasty Bastard's words weren't the only ones she'd kept. She felt as if she were spinning in the outer reaches of a tornado of her own creation, gradually slowing after months of needless speed. As she turned, she thought of Mira, and of their reputations. Who would ever ask her to make another film? She spun these questions until they became like a web; then, eventually, exhausted by the possibilities and encased, she rolled over and slept.

—

By the middle of June, the empty days were threatening to flatten her. Her only commitment was to find a new gynaecologist. Not that it mattered now – her endometriosis and that stabbing abdominal pain. Interviews with the networks, broadsheets and radio had come and gone, without her; Doris had knocked and given up; Mira's calls had risen to a climax and petered out. Her mother had even called once. Her lawyers would be scurrying . . . But it didn't matter. By now her film's run at the multiplexes would've begun and would soon be over. Gamely she'd crept twice to her laptop, only to have her suspicions confirmed. 'Plodding and below-par, with spectacularly lacklustre performances,' said *The Age*; 'Diabolically unfunny,' said *The Australian*, 'and an awful title.' Soon, her film would slip off the screens completely. Perhaps on DVD it might live a long and quiet life.

Late in the afternoons, when time was elastic and infinite, she found herself pining for Freeman & Milne. For the stupor of work gulped blindly and the allure of other people's stories and poor judgement. As the hours stretched, she pined for a life beyond that of her own making. She was worn out by the effort it had taken her to fail so spectacularly. She knew that if she didn't get up soon, her misery would become entrenched and she'd never get up again.

By early July, she felt herself restoring, regenerating: her skin clearing, her hair returning gradually. Her vagina lost its odour. There was no one with whom to discuss these anatomical shifts, the altered state that was her body. She told herself to accept that solitariness, for perhaps she would never know another way. So she charted herself and took heart from what she saw. Her anxiety, at least, was abating. And, slowly, in its wake was coming relief. Her fall, she thought, was over.

His calls continued to tempt her: eighteen times the first day, five times on the thirtieth. With each call, she debated. Despite her trepidation, the hard-headed part of her refused to admit defeat. Her hope was resilient and had been well-nourished, fed by the clichés of her genre. Always, at the climax, the dramatic rush – to the airport, the bus stop, the packed-up apartment; always, the hero running in the street, puffing and transformed. Perhaps it was possible, and David could do it. Perhaps she'd been right about him – despite the evidence. Then she remembered: what he'd done. What had come before this split. What, no doubt, would come again.

In a weak moment, she read his emails, half a dozen in all. They were jammed with concessions that he had made many mistakes, had a lot to learn, was seriously committed now to professional help – if she would take him back. He wrote that he missed her more than he'd ever missed another person, even Nat. He wasn't sleeping or eating, didn't want to drink. But his prose was contorted. It contained bitterness and recrimination, and only one apology – for that push and slap. Hunched over her laptop at two in the morning, it occurred to her that, sometimes, apologies came so late they were worthless. While his words were the ones she wanted, she didn't hear in them a shift. The underlying melody was the same. And she found it unbearably sad.

At 6.10 one Monday morning, her mobile rang again. She could see that it was him and knew that she shouldn't answer. But, perhaps because she was feeling stronger, or perhaps because her curiosity was growing apace, she succumbed. The contact was as tentative as a first date. Except this time, she suspected that his voice wouldn't hold an invitation; this time, there would be a demand, as though something was due. Answering, she felt that hint of apprehension.

'Hey, Elle Nolan, is that you? You're actually there.' His light touch, his masquerade, irked her.

'What do you want?' In her tone, she could hear disappointment and it unsettled her.

There was a bottomless pause. She felt drawn towards it, sucked into it. As if she alone was responsible for filling it. An ingrained habit, this desire of hers to overextend. She held herself in.

'Guess what? I've finished up at Freeman & Milne.'

It was far too late, she thought, and cruel. Once she would have celebrated and congratulated him. But today, it wasn't his due; it was, most likely, Alex's.

'I was thinking of dropping in. Will you be there in twenty?'

'No.'

Another pause. Again, she resisted its pull. And, to her astonishment, she saw into his furrowed brow and gleaned that he didn't understand; he was searching for the true reason for her behaviour. As if the previous twenty-two months hadn't been cumulative. As if every conversation she had tried to have was irrelevant, forgotten, a whim or passing fad, or a creation of her cycles. As if assault was something that could be overlooked, a minor trip.

'Ginger, why haven't you answered my calls? Or let me in? Don't you think you're overreacting here?'

She sucked in cold air. 'I want your stuff out of my house.'

'Sweetheart, we had a fight, all couples fight, it's —'

'Everything will be delivered to Head Street on Friday morning.'

'This is crazy; why are you being so unreasonable?'

'Someone will need to be there, to let the removalists in.'

A pause. 'Okay, okay, listen, I'll get it myself – on Saturday, we can have breakfast —'

'No. I'll email you the details.'

'Fuck you, then!' he said, his voice rising, as though caught in his throat. '*Fuck you.*'

As he hung up on her, she laughed at his outed panic. Within the hour, the phone rang again and she hit the red button. She imagined him hearing the harsh repeating beep of the engaged signal, imagined it bouncing off the white walls of his mansion like squash balls. She stood up and opened the blinds. The phone rang again but she didn't answer it, didn't end it; and it rang again, until, finally, she leaned across her bed and turned it off. Lying on the mattress with the phone in her hand, she was on a boat, lifting the anchor from the seabed, to let the insistent current take her.

After that, David desisted. A hiatus, as it turned out. Still, a shard of her was disappointed that he had stopped. And that in itself was disappointing – that her delusions lingered even now. It set her back a day or two.

Around that time her mother rang again, and she ignored the call.

On Wednesday, she finally finished Katharine Hepburn's autobiography. After almost three decades with Spencer Tracy, the great Kate hadn't known why she stayed with him. She hadn't known his feelings for her. But she'd tended to him happily and tried hard not to ruffle him. She'd even tried to forsake some of her best qualities because she suspected he didn't like them. Because what they had, for her at least, was bliss.

Shutting the book, Elle felt unsettled, but also comforted.

On Thursday, she decided to get up.

Upon leaving her bedfellow, misery, on her pillow, she found anger awaiting her in the shower. It coursed through her as she washed and she felt it prick her skin as though it were alive in the scorching water. Fully dressed for the first time in weeks, she strode through her house and realised that this anger of hers needed to get out.

She took to walking.

Her first day outside was arctic and windy and the sea at Williamstown was broken into peaks. It reminded her of a blanket of meringue but more ominous – poisoned meringue, perhaps. The temperature compressed the air from her lungs. She walked with the wind in her eyes and felt an empathy with the brewing sea. The water was carved up by forces she couldn't name but knew, and she sensed that she was heard and understood. Reflected and refracted by what her eye could see, all the way to the black inky line.

She packed him into boxes scavenged from the supermarket. His orange sneakers, his misery memoirs, all that Latin jazz. She sealed them with tape, as if to leave the flaps open was a sign of ambivalence. As she packed, she was fuelled by remembered images and sensations. It was not the fiasco in that laneway beside the Regent Theatre that fuelled her most. It was the rest: the on-off, hot-cold sensibility of his moods; the way his face snapped shut. How, watching television, he could create pure menace. How, naked on the couch, he engendered such extreme and warring emotions in her.

She hated him so intensely that it scared her. She spent her waking hours reliving humiliations in disbelief, like tracing wounds, trying to fathom how they came to be so deep. Gradually she cobbled together a theory: when a body is dealt a series of blows, it falls into shock and doesn't feel pain – just as she had, lashed by him over the months, lost the ability to feel rage. And rage, like pain, was crucial. A part of her body's natural self-defence.

Tossing his belongings to the removalists, she shouted at herself: *How did I get him so wrong?*

22

There are cars on the West Gate Freeway now, travelling from Melbourne, and Mira is heartened by them, even if they're going in the opposite direction. As the bridge curves ahead of her, she veers off the highway onto Williamstown Road. Passing the roadblock on Francis Street, she feels a nervous sense of homecoming. This is Yarraville, a place she loves, a place, after tonight, she won't view the same way again. The slender streets and rear lanes, the picket fences and lattice work, the bustling cafes and retired Italian men in the parks; all will now be tinged grey in her memory. Shrouded in soot.

Please, she thinks, approaching Seddon, *don't make tonight any worse than it already is.*

She's been gone three hours. A dangerously long time . . . *But*

Elle's a fighter, she tells herself, *and hardy*. Hardier thanks to her time with *him*.

She tries Elle's phone again. But again it rings out. *Oh shit*, she thinks. Next, though it was to be her last resort, she calls the police. So what if they are busy or dismiss her fears? To her bemusement, she's placed in a queue. *I can't bear this*, she thinks. Surrendering her position, she tries Elle's phone again but it gives her nothing.

Parking on Gamon Street, Dave leaps out of his car and bolts across the corner. He runs the length of Elle's street. There's no fleeing now. He's running, in the mad hope he might somehow save her life and maybe redeem his.

Until tonight, he'd only seen one other dead person. His dad had been dead barely a minute when Dave arrived in the South Caulfield hospital room. His mum was bawling at the icy window. His dad, on soiled white sheets, was a weathered but intact shell. Dave could see he'd gone and was glad. He hadn't wanted to sit by his side, as his mum had done, and count his last breaths. That death didn't fit a man of quick temper and fiery exits. His dad would've hated it, raged at it. 'Hold his hand, say something to him,' his mum had said. 'He's still here in the room.' But Dave had shrugged. Their conversation had never started.

His Elle, though – she was something else.

Outside her darkened house, his run crumbles. He rubs his forearms as if to warm them. Takes a step forward, then a step back. With no streetlights, the night's too dark and he's spooked. Somewhere, a dog's bark is answered by sirens. He steps forward again. Stops. Swears. Maybe he can't face it, doesn't have the balls.

He lights up. *Come on*, he thinks, *she could be alive*. He takes a step across the road. Now he's here, he should call the cops. Own up to the lot. No mitigation, no justification. She deserves that much. Once on that path, he should continue. Make up with his mum. Set up a trust for Natasha and Amelia. Accept the end of his legal career. Talk to a male shrink in the fucking slammer. Draw.

He exhales in shudders. Living like that's going to take a lot of stamina. Guts. And that sort of responsibility's the opposite of the intensity he's been craving. And destroying. His chin trembles. Whether she lives or dies, that intensity's gone. It occurs to him the intensity he felt the night they met has been unmatched – until tonight.

A shitty thought.

He hesitates. Her house rises up before him. Its porch is covered in that tangled, flowerless vine. Its bay windows like two closed eyes. Between them, that door behind its screen. If he were agile, he could climb in her bedroom window. But he's not agile. He's spread over the last two months; his drinking has poured over his belt. Someplace along the path of losing her, he's lost his health. The least of his worries now is constant head pain. Most likely, he'll have to smash a window.

He watches his cigarette burn. He sucks hard, drawing the ember close. Once the heat bites, he flicks the butt. It lands in the gutter among a puddle of other butts, like those left by office workers. Except these others are his. A dozen times, he's stood on this spot, in the early hours. *Is she asleep? Is she dreaming of me?* The stubby remnants of his wasted hope taunt him. Whatever he does, it's always too late.

When he'd arrived that afternoon, it'd been 4.30, cool and sunny. A typical wintry Melbourne afternoon. He was late for a meeting in the city with his lawyers. He'd been late a lot lately, forgetting his phone, losing his keys. He'd been living those moments that other people only dreamed about: the unprepared student sitting the exam; the near-naked actor on the stage. He'd been stumbling through his days, hungover, unslept. Four times already that week, after midnight, he'd taken a drive and found himself in Seddon. And, at 4.30, braving the daylight for once, he'd been there again, dreaming of reunion.

The secrets of that blind spot come to him then. The plunge of the blade. The puny resistance of her flesh.

Awash with shame, he doesn't move. His courage pisses away. He's been here before too. But why can't he do it? Why can't he redeem himself? Or save her? He groans. What would it fucking take?

Somewhere in the shrubs is the kitchen knife. He should find it. Since using it he's been improvising, badly. He thinks then of Reg – poor, kind Reg. *Jesus.* Maybe Elle was right. He is sick in the head.

23

One Monday morning in July, Elle finally visited her new gynaecologist in a grey concrete building in Carlton North. In a windowless box, she wept as she described her medical history. Together, they discussed the psycho-sexual possibilities of her symptoms, as well as the merits of a laparoscopy. Then Dr Littlemore examined her and proposed a series of tests. Three days later, the gracious doctor herself called. It was unlikely, she said, that Elle was ravished severely by the disease – if she had it. And, most certainly, she was fertile. Elle was trying to understand this diagnosis when Dr Littlemore cleared her throat. There was more. By the call's end, Elle had made another appointment, stunned; touched by something other. Pregnant.

Afterwards, she rode directly to Williamstown, where the sea was liquid steel. Overwhelmed, her thoughts rolled in with the waves. Disbelief, worry and embarrassment; joy and awe. Back and forth. She leaned against the bow of a slender tea-tree, which curved alone on the foreshore. The wind rattled around her as the charcoal sky rumbled. She knew she ought to move. The storm was shifting inland quickly. Lightning forked on the grey stage. Elle watched, feeling invincible. She'd survived David; she could survive anything. She waited, captivated. She was the tree now, bent from the wind but still growing. The first dollops of rain splashed onto the branches, onto her nose. She laughed. The storm was like her news: a universal miracle.

Within an hour, the storm had been replaced by sunlight. She emerged from under her tree and took in the born-again day. On that glistening foreshore, a coil of energy swirled inside her. It spun, its arms raised, its legs kicking, a happy, feminine tornado. It sounded absurd but that was how she felt. As she headed towards her bicycle, she was conscious of her body, her chest, her stomach, her womb. Amid the surging energy, she walked slowly, savouring it, knowing that she alone was in charge of her pace, the mode of her travel and the mood at her destination. She wasn't anticipating his call, not tiptoeing through her day, or second-guessing his Friday night. There was nothing to crave, nothing to challenge, nothing to rise above or hold together. She could stay like this for as long as she liked.

How she'd deal with him and what she'd say could wait.

As her bike glided forward, she felt so light, she could soar.

That the facade of Mira's worker's cottage on Hyde Street was unchanged surprised her. She felt as if the entire planet ought to have shifted to reflect the shift in her.

As she knocked, she strained to hear the life within, knowing it would be anchored to the rear. Mira would be immersed in the boys' dinners and bath, stories and bed, and the intervening, unpredictable mayhem, like an upturned bowl of beans or puddle of sand. Not a good time to visit, but perhaps exactly right.

She knocked again. Far above, orange-clad figures were working on the West Gate. She could see the flashing lights of crawling rollers, the wagon train of construction vehicles. Impossibly, yet another lane was being drawn onto the bitumen.

The door pivoted inward and Elle grinned.

There was Mira – smiling, singing out, dressed in heels and a frock. Over her bare shoulder, Elle could see Troy in the kitchen: Troy, the mousey-haired, sunny-eyed real deal. He waved a wooden spoon at Elle and smiled politely. Two heads edged the doorframe in the living room. Jesse and Max, already in Scooby-Doo pyjamas, damp-haired, grinning. Both boys looked longer, finer, yet still so new. Springing about behind them were two strawberry-blonde girls. And Jude, her grown brother.

Elle blinked tears.

'Well, hello,' said Mira. 'You seem better. Still shattered-looking but not so tender.'

'That sounds about right.'

Elle tugged a curl of dry lip, wondered whether Mira was going to invite her in. The traffic noise ebbed with a receding set of cars.

'I'm sorry I went to ground.'

When Mira sighed, the light in her face faded. 'It didn't help.' After a beat, she said, 'And it wasn't easy. We stuffed up. But we can recover.'

Elle nodded, cherishing the pronoun. But a question mark

was poised between them, flashing amber. She put some anger into her voice.

'He's gone.'

A grin sprang from Mira's face, wide and lovely. Elle could see her try to make it respectable by drawing across it a shadow of scepticism.

'It's been almost two months.'

Mira threw her arms open, like an invitation, and Elle didn't hesitate. When the women separated, they were moist-eyed and tipsy with emotion.

'Come in and celebrate.'

Elle shook her head, laughed, despite a twinge of misgiving. As much as Mira had her best interests at heart, as much as she wanted to share her news, she hesitated. In the kitchen, she could see Jesse coiled around Jude's leg. Elle could remember that sensation exactly – the grip of her nephew's twiney legs, the weight of him almost toppling. She'd felt like a tree clambered by a monkey.

She clasped Mira's arm. 'Not tonight. I'll call you.'

'Call down the coast,' said Mira.

Back on the footpath, Elle glanced up to the workers on the bridge. Their lights were brighter and they had moved a centimetre. Her cautious excitement ebbed as she thought of those men who'd perished, over four decades ago. Some things, she thought, were transformative: negligence, tragedy, divorce; more rarely, for the lucky – love.

Perhaps, at last, her luck was back.

A week later, on the Wednesday, she found an envelope on her mat. It bore a single word: 'Ginger', entwined with flowers. Picking it up, she felt uneasy that he'd been so close. She examined her street, the parked cars and empty footpath. Then, relieved he was gone, with the paper in her fingers, she calculated the risk of letting his words back in. One thing was certain and it shocked her: she was tempted to read what he had to say.

Even now, wisps of hope remained. Her faith was defiant, refusing to admit defeat. Fingering the stiff white paper, she promised herself that while that temptation existed, she would avoid him. Her faith needed to be fed by more than romantic comedies and his unsatisfying words. Romantic comedies were, after all, penned by people like her. But, despite her resolve, she slid the letter into her handbag and carried it with her like a talisman.

One day she would read it, when her resilience was a given.

By early Thursday evening, she had visited three real estate agents. When she stepped out of the third, her house was on the market. With the decision made, her energy multiplied. She scrubbed her home, removing the last film of him with the tobacco stains from her walls, and took stock. She owned too many things. Lamps, fruit bowls, side tables. Paintings. She scheduled a garage sale to sell the mementos from her life. She studied maps of regional Victoria and drew circles around Castlemaine, Point Lonsdale and Macedon. On Friday morning, when she dressed, she stopped: gave thanks. The underbelly of those thanks, though, was ever-present and dangling like a question: David. The honourable thing would be to tell him. But being honourable with him would make her vulnerable. On balance, it wasn't worth the risk. Not yet.

At twilight she arrived home, relishing the prospect of a nostalgic viewing of Alexander Payne's *Sideways*. But as soon as she entered her silent house, she knew. She could feel the remnants of his presence as surely as if he'd painted his moniker on the walls. In her bedroom, pillows had been spun across the bed. A collection of short stories had walked from her side table. A bottle of her new citrus scent, too. Seeing her strewn belongings, she was needled, as though they were splinters of David himself. This homecoming in her absence wasn't in the script. But then again, the script had changed. No doubt, somehow, he had sensed it.

She flicked on lights, slipped off her shoes. Remembered again her hunger. If she didn't eat soon she would feel ill, gag. A pot of simple marinara awaited her on the stove; all she needed was the patience for the boiling water. She studied her bedroom for further traces of him and found none in the half-packed boxes. As she scanned the dining room, the locked-up study, she felt herself frowning. That he could ambush her like this made her uneasy. She hadn't thought to change her locks.

She heard a noise from the kitchen, like a cup upset.

Fear raised the hairs on her arms and quickened the thud in her ears. She thought to retreat, to hover at Doris's – until he had gone. But she needed to eat and this was her house. For too long, she realised, she had lived with fear. Accommodated it into her psyche as she had accommodated him. Without ado, she swept down the hall. Her navy woollen dress was like a sheath; it clung to her, accentuating her shape, and she plucked it from her curves. When she reached the kitchen, she squared her shoulders, collected herself. He was bending over her laptop with a glass of red wine in his hand and a tea towel over his shoulder. On the bench, her tzatziki was out and crackers were scattered. On the stove, the lid was off her marinara, a wooden spoon balancing across it. As he straightened, jazz began to play from her laptop, something Cuban.

Her fear and exhilaration tripped into anger. It ignited within her – like a cinder in a drought – and its force shocked her. Even two metres away, he could see it and he edged backwards towards her glass doors and the garden. As his eyes flickered outside, she was struck by his feebleness. The odd, blue-black socks were back, the crumpled suit, the brown and ginger bristles on his cheeks. What once had been intoxicatingly vulnerable was now pathetic. Whatever clinging hopes she had were severed at the sight of him. With a heartbeat of disappointment, they were gone. And she was unafraid.

'What are you doing?'

To her surprise, her tone was breathless, her anger aerated. But he didn't respond. Beneath his gaze, she was aware of the dust motes alight around her in the last of the sunlight. She wiped strands of hair from her face, damp from her ride, and straightened her dress.

'Well, look at you,' he said.

She felt his stare linger on her swollen cleavage, her subtly protruding belly. She saw that there was no chance that he would miss what she had, so blithely. Somewhere, beneath her hostility, she was flattered. On some level, he had known her. It was a nod to the intimacy they had shared. She was both flattered and besmirched by it.

She stirred her pot of marinara and watched his face in conflict. In his eyes she detected a searing anger-hurt. The tea towel in his hand was damp where his fingers clenched cloth.

She entwined her own hands on the slight shelf of her belly. 'I want you to leave.'

'How far gone are you?' His voice was a rasp.

She hesitated. She was too tired, not ready, but it felt unfair.

'How far gone?' His voice rose, with that hint of panic.

'Another time, David; I'm tired.'

'I deserve a conversation.' He spat the words.

'You don't have any claim here,' she said. 'You forfeited your rights months ago.'

She saw a blatant flare of hatred shoot across his eyes. It riveted her and she understood: no matter what happened between them he wouldn't take responsibility, look within. He was flush against the glassy surface of his own limitations. She felt her fear returning. The only thing between them now was a stone bench.

'This's bullshit.' His eyes narrowed. She imagined him trying to separate his legal entitlements from the emotional debris entangling him. And from his rising anger.

She crossed her arms to make a fence around her belly; her resolve set like concrete. She would do whatever it took to keep him away – from intervention orders to disappearing interstate.

'I want your key,' she said, stepping towards the hall.

After a beat, David fossicked in his left pocket, then his right. Warily, she watched, wondering if he was play-acting. It was hard to tell; he seemed so shocked, so lost to his own reactions – perhaps the contents of his pockets were a mystery too. He stood for a moment, staring, as if undecided, and then he searched his left pocket again. This time he found his mark. He flung the silver key onto the stone bench. It caught the light as it ricocheted. An incongruous moment of beauty.

She was watching its spinning dance when he lunged at her. Her head was first to the floorboards. Pain erupted in her skull and shot tears into her eyes. What was he doing? The question exploded in her head like a blinding firecracker, eclipsing everything. She heard him cursing into her right ear.

'You selfish cunt.'

She shoved him, using all her might. 'David, get off me.'

When he eased back from her she thought that he was done, until she saw his face. There was none of the man she had thought she'd loved. None of the laughter or warmth or wit. It was stripped back to its base elements and she saw his naked fury. She saw his intention in it: ugly and determined. And it galvanised her.

She kneed him in the groin, as hard as she could. When his back arched, she pushed backwards like a scrambling crab. But before she could find her feet he charged, slamming her into the kitchen wall. The force jarred her left shoulder and sent pain driving down her neck.

'David, let me go!' She searched his eyes, trying to find him. At the same time, she felt that other-worldly flutter in her stomach, like wings spreading. Her thoughts jammed again. She was carrying a child. This could not, must not, happen.

As if reading her, he pinned her arms and, slowly and deliberately, sat on her belly. The pressure caused by the full weight of him was overwhelming and intense and nauseating. And she screamed. She tried to flip him, bucked and thrashed. Tears were spilling down her cheeks, pooling on her neck. She gave him everything she had.

'Listen to me!' she screamed. 'Listen! I call her Rose. I'm twenty-two weeks gone.' She thought she saw him listening, the cock of his eyebrow. 'I've only known for a fortnight; I was going to tell you and I'm sorry I didn't. Please, David, get off me. Please. You're not this person.'

She spoke to him as if he were capable of listening, of reasoning, retrieval. As she spoke, in great, unwieldy sentences, her mind was trying to grasp what he was doing. This man was once her David.

How much she had overestimated him. And underestimated him. The depth of it was inconceivable.

'Please,' she said into his smouldering stare. 'David, please. Stop!'

He rose up from her and she felt an instant's delicious relief – before his hands clamped her throat. It took her a second to understand. She was conscious of his fingers overlapping at the top of her spine, his thumbs meeting over her windpipe: pushing downwards. It was not until she felt their clenching pressure that she grasped what he was doing, his absolute intention, and another wave of disbelief took her down. He was watching her, wanting her acknowledgement of what he could do with his bare hands, his thumbs. She tried and failed to suck in precious air. She dragged her fingers down his hands, taking strips of him beneath her fingernails. She thrashed and bucked again. At the last, screens of silver slid over her eyes and brought with them a desperate sadness.

24

There is a child, aged five or six, kneeling beside Elle's body. The girl's narrow, heart-shaped face is furrowed as she tugs urgently at the soiled towel. Up above, in the midst of raging emotions, Elle can hear the pleading, singsong voice. And she can feel the urgency, though she doesn't understand it. Images are colliding around her but not like before. Not causally, not logically. This time, waves crash over her dining-room chair, semitrailers surround her on a traffic island, and she is flailing in the Maribyrnong, gulping brown muck. Then she hears the distressed child again.

'Wake up, wake up.'

The reedy voice pulls her downward.

'It's not your fault! It's not your fault. You have to wake up!'

—

Abruptly, Elle is back. The first thing she notices is the wet. It's the contents of her bowels and something else. Something thick and sticky. She knows not to move, and standing is out of the question. As she blinks, random flashes from her life linger but she can't make sense of them. She tries to concentrate on her breathing. But what she hears is whistling, unearthly and close. Her emotions distil then into worry and shock. She opens her mouth, tries to speak. Her lips move and her tongue responds, but nothing comes. Not even a whisper. She tries again but hears only that dreadful whistle. Gingerly, her fingers reach to her neck and it rises to meet them: hot and tight. The touch fixes her mind on an image: David, straddling her, his full weight on his hands, around her neck.

Unnerved, she banishes the memory, focuses on her bearings. In the dark, she's horizontal and twisted. In front of her, she can make out a smooth surface. Below, she feels rather than sees hard ceramic tiles. On her tongue she can taste fine soap powder. Her world is almost unrecognisable from this angle – the tiles, her washing machine, even the wall – such everyday sights; she's seen them a thousand times but not from this perspective.

She lies still, breathing noisily, and listens. Her house, usually so bright and warm, is jet-black and otherwise silent. How long has she been gone? She guesses some time: the tiles beneath her are wet and her flesh is cold.

Her fear takes hold then and she begins to tremble. But as much as she doesn't want to, she needs to move. Days could pass before someone comes looking for her again. Scared or not, she refuses to die that solitary, clichéd death, observed by a basket of pegs. *No.* There will be no dying, alone, tonight. She untwists her legs, which feel new and stiff. Then, carefully, she tries to rise. But messages sent from her head to her torso are lost en route. Nothing in her mid-region moves. Not a millimetre. She blinks hot tears. Her body, her mind: she's always assumed they would not fail her, at least not for decades. Her nose drips. She manages to raise her arm to wipe it with the back of her hand. Relieved that something works, she closes her eyes to better focus. Partially on her side, she wonders if she can inch onto her hip and lever herself up, bypassing her stomach. Bracing herself, she tries. To her relief, she rises into a sideways curl. She stills to catch her breath.

Perhaps only thirty centimetres from the floor, poised on one elbow and hip, she pauses. She hears a siren in the distance, growing faint. Beyond her house, lives go on. Cars crash. Traffic snarls. She can't take it in: her absolute disconnection from everyone and everything. She is a small island of woman on her tiles. The thought drains the last of her resolve. Even if she did make it to her telephone, what could she say – with a whistle? Her call would be dismissed, a prank, a nuisance. Her thoughts threaten to run on, taking her further from herself. An image pops into her mind of a child's face, soft and fleshy. Vaguely familiar. Jesse or Max? Those beautiful boys. The image steadies her. She breathes, whistles . . . waits . . . What she needs to do is not complicated: get to an external door, wave down a passer-by. The front, she decides, would be best, with the most chance of traffic, though it's the furthest. Simple enough, when you can walk and speak, in daylight. Her galley kitchen, her long hallway; she has to survive them. It's as if her humble home has become the front line.

She inches closer to her washing machine and raises her right arm across her body. Carefully, she turns herself onto her hands and knees. She becomes conscious of the lack of pain and its absence is a gift. Staying on all fours, she's conscious too that she's almost up; coping. As she steadies, she becomes aware of something hanging. Heavy and loose. Reaching down, she touches warm, wet meat. Panic surges again in her chest. What has he done? Her arms tremble violently and their shaking threatens to spread. When she closes her eyes, she sees David's face too close to hers, his expression raw and enraged. A matching burst of anger begins to clear her thoughts. Pushing the slippery stuff back inside her, she wraps the ugly green towel around her waist, like a corset. Using the washing machine, she pulls herself to her feet and, upright, tries to gather her circling thoughts. It's almost beyond her. Anger, shock and disbelief whirl within her, carrying round and round the same questions: *How could he do this? Why? Why!*

It is not until she feels the distant flutter in her stomach like the touch of wings that she *remembers*. And she lets out a long and soundless wail.

25

Within minutes, Mira will be outside Elle's house again. She feels unbearably hot. Why didn't she squeeze through that window? Speeding towards the intersection of Gamon and Somerville roads, she'd plagued by images of Elle injured and prone.

Please, she thinks, bartering with the divine. *If Elle is unharmed, I will never be judgemental again. I swear.*

When the lights rise to red, Mira hits the redial button. *Please, please, pick up.*

Halfway down her hall, Elle is slipping under again when she hears the chiming. The sound is so loud; at first she can't place it. Cold is seeping into her bones and she can hear her teeth chattering along with that horrible breathing. The wetness of that towel around her abdomen is bothering her too – that and the tiredness. So far she has blacked out three times. Each time she's awoken disoriented, her fear escalating a notch, her fragility that much more obvious. Inescapable. Rose's survival is the only thing driving her forward now. The infant's face keeps popping into her head and she tries to hold it, to memorise it. But Rose slips from her, like a fragment from a dream. As the chiming persists, though she can't place it, she wills herself to push on. She is stooped, as one foot and then the other scrape the surface of her floorboards. She is, she fears, barely progressing. A metre feels like an hour and her front door, her finish line, is six metres away.

Then she sees it: her mobile phone, in a green fruit bowl on her hall table. A moment later, it falls silent. The effort it takes for her to reach the midpoint in her hallway leaves her faint. If only she could close her eyes, slip back to that floating peace. Only for a moment. Against the wall, she's creating a smudge on the plaster, like a bleeding shadow; it takes all of her will not to look. Elle feels herself slipping. Down the wall she goes, heavily, like a bag of bricks. Into the blackness, she thinks: *If only I never met him; if only I didn't relent, again and again.* As her ears ring, her final lament: *If only I didn't tell him.*

Seconds or maybe minutes later, the phone starts again and pulls her back. Leaning into the wall, Elle raises herself and then pushes off: one foot and then the next. Reaching the narrow table, she glimpses her friend's name lingering in the screen and draws strength from it. But, as she picks up, the name disappears. Confused, she retrieves the missed call. With her heart pounding in her throat, she hears the ringing signal and then that deep, rich voice, and she hisses. Whistles. But her tongue, her voice box, will not give. Words jam in her throat. Snared. Too big for the tiny space that he's left.

'Is that you?'

Hearing Mira's concern she wants to weep, to crumble like a child into the arms of her mother.

'Elle, are you all right? Say something, please, you're scaring me, where are you?'

She bangs the telephone on the hall table. *A text, I'll text.* But as she cuts the call, the telephone beeps, the screen fades and it's as flat and useless as a tile. This time, she closes her eyes and slides onto her haunches. She hears her father's voice: 'Ellie,' he's saying, 'don't stop.'

But she is sorely tempted. She waits, slumped against the wall, for the decision to be made. She waits, breathing noisily, shivering, almost impatient with it. But it doesn't come. She's as grounded, as earthed, as her house on its timber stumps. In the hiatus, as the minutes pass, she finds herself listening. For that delicious flutter, otherworldly yet within. She was only just learning to identify it – not a rumble, not wind, not pain. Rather, a delicate, internal tickle. Consciously pregnant for only two weeks, she hasn't had the time to get accustomed to that thickness around the waist, the need to slide doors open wider, the need to rest. But she'd known, right away, to savour that flutter. To celebrate and cherish it.

Her gaze shifts to her locked-up study where, inside, a white cot stands, pristine and already made up with sheets the colour of the sky, topped with a pale pink teddy. When it had arrived, two days earlier, she'd hummed 'Mary Had a Little Lamb' as she'd tucked in edges, smoothed crumples, in unrivalled delight. She had not known love like it.

She listens, but beyond the chattering of her teeth and the rasping of her breath, nothing comes.

Dave is bent double on the bitumen when he sees movement in the house. He stares, slack-jawed, through the darkened windows. Without streetlights, without a moon, the night isn't helping. But he's convinced a shadow's moving. He barrels across the nature strip to her gate. There he halts, as if it were electrified. Is that really her, or a trick? Is the night, this crazy night, playing with him?

Maybe, but there it goes again, growing closer, in the hall. Any second now the locks will click. His body jerks. It's fucking unbelievable. But then again, it isn't . . . If anyone could survive that – survive him – it'd be her. He grabs the gate's pickets. His palms are wet. The window is black again, the shadows still. He waits.

Slowly, he buckles. He stays on his knees: folded out of sight. He can see the months ahead now. Wherever he is, she'll come for him in the dark, as she is tonight. Dead or alive, she'll look at him with those big, cold eyes. That her feelings for him are gone astounds him. He pictures her as she was in her kitchen: content, self-sufficient and aglow. Unscathed without him. No desire left in her. Definitely no love. His power over her, which he'd never fully understood, gone. And now, the possibility she's alive somehow makes all that worse. The baby too . . .

He tugs his telephone from his pocket. His thumb presses firmly, three times. His sore, obedient thumb: how he hates it.

—

Shoving open the flywire screen, Elle is accosted by the close sky and its chemical odour. And then she sees him. He is crouched on the footpath like a huge, stalking cat. *Oh fuck.* She clings to the edge of the flywire, steadies it, and pulls it closed. Thankfully he doesn't hear, isn't looking. Though it has taken an aeon to get to the threshold, the possibility of his return hasn't occurred to her. She shrinks into the shadowy reach of her hall and waits, her heart thudding in her throat. Her mind can't latch on to a lucid thought. Closing her eyes, she sees that cherubic face again. This time the wisps of honeyed hair, gummy smile and enormous blue eyes become the narrow, heart-shaped face of a six-year-old; and she tries to draw strength from it, from *her*. Inching to the screen door, she nudges it open again.

As if sensing movement, David's head swings her way and he stands. On the footpath, he is only two metres from her porch, an arm's span from her low picket fence. Confronted by the size of him, she scolds herself for moving. She waits, knowing that he could stride over her knee-high gate . . . Knowing that if he struck, she would go down like a felled tree. She waits, shivering, that towel around her waist wet and cold. But he doesn't move, doesn't speak, simply stares at her. The embers in his red-brown eyes are alight again. In them, she detects shame and something new: bewilderment? At the sight of her, or his predicament, she isn't sure. He looks so broken and so lost to himself; it's ridiculous. She feels him trying to extract something from her – an emotion, perhaps. But she is dry. In him, she doesn't recognise herself at all. The only thing that matters now is inside her. What she's learned and what she's carrying. She holds his gaze to let him glimpse it. No matter what she has done or said, she doesn't deserve what he did to her tonight.

His head drops, chin to chest.

An edge is shaved off her dread. She wills herself to keep upright. It is so good to be outside, despite that cloud. She props herself against a vine-covered pillar. Warily, she observes him. Though the relief she feels is real, she cannot trust it. Not until he's gone. Then, unbidden, her future plays in her head: her gradual recovery, a court case, a jail term. She realises that, regardless of where she is, there will always be the unavoidable prospect of him. If what she hopes is true, her baby is alive and, inevitably, he will know. And, one day, he will be sitting at a desk in a low-security jail: a father. Writing confused letters, briefing advocates, exploring his rights. And what are his rights? Would they survive this? The glorious relief she felt when that flutter returned to spur her on is eclipsed now by a new pragmatic fear.

She peers at his pathetic bowed head, as from the depths of her memory news stories erupt. A father on an access visit driving his three young sons into a dam . . . Another estranged father tossing his precious four-year-old daughter off the West Gate Bridge . . . The frailties of the legal system rattle at her. Terrify her. Yet again, she's reminded of the never-ending consequences of her recklessness.

Her heart thuds and she fears she may black out again. On the footpath, David is fussing with his trousers. His trousers purchased one horrid shopping day in the city and soiled now with her blood. Chilled and faint, she watches him, this man to whom she's bound herself. His face has altered, drawn inward, and he seems to be frisking himself. Patting his body down, as if to check he is all there. She notices then his terry-towelling dressing gown. What is he doing? He is to her left, on the road now, but far too close.

She watches him pace, while in the background a car grows closer. She is shaking too much, her teeth chattering; but help exists – somewhere. A moment later, headlights swing around the corner at Hamilton Street. A police car. The sight of it is so wonderful she wants to weep again. She looks to David, and tries to grasp what he is doing and what he has done. He seems curiously unsurprised, turning his back to the car. Something glints beneath his robe. A blade.

26

Poised on the kerb, Dave is searching the faces of the young women in their car. Searching but not seeing. *Finally*, he thinks, *you're all here*. Even Mira, hopping out of her old Saab, midway between him and the cops: blameless, loyal Mira.

He takes a step onto the road and the cops get out of their car. They share a look as an ambulance pulls up. The driver looks at him then, hard. Her broad face changes, maybe in recognition. She's pretty, with a blonde ponytail: familiar. She hasn't seen his knife. The other one, a stocky redhead, eyes Elle, and her face changes too. Her gaze is steady on the bloody green towel.

'It's okay,' she yells to Elle. 'You're going to be okay.'

The redhead calls to the ambos. No one moves.

Dave fingers the tape in his pocket. It's a shame he can't listen to it, relive their first date at Middle Park: her wild urchin hair and all-seeing pale eyes. Her breathless arrival at his house and the glorious colours of her face. That first night at Alex's gallery, her poise and spunk. Her shining eyes, urging him to draw a frigging picture.

He's stopped on the bitumen now, a bushfire roar in his head. He's been the worst kind of idiot: privileged and wasteful. Fucking up everything he cares about. And, tonight, he's trashed the only thing that was left to him: his future. He can't bear to think of his daughter living without her dad; worse, living with the knowledge of what he's done. And with the shame. His eyes shut. His grief crescendos, bitter and intense. Thick with it, he raises his arm.

Elle sees, high above his head, her long kitchen knife. Forgetting her useless throat, she screams. Only a gust of air and searing pain eventuate. Time is suspended, inching, eternal. The police officers shout, their hands find their guns and raise them. Words of caution and appeasement fall like blanks at David's feet. The blonde woman's face glazes with panic.

To Elle, the seconds seem to creep.

David locks his eyes on hers, and takes a step closer. To her dismay, she glimpses his regret. It confuses her that remnants of the man she'd loved endure. That he has chosen now, this late hour, to reveal them to her. But his regret is no match for hers. *Please*, she thinks, *let us go*.

David turns and charges – at Mira. He is yelling a command that Elle can't make out. Mira screams, her mouth a large black hole, as she scrambles to her car. The redhead hollers. David is almost within striking distance, shouting wildly with the knife high. The driver shoots.

A volley of five shots strikes him, at short range, in the chest. The exit wounds in his back explode fireworks of red across the white sky of his towelling gown. Bloody jags of flesh and fabric merge and flap. He sinks to his knees, slow and heavy, like a beast of burden: plainly, instantly, lifeless. Elle reads the two young women's faces: matching contortions of duty and grief, fear and comprehension. And then she understands the extent of it.

Tears swamp her eyes. *Oh, David.* She stares at him, willing him to stay down. Get up. Stay down. The last of her anger leaches away. Mira emerges from behind her car door. She's whiter than china, her head shaking. Elle sees but doesn't feel Mira's confusion. What she feels is reprieved. And shocked. And crushingly sad – for him, for her, for them.

Around her, a wind picks up: clean and cool. The movement releases the people on the road; more cars arrive, flashing blue. A policewoman tends Mira while a spectacled paramedic strides across dancing leaves to Elle, saying, 'Here's hoping that blows it out to sea.'

Other voices fill the night now; neighbours, the curious. Doris. Elle is faint with relief. If she's not careful, she could slip beneath the voices and float again. Perhaps find David hovering above the telegraph pole. She plunges her fingers through the vine and towards the pillar, like ten slender anchors, and wills herself to stay earthed. The paramedic bends to her, calls her Elle, slides a needle in her arm. When her eyes close, for the briefest moment, she smells David's melon scent, hears his giggle. She blinks, half expecting to see him afloat, or standing over her. The good David. But there is no trace of him in the night or the shape on the bitumen. *Farewell, you*, she thinks. The paramedic is squeezing her hand, talking gently, confirming what they already know. Within, underscoring his words, is that flutter. Tiny fingers tapping out their otherworldly morse code: *I am still here.*

Yes, she thinks, smiling, *we are still here*. And then, on a stretcher, she's passing Mira, passing David, facing the sky, taking in its sweep.

ACKNOWLEDGEMENTS

What Came Before has gone through several incarnations. Thank you to everyone who read the manuscript and gave feedback – from those in the legal profession and film industry to fellow writers, editors and friends. Specifically thanks to Alison Girvan, Sam Everingham, Zoe Odell, Sarah Barton, Bruno Moro, Clare Kennedy, Sally Hepworth, Cristina Pozzan and Nicola O'Shea. I'd also like to thank my family; my agent Tara Wynne at Curtis Brown Australia; and the editorial team, Cate Blake and Ben Ball at Penguin.

Finally, my biggest thank you to Jason for his unwavering support and faith.

It took me over a decade to write *What Came Before*. During that time, I read countless news stories of women killed by their partners or exes. I'd like to acknowledge those women, as well as the women and children I've alluded to in this book, whose lives were so devastatingly cut short.

ACKNOWLEDGMENTS